Praise for Debra Webb

"Wow! Those that crave adrenaline overflow must read this book. From page one, the characters explode off the pages with their highly intense action.... Very highly recommended."
—*Myshelf.com* on *Silent Weapon*

"A fast-moving, sensual blend of mystery and suspense, with multiple story lines, an unusual hero and heroine, and an ending that escapes the trap of being too pat. I thoroughly enjoyed it."
—*New York Times* bestselling author
Linda Howard on *Striking Distance*

"Debra Webb delivers page-turning, gripping suspense, and edgy, dark characters to keep readers hanging on."
—*Romantic Times BOOKclub* on
Her Hidden Truth

"Debra Webb's fast-paced thriller will make you shiver in passion and fear."
—*Romantic Times BOOKclub*
on *Personal Protector*

"A hot hand with action, suspense and last—but not least—a steamy relationship."
—*New York Times* bestselling author
Linda Howard on *Safe by His Side*

Dear Reader,

First let me thank you for all your amazing letters and e-mails about Merri in *Silent Weapon*. I can't tell you how much I enjoyed each and every one. This book is in large part due to your tremendous response to her story. I hope you will enjoy Merri's newest exciting adventure as much as I enjoyed writing it.

Please visit my Web site at www.debrawebb.com and let me hear from you as soon as you've finished the book! I can't wait to see what you think of Merri's developing relationship with one sexy cop.

Look for my next Bombshell book coming in June 2006. I promise you many more intriguing adventures with my kick-butt ladies. And who knows, maybe you'll be seeing more of Merri as she makes her mark as Nashville's sexy, silent weapon!

Regards!

Debra Webb

DEBRA WEBB
SILENT RECKONING

Published by Silhouette Books

America's Publisher of Contemporary Romance

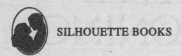

SILHOUETTE BOOKS

ISBN 0-373-51386-0

SILENT RECKONING

Books by Debra Webb

Silhouette Bombshell

‡‡*Justice* #22
††*Silent Weapon* #33
††*Silent Reckoning* #72

Harlequin Books

*Striking Distance
*Dying To Play
‡*Colby Conspiracy*

Code Red
Tremors

Forrester Square
Nobody's Baby

Double Impact
"No Way Back"

Mysteries of Lost Angel Inn
"Shadows of the Past

Whispers in the Night
"Protective Instinct"

*A Colby Agency Case
†The Specialists
‡Colby Agency: Internal Affairs
**The Enforcers
††Silent Weapon
‡‡Athena Force

Harlequin Intrigue

*Safe by His Side #583
*The Bodyguard's Baby #597
*Protective Custody #610
Special Assignment: Baby #634
*Solitary Soldier #646
*Personal Protector #659
*Physical Evidence #671
*Contract Bride #683
†Undercover Wife #693
†Her Hidden Truth #697
†Guardian of the Night #701
*Her Secret Alibi #718
*Keeping Baby Safe #732
*Cries in the Night #747
*Agent Cowboy #768
‡Situation: Out of Control #801
‡Full Exposure #807
**John Doe on Her Doorstep #837
**Executive Bodyguard #843
**Man of Her Dreams #849
Urban Sensation #864
Undercover Santa #879

Harlequin American Romance

Longwalker's Child #864
*The Marriage Prescription #935
The Doctor Wore Boots #948
*Guarding the Heiress #995

DEBRA WEBB

was born in Scottsboro, Alabama, to parents who taught her that anything is possible if you want it bad enough. She began writing at age nine. Eventually she met and married the man of her dreams, and tried some other occupations, including selling vacuum cleaners, working in a factory, a day-care center, a hospital and a department store. When her husband joined the military, they moved to Berlin, Germany, and Debra became a secretary in the commanding general's office. By 1985 they were back in the States, and finally moved to Tennessee, to a small town where everyone knows everyone else. With the support of her husband and two beautiful daughters, Debra took up writing again, looking to mystery and movies for inspiration. In 1998, her dream of writing for Harlequin came true. You can write to Debra with your comments at P.O. Box 64, Huntland, Tennessee 37345 or visit her Web site at www.debrawebb.com to find out exciting news about her next book.

This book is dedicated to a very special
young man, my son-in-law, Mark Jeffrey.
Thank you for making my daughter happy.

Chapter 1

I read an article once that championed the legalization of prostitution. After all, the writer insisted, it is the oldest profession known to civilized man. At that juncture in the article I had paused to frown at the use of *prostitution* and *civilized* in the same paragraph. No offense to ladies of the night, but there is absolutely nothing civilized about *the profession*.

Case in point: I, Merrilee Walters, am standing here on a Nashville street corner way east of 2nd Avenue and Broadway, not exactly the ritziest section of town. You know the section I mean. Friday-night traffic is heavy. The weather is unseasonably warm for late March, so the convertible tops and windows of cars are down, allowing drivers to enjoy the first previews of summer.

The hot pink skirt I'm wearing barely covers my

rump. The fishnets are making my legs itch and my feet are absolutely killing me in these damned thigh-high stiletto boots. As if that isn't bad enough, the matching pink tube top keeps creeping down to give a preview of its own.

I can't believe I agreed to this. What self-respecting redhead would wear hot pink?

If the outfit isn't barbaric enough to make you shudder, I have to put up with all the wolf calls and lewd comments shouted at me from the passing cars. I don't have to actually hear the words. I see the faces leaning out windows. I can fill in the blanks. And, well, lipreading is my specialty.

Don't let anyone kid you. Prostitution is pure hell. And I haven't even gotten to the part with the johns yet.

My mother always told me that bad girls—translation according to the Southern Mothers' Dictionary: any female who has sex outside marriage—went to hell. Well, I'm here to tell you, she's right. This is surely hell.

Actually I'm not a hooker. I'm a detective in Metro's Homicide Division and this is an undercover operation to nail a scumbag who likes to damage prostitutes, to the point that two have died. As if that isn't bad enough, he's suspected of having killed a cop—one of Metro's finest. I can tell you right now, I wouldn't want to be him when he's finally caught.

With the creep in hiding, there is only one way to lure him out.

I shifted my weight to the other foot and watched

the woman across the street. Tall, smooth dark skin. Very pretty with sleek black hair cascading around her shoulders. Shameka had survived an attack by this low-life. She'd escaped certain death by the skin of her teeth—and plain old street smarts. Once she'd gotten over the initial fear, she'd marched into Metro and demanded to be used as bait to catch him. A gutsy move from a gutsy lady. And exactly the break Metro had been looking for.

She was scared tonight though. I could tell. But she would die before she'd back down. She wanted to get this guy almost as bad as we did—we being the cops.

I haven't always been a cop. Just over three years ago I was an elementary school teacher. Really, I was. The only four-letter words I used on a regular basis were Spot, Dick or Jane. Well, okay, truth is, that hasn't changed. As much as I try to fit in, foul language just doesn't work for me. Now my colleagues, well, they go into a bar and five minutes later sailors come running out. But they watch their mouths around me out of respect. I like that.

And I love being a cop.

Getting back to how I ended up on this street corner…

I grew up in a houseful of boys, all cops or firemen—except my dad, he's a CPA, weird huh? Anyway, three years ago I lost my hearing. I don't mean it faded so that I needed a hearing aid. I mean, I came away from a merciless infection with profound loss. I hear nothing at all. Not a single sound. Sometimes I think

I do, but my doctors say I don't really hear, I simply remember what things sound like so I think I'm hearing when I'm actually recalling.

At first I was totally devastated. I locked myself away at my parents' home and felt sorry for myself. I lost my job, and my fiancé—who wasn't such a loss as it turned out. My life felt as if it were over.

With my family's support I went into counseling and intensive training for the hearing-impaired. I learned signing and, more important, how to read lips. I got myself a job in the historical archives of Metro and then I developed an interest in solving cold cases.

Since I knew no one would want to hire a deaf policewoman or detective, I did my crime-solving on my own. Bringing down a murderer who had escaped justice landed me in lots of hot water, but also garnered me lots of attention. The Chief of Detectives at Metro offered me a position with Homicide, and I brought down mob boss Luther Hammond by using my own unique weapon—reading his evil plans off his own lips.

So here I am. One year later.

After a couple of months on the job, I went off to the police academy. Eight months later I was fortunate enough to be accepted at the Tennessee Forensics Academy. I got back on the job a couple of months ago. Metro wanted to assign me to profiling or forensics and, at first, that's what I thought I wanted. But I was wrong. I couldn't make the difference I yearned to make behind the scenes.

This is where I wanted to be—out here in the

trenches. My life is all I could hope for on a professional level.

On a personal note, my family finally accepted my new career. I have an on-again, off-again romantic interest, but don't tell anyone—because he's my boss now.

His name is Steven Barlow. We worked together on my first official case, bringing down a local mob boss. It's true. Even Nashville had a mob circuit.

Barlow is the Chief of Homicide now so this thing between us has pretty much been slipped to the back burner. But I would be lying if I didn't confess I still get tingly whenever he's around. Except when I'm pissed off because of some decision he has made. He likes attempting to keep me away from danger. I understand his motivation on one level, but I hate it on all others because more often than not, it cramps my style.

He's not happy that I'm working this sting, but he'll get over it. Truth is, he's not thrilled about my change of heart where profiling and forensics are concerned. Most of Metro's brass would feel a lot better with me working crime scenes the way folks on the television program *CSI* do. But then I'd miss all the real fun.

Barlow and the rest need to get real. This is where I want to be. And it's homicide…the work revolves around unlawful death. Can't have unlawful death without a little danger.

Enough of the reflecting. Shameka still looks nervous. But she's hanging in there. I didn't feel totally comfortable about being across the street from her but the operation commander insisted it was the best strategy.

Still, my instincts were humming. *My gut says I should be over there with her.*

No sooner than I had taken two steps to put the thought into action than the watch on my left wrist started to vibrate. I glanced at its face, read the frantic message: *What the hell r u doin???*

You see, since I can't hear, the op commander can't communicate with me through the typical earpiece. Metro had this special watch designed just for me. It isn't just a watch, though it does show the time. It has a display for text messages similar to that of my cell phone for the hearing-impaired, only smaller.

The watch vibrated again, the same message flashing in warning.

I ignored the question. Just kept swaying my hips, the way I'd seen the other ladies of the night doing, and moving toward my destination.

"Hey, Shameka," I called out.

What's up, girl? She smiled, but her lips trembled with the effort, making reading her words a little tougher.

I sidled up next to her and flashed her the widest, most encouraging smile I could summon. "I was lonely way over there all by myself."

She looked directly at me and said, *Thank you.*

Her relief was palpable. She'd willingly put herself out on this limb to help capture a murderer, but she's only human. The fear wouldn't be denied. Has something to do with that danger Barlow likes me to avoid.

We chatted and laughed for nearly an hour while nothing happened. Understandably the rest of the team was getting antsy. The op commander would likely blame me if this whole effort turned out to be a bust. If I'd stayed on my side of the street...if I hadn't done this or that.... At least he didn't send me any more messages. I might not have a potty mouth, but I do have somewhat of a reputation for being obstinate. So shoot me.

Shameka is a civilian. She has feelings and I can't ignore those, not even to catch a suspected cop-killer.

The traffic had thinned for a bit but now it picked up again as folks left clubs and headed for all-night restaurants. Others were just beginning their nights at the bars and clubs. Within another hour the op would likely be shut down. As much as we all wanted to get this guy, this many resources couldn't be focused on one case forever.

My nerves jangled with anticipation. I surveyed each vehicle that approached our position while doing my level best to maintain a broad, inviting smile. I kept one hip cocked, showing off every inch of fishnet-clad thigh exposed between the hem of the micromini skirt and the top of the black leather boot.

God, the shoes were killing me.

Women who wear shoes like this have to be masochists. It just isn't normal.

The band on my wrist vibrated. As I started to

glance down at it, something in the edge of my peripheral vision snagged my attention.

Black pimped-up Caddy, moving slow.

The car swerved into the lane closest to our position.

My gaze collided with Clarence Johnson's at the exact instant that his weapon leveled in our direction.

"Get down!" I shouted.

I slammed my full weight into Shameka, forcing her down onto the sidewalk at the same instant that fire flew from the barrel of the sawed-off shotgun the perp wielded.

I snagged the weapon I'd tucked into my right boot and fired six times at the Caddy as it spun away, smoke boiling up from the rear tires.

I didn't have to hear the sirens or see the lights to know that Metro would be on that Caddy's tail. Unmarked cars came out of a dozen hiding places.

"You okay?" I surveyed Shameka as I scrambled up onto my hands and knees. The burn of scraped skin registered vaguely but I was more worried about her sluggish movements.

Shameka nodded as she struggled to an upright position. I'd hit her hard, but there hadn't been any time to do anything else. She moved disjointedly now and worry gnawed at me.

Then I saw the blood.

Darkening her red skirt from somewhere in the vicinity of her waist.

"Oh, God."

Shameka stared down at herself then at me in surprise. *He hit me.*

"You'll be all right," I promised.

People were suddenly all around us, beat cops as well as detectives. The paramedics on standby for this op pushed me aside to clear a path to the victim.

I maintained eye contact with Shameka until whatever they'd put in her IV for pain dragged her into unconsciousness. And then I just stood there, watching as they loaded her into the ambulance and drove away.

If she died…

No. I would not think that way. That dirtbag couldn't win. I shifted my attention in the direction where I'd last seen the Caddy. They had to catch Johnson.

Anything else was unacceptable.

The next morning I dropped into the chair behind my desk and attempted to focus on reports. It didn't matter that it was Saturday. Cops were cops 24/7.

I'd spent most of the night at the hospital.

Shameka was in stable condition. She'd made it through surgery with no problem. The surgeon had assured me she would fully recover. Two cops were stationed outside her room for protection.

Clarence Johnson would learn that she had survived.

The scumbag had gotten away.

I couldn't believe it.

Metro had found the Caddy. Apparently I'd hit him since there was blood in the front seat. Good. I hoped he died a slow, painful death and I didn't even feel guilty for thinking it.

Someone tapped me on the shoulder and I looked up to find Jesse Holderfield hovering over me.

Chief wants to see you. He rolled his eyes. *He's in a mood.*

"Thanks, Holderfield."

Jesse Holderfield reminded me a lot of my dad. Quiet, reserved. Nothing like you'd expect a homicide detective to be. But he was good. He had thirty years under his belt in this division.

I got up and headed toward the Chief of Homicide's office. His domain was down a long hall, just far enough away from the bull pen to maintain some of its dignity where decor is concerned.

Not that the bull pen was that bad. The place had a decent paint job even if the off-white color lacked creativity. The carpet was commercial-grade and beige. Each detective had his or her own cubicle, also beige. Standard-issue metal desks, each topped with a computer only one generation behind the current technology.

But the chief's office, now that was a different story. A plusher grade of carpeting. A nice cool blue color on the walls. To match his eyes, I mused.

But then I wasn't supposed to be noticing his eyes anymore.

And I knew exactly what Holderfield meant when he said the chief was in a mood.

I tapped on the door and stuck my head inside. "You wanted to see me?"

Have a seat, Detective.

Not Merri, like he used to call me, or even Walters.

Just plain old Detective. This was the game we played now. The vibes he gave off confused me—at times, it felt like he wanted to pick up where we left off after our first case, with a budding personal relationship. Other times, I was almost convinced he'd never felt anything for me at all.

I stepped into his domain and sat as ordered.

Steven Barlow had risen to the position of Chief of Homicide because he was most assuredly the best man for the job. His reputation as a detective was unparalleled, though I'm working on matching that record, and his dedication was legendary.

He looked great. Still wore his dark hair regulation short and no one, I mean no one, dressed as classy as Barlow. I had to smile. Yep, he looked amazing. Made me feel a little warm and fuzzy inside. I did so love to look at him.

And then his gaze connected with mine.

Amazing morphed directly into angry. He was not a happy camper, his expression reflected the mood Holderfield had mentioned.

We've spoken about this before.

The warm, fuzzy feeling evaporated.

Here it comes, the talk.

"Yeah, yeah, I know," I said, in an attempt to derail his momentum. We'd been through this a dozen times in the past year. "I take too many chances. I shouldn't have moved out of position. I had my orders and I didn't follow them. Let's cut to the chase here, Chief. Am I in trouble?"

God, I hoped not. I didn't want to get suspended or worse, fired. I hadn't come this far to throw it all away. I had done what I had to do. Any cop worth his or her salt would have done the same thing.

You understand that disobeying orders is a serious offense.

I understood, but I pretended not to notice. I'd found that feigning ignorance often got me off the hook.

Didn't appear to be working this time.

I swallowed, tried to read his expression. I shouldn't have bothered. Seeing more than what he wanted me to was impossible. He was too good at putting on the poker face. Just another skill that made him a good chief.

Made for figuring out this thing between us extra tough, as well.

"Yes, sir, I understand."

His expression changed ever so slightly with my response. Not quite a flinch but almost. Did it bother him that I didn't call him Barlow? At least I wasn't in this alone. We were both still adjusting to the roller-coaster-like changes in our relationship. Sometimes it felt as if I was the only one frustrated and confused…it was nice to know he felt it, too.

Your instincts were on target, he admitted as he shifted his gaze away from me. *The operation commander and I have discussed the issue and no formal disciplinary action will be taken considering the way things turned out.*

Relief surged through me. Though I didn't feel the

least bit repentant for what I'd done, I recognized the need for a chain of command.

This time, Barlow added.

"Thank you, sir." I would do better next time, maybe even ask permission to make an unexpected move. I chewed my lower lip. I hoped.

That intense gaze reconnected with mine and a brand-new flicker of fire shot through me. I shivered, hoped like heck he didn't notice. Those awesome lips parted and for a few seconds I thought he would say something like, I worry about you, Merri, or I couldn't live without you. He didn't.

For a couple of months now, he said, *we've been using you as a fill-in.*

Oh, well. I focused my mind on his words. It was true. Since coming back on board at Homicide after attending the academy, I hadn't been assigned a partner. Instead, I'd worked as a kind of floating detective, filling in wherever needed. It wasn't that bad. Gave me a chance to get to know all the detectives in my division. But I couldn't help feeling that I wasn't *official*…in a sense. I didn't complain, just went with the flow.

We're going to change that today.

'Bout time, I didn't say. However, I couldn't help wondering if this abrupt decision had anything to do with my actions last night. Maybe they thought I needed more structure. Someone to keep me in line.

I still didn't regret what I had done.

A new detective just transferred in from Hendersonville, Barlow explained. *He spent three years as a beat cop before taking the detective's exam. He graduated from the Forensics Academy just two weeks ago.*

Finally, someone newer than me. Sure he had the beat experience I didn't, but at least he didn't have a dozen years of homicide experience over me like everyone else around here. Metro also liked for all detectives to go through the ten-week course at the forensics academy, so the new guy was ahead of the game on that score, something we had in common.

"That's great. When can I meet him?"

I watched Barlow's lips as he responded, but I didn't miss the glimpse of something like reluctance in his eyes. *We'll get to that.*

Uh-oh. That didn't sound good. What was wrong with the new guy? Maybe he was physically challenged like me. You know, lame or mute or something. That would make us even. I could live with that.

Apparently he has some reservations about the assignment.

Fury whipped to a frenzied froth inside me before I could slow it down. So the new guy didn't want to work with the deaf girl. Another wave of anger washed over me on the heels of the thought. No matter how well-adjusted I appeared or how I told myself what other people thought didn't matter, my temper always flared whenever I encountered prejudice.

"Just because I'm deaf doesn't mean I'm not every bit as capable as he is," I argued. Just let me at the guy, I fumed. I'll show him.

Barlow looked away briefly but not quickly enough

for me to miss the abrupt amusement that flickered across his handsome face. Oh, yeah, I wasn't supposed to notice that he's handsome anymore. I tamped down the longing that had started building the moment I walked through his door. No matter that I tried to ignore it, it was always there, waiting to pounce on me whenever we shared the same airspace.

Oh, well, old habits were hard to break. I couldn't not notice how he looked…how he smelled, for Christ's sake. A new kind of confusion made me frown. Why would he find my feelings on the matter amusing?

He doesn't have a problem with your being deaf, Merri.

Merri. I melted a little more inside. No, no, I wasn't supposed to do that, either. Tough stuff. I couldn't stop the reaction. Just watching his lips form my name was a big-time turn on.

Then the rest of his words assimilated in my brain. "Then what does he have a problem with?" Jeez, it wasn't like I was incompetent or lazy. I worked hard. Graduated in the top five percent of my police academy class and the top three percent at the forensics academy. He was lucky to get me as a partner. Darn lucky.

He would prefer a male partner, Barlow said, his gaze reflecting the frankness no doubt in his tone.

Shock rumbled through me as realization penetrated the automatic denial. The new guy didn't want to work with me because I didn't have a penis? What century was this guy living in?

"Tell me you're kidding," I said, making my voice as flat with disbelief as possible. "That mentality went out with the seventies. Where's this dude been living?"

I liked the amusement I saw in Barlow's eyes but I was a little too ticked off to enjoy it as much as I should have.

Originally, Mr. Patterson is from Georgia.

Well that explained everything. Bulldogs weren't the only things Georgia boys were known for. They could be bullheaded, too. Not that I actually had anything against guys from Georgia, but my ex-fiancé was from Atlanta. Enough said.

"So, why not shuffle one of the other detectives to work with him," I offered. Heck, I could think of half a dozen of the detectives already in the division who would be happy to partner up with me. So far I got along with everybody except the folks in charge.

That's not the way I do things, Barlow said, all signs of amusement gone now. *Mr. Patterson will learn to fit in or he'll be gone.*

Another thought occurred to me. Barlow was big on the whole team-player motto. Maybe someone else would spend some time in the hot seat besides me. I could handle that.

I shrugged. "Bring him on. I'll teach him some proper manners."

Barlow let a smile peek through his stern expression and, well, let's just say that my heart did one of those tricky maneuvers best called a triple flip.

I'm certain you will. I'm counting on you to teach him the way we do things here.

"No problem. Remember, I grew up with four brothers. Patterson should brace himself." At this point I looked forward to the challenge.

As I watched, Barlow pressed the intercom button and asked his secretary to send in Mr. Patterson, which, of course, drew my attention to his hands. Long, strong fingers; wide, masculine hands.

Focus, Merri. You're about to meet your first partner and he's one of those macho types who thinks women can't do a man's job.

I found myself holding my breath as the door opened. I forced myself to relax, refused to be the slightest bit nervous as I shifted just enough to look back at him as he strode into Barlow's well-appointed office.

Tall, young...really young, maybe twenty-five or -six. Good-looking. But my grandmother had a saying, pretty is as pretty does. If he insisted on being a jerk about working with women, then that attitude would greatly depreciate the value of his handsome face.

Barlow stood. I did, as well, though I thought about keeping my seat just to remind him that ladies didn't have to stand when a man entered the room. Notice I didn't use the term *gentleman*.

Barlow shook Patterson's hand, then gestured to me. *Ray Patterson, this is Merri Walters.*

I thrust out my hand. "It's nice to meet you, Mr. Patterson." I plastered a smile into place.

He took my hand and shook it firmly. *Call me Ray.*

Okay. I don't know exactly how they do things in

Georgia, but up here in Tennessee when someone says, "Nice to meet you," a person generally says something like, "The pleasure is mine" whether they mean it or not. That he didn't only lowered my impression of him.

Ray turned to Barlow and I did the same, just in time to catch something about seat or seats. Barlow gestured to my chair and then I realized he'd said that we should take our seats.

Before I could settle back into mine I realized Ray had spoken to Barlow. I swung my attention back to him as he said *my position clear.* Man, I was a little slow on the uptake today. I'm generally much better at keeping up with a two-, even a three-way conversation.

I would prefer a male partner. Ray looked from Barlow to me. *I don't mean to offend you, Miss Walters, but in my experience women are too emotional. That natural fault makes female detectives too unreliable for my comfort.*

I told myself to think before I responded, but it was already too late. My mouth was in motion before my brain jumped into gear.

"I understand completely, Ray," I said with all the feigned patience I could muster. "But we all have our faults. If you won't hold being a woman against me, I'll try my best not to hold your stupidity against you."

Chapter 2

Sunday morning I slept in.

I'd stopped by the hospital after my shift ended yesterday. Shameka was out of the woods. Looked pretty damned good for a woman who'd been shot the night before. She thanked me repeatedly for saving her life. But she was the one who deserved the respect and gratitude. It had taken mega guts to put herself out there like that. And, though Johnson hadn't been caught yet, Shameka's efforts were not for naught.

Having drawn Johnson out into the open again, Metro now had hard evidence against Clarence Johnson, drug dealer, on-again off-again pimp and perpetual scumbag. Not to mention we had an eyewitness regarding Johnson's intentions on Friday night. A witness whose credibility would be impeccable with the DA as well as any judge on the circuit.

Me.

Up to now he'd been a mere suspect. All of Metro had been pretty darned sure he was their man, especially considering Shameka had insisted that Johnson was the one who'd shot the cop. She hadn't witnessed the shooting but she'd heard him brag about it. But still, we hadn't had the evidence we needed until now.

The man who'd killed Officer Ted Ferris had left some DNA evidence at the scene of the shooting. Apparently Ferris had injured his attacker. Blood not belonging to Ferris had been found on his uniform. The crime lab had stopped everything to run the needed tests on the blood they'd found in the abandoned Caddy.

I smiled. Clarence Johnson was a match. The blood wasn't proof positive that he'd killed Ferris, but it was solid evidence that he'd been there when Harris died. The scumbag was going down. All Metro had to do was find his sorry hide. Then again, maybe he'd crawled into some hole and bled to death. That would save the taxpayers having to foot the bill for his trial.

I still felt furious at my new partner. But I would have died before I'd have let him see how he annoyed me as we'd muddled through the day yesterday.

Introducing him around and showing him all the important destinations, such as evidence lock-up, the Chief of Detectives' office and the archives, my old stomping grounds, had been standard procedure. Ray

Patterson smiled and shook hands with everyone he met. He played the good-old-boy charm to the hilt.

Mostly I wanted to puke.

The guy was a fake. He pretended to be cool with his new assignment, specifically with me as his partner, and yet I had been in the room when he'd made his position more than clear to Barlow. He was the quintessential male chauvinist. A pig, no pun intended.

As I'd tossed and turned last night I'd considered why Barlow had decided to partner me up with a dinosaur mentality like Patterson. He could have easily shuffled someone else around. It wasn't unheard of. There might have been rumbles of complaints but it would have passed.

I knew Barlow. He was a smart man. His first loyalty was to the job. He had his reasons for doing this the way he did. I just wasn't privy to them yet. As much as I disliked the idea of working with a guy who considered himself a better cop than me simply because he was a man, I trusted Barlow's judgment. We might not be able to work out our personal feelings but the guy had it on the ball where his work was concerned.

I felt totally confident that his reasons would be revealed eventually. And all would have been for the best for all concerned. The question was, would Patterson live to see it?

My lips quirked.

I padded into the kitchen for more coffee. As I surveyed the room I considered whether or not I really

wanted to jump into a kitchen renovation. I'd been
thinking about it since I returned from the academy.
My whole house could use an update. Though I liked
the cottage-style, it was getting a little worn. New cab-
inets and countertop, definitely new appliances would
be good. The hardwood floors throughout I would
keep, but a fresh coat of paint and maybe some new
slipcovers for the living room furniture. Maybe.

I thought about calling my mom to see if she'd heard
from Sarah or Michael this weekend.

Michael is one of my brothers. He's also a fireman
in Brentwood. His wife, Sarah, was my best friend all
through high school. We've always been like sisters,
which is great, since I never had one for real. She's also
the Chief of Detectives, Barlow's boss', secretary. But
more important, she's pregnant, due any second. This
was actually her second pregnancy—she'd lost the first
baby at six weeks. That was a tough time but she and
my brother had been determined and they'd gotten
through it. Her maternity leave from work had started
a week ago. I missed her smiling face around Metro but
I sure was happy for her.

The arrival of the first grandchild in any family is a
monumental occasion. But in my family it ranked right
up there with the second coming of Christ. We could
hardly wait for this baby to come.

I would be turning thirty-one in a couple of months
with no prospects of marriage, much less childbearing. I don't have a problem with that. I love kids.
I definitely love men and sex. But I'm still enjoying my

second career and my newfound independence. Besides, staying unattached was so simple. Love was too complicated…still, the sex part would be nice. Truth is, like most women, I told myself what I wanted to hear. I didn't have any offers, so I focused on my career and, for now, that was for the best.

Besides, whenever I thought of sex…I thought of Steven Barlow and what it might be like to have hot, frantic sex with him. We'd kissed, but nothing else. And every time I let myself dwell on how much I wanted him…well, it wasn't good. I got all frustrated and then I started thinking about another man, one as equally forbidden, or maybe more so, as Barlow. Mason Conrad. He was totally off limits. I'd been undercover to take down that mob boss I told you about and he'd been one of the bad guys. But that didn't stop us from connecting in a big way. What we'd shared, which wasn't actually sex, but had the same result, had rattled me, still did, when I obsessed on the memories. Hanging on to my feelings for Barlow was probably all that had saved me from a monumental mistake.

The smell of overheated coffee made my nose twitch and dragged me away from thoughts of my lackluster sex life. I should make a fresh pot. Feeling lazy, I tightened the sash of my robe and opted for taking my chances with the already brewed stuff. If I could drink the junk at the office I could handle anything.

Getting back to my personal life—I've always been an independent woman…to an extent. I guess I didn't realize how cautious I'd actually been or how far I'd gone out of the way to avoid risk in my professional life until the hearing loss happened. In the process of relearning to live my life, I'd come to understand there was more I wanted to do.

Much more.

This was right where I wanted to be.

Ray Patterson had better watch out. I had every intention of showing him what a woman could do. Including leaving him in the dust on our first assignment.

The light above the door leading from the living room into the kitchen flashed, alerting me to another phone call.

I missed the little things, I considered as I made my way into the living room. A ringing phone, a dripping faucet. All those irritating noises you wished would go away forever. Guess what? You missed them.

This time the caller ID showed Metro dispatch. Not a good start to a Sunday morning. I should have gone to IHOP. Now I would end up going to work hungry.

"Walters."

I watched the display as the words spilled across. A possible homicide victim had been discovered. The location came next. I recognized the Green Hills neighborhood. Patterson and I had our first case.

Now we'd see what the guy had to back up all that macho bluster.

I headed to my bedroom to change. Thank God my usual uniform didn't include fishnets or stilettos.

To my surprise Chief Barlow waited at the crime scene.

The lessons I'd learned at the forensics academy immediately kicked in, drawing my attention to the grisly details of the scene that had been cordoned off by yellow tape.

According to the uniform who filled me in, the body had been discovered by a young woman walking her dog. A walking trail between a swanky residential area and a shopping mall provided the background.

The techs were already in place, marking potential evidence and snapping photographs. The medical examiner's van arrived as I walked over to speak with Barlow.

I wanted to see the body but since he stood between me and it, I took that as my cue.

"What've we got?" I can't tell you how many times I've heard detectives in movies ask that same question. God, I'm turning into a cliché.

Just like the Harrison murder, Barlow told me.

It wasn't necessary to analyze the grim expression on his face or the statement to understand what he meant. I had worked the Harrison murder, which was still unsolved.

Reba Harrison had been found scarcely a block from her upscale home. The primary detail that stood out in my mind about the case was the brutal way in which she had been raped.

Most of the sexual activity had taken place while she was still alive, but not all. The foreplay leading up to murder had lasted several hours. The bruising around the wrists and the ankles indicated she had been restrained most of that time. She'd been strangled with the same type of cord used to restrain her.

Finally, her body, adorned with nothing more than exaggerated makeup and a tiara, had been dumped in the meticulously landscaped bushes along her street.

"Has the victim been identified?" As I asked this question my new partner strolled up next to me. I didn't bother saying good morning. Clearly it wasn't going to be one.

Barlow acknowledged Patterson's presence with a nod then said to me, *Mallory Wells. Twenty-four. Single. Moved to Nashville three years ago to break into the country music business.*

Just like Reba Harrison, only Reba had been a life-time resident. She'd had the same professional aspirations.

Looks like we've got ourselves a serial killer.

This from Patterson.

I resisted the urge to say *duh.* What he didn't know was that we had already made that connection when Reba Harrison died. Almost every step of her murder matched those of a suspected serial killer from four years ago, before my time. The killer had murdered six women in the Nashville area, all involved with the country-music business on one level or the other, then he'd apparently disappeared. The case was still unsolved.

Perhaps, Barlow allowed. *The evidence will confirm or refute that conclusion.*

I knew Barlow was thinking the very same thing I was, this guy is back, but I couldn't help reveling in his noncommittal response to my cocky partner. Before I had time to fully enjoy the moment, Barlow shifted his full attention back to me.

I'll need you and Patterson to focus solely on this case, in the event the two murders are connected to each other or to any past cases. I'll be passing the Johnson case to Holderfield.

I opened my mouth to argue and Barlow motioned for me to follow him away from the fray of ongoing activity.

Patterson had the good sense to make himself scarce.

"You know that's my case, too," I said the instant Barlow stopped and shifted his attention back to me. "Shameka is my witness and Johnson is my perp. It's my job to help find him." It was the least I could do after what Shameka had gone through.

Those analyzing blue eyes studied me a moment before he spoke. Barlow did that a lot. He liked to mull over what he wanted to say before he opened his mouth. Saved him the taste of shoe leather quite frequently, I reasoned. I should take a page from that book. But then, I had pretty much acquired a taste for the stuff. Why change now?

We're going to get Johnson. He's made. Every cop in the city wants him. This one— he glanced toward the victim and the crime-scene techs circling around her —*is going to be different. If it's connected to those old murders, I don't want the killer to get away this time. I want your keen eye on this one, Merri. I need my best and freshest on it.*

Okay. He'd earned himself some major points with that monologue. Still, I couldn't help thinking he was only doing this to get me off the Johnson case. It seemed like every time I got close to nabbing a perp he hustled me out of harm's way. This turn of events sounded suspiciously like that. Johnson had seen me just as clearly as I'd seen him. He would likely want revenge for those who set him up, and it wouldn't take a scientist to figure out I'd been part of a sting. I knew how guys like him thought. He was going down, he had nothing to lose. That put me in the line of fire right along with Shameka.

Irritation niggled at me. I'll bet if I checked the roster I would find that a unit had been stationed outside my house since the op to take down Johnson went sour. Part of me understood that was a reasonable move, but another part, the side that worried my hearing impairment would be considered first and foremost even before my skill level, didn't like the idea that he thought I couldn't take care of myself.

"I guess I should be flattered," I said, allowing him to hear the skepticism I felt. "I'm assuming I'm lead." I had seniority over Patterson so that should have been a given, but I wanted the point clarified.

You're lead. Patterson will fall in line.

Maybe he would and maybe he wouldn't, but either way this investigation would be conducted my way.

"I'll let you bring him up to speed," I offered charitably. He was here, might as well make himself useful. I had a crime scene to analyze. "You know more about the old cases than I do."

Barlow held my gaze for a few pulse-pounding seconds and I was certain he wanted to say something more, but he didn't. That's when I walked away. If he could let it go, so could I.

After slipping on shoe covers and latex gloves, I moved beyond the yellow tape that visually declared the boundaries of the scene.

The shrubbery appeared undisturbed. The path was decorative gravel, which basically ensured there wouldn't be any usable pedestrian or vehicle tracks.

Like the first victim, Miss Wells was nude. The bruising around the ligature marks on her wrists and ankles indicated she had been forcibly restrained. The additional bruising apparent on her thighs suggested rape or some seriously rough sexual activity but the M.E. would confirm that conclusion once the body was in his territory at the lab.

Her eyes were open, a frozen mask of terror on her face, also like the previous victim. Makeup had been applied to the point of appearing grotesque and clownish. The tiara sat atop her head as if it had been carefully placed there after her body was dumped. Probably had been.

Any jewelry she had worn had been removed, either for the purpose of financial gain or as mementoes of the deed. Dropping into a crouch I leaned closer and peered at her fingers. She'd worn something on her right ring finger. Maybe a high-school ring, judging by the width of the tan line. Any other personal items, including clothing, she'd had in her possession at the time of death wouldn't be found if this murder followed the same MO—modus operandi—as the Harrison murder.

There was no way to know just yet whether the guy collected the items or disposed of them, either to prevent the possibility of leaving evidence behind or for cold hard cash since nothing had been recovered. I had to operate under the assumption that this case wasn't related to any other…until something proved otherwise. The similarities to the old cases were becoming glaringly more obvious.

For example, the last victim, Reba Harrison. Though she had been repeatedly and savagely raped, not a single speck of semen, not one body hair, not even a trace of saliva that didn't belong to the victim had been recovered from her body. It was as if a phantom had carried out the horrific crime.

Considering the hours the perp took to do the job, it was outright amazing he didn't leave behind so much as a molecule of evidence, physical or biological.

The tech working on the other side of the body looked up abruptly. I did the same. Patterson stood behind me and had apparently spoken.

Time for him to understand the situation.

"I should explain something to you," I said as I pushed to my feet. I moved a few feet away from the body and the nosy tech still doing his job. Patterson followed somewhat reluctantly.

Yeah?

"I'm deaf, Detective Patterson." I didn't call him Ray as he'd insisted I should do when we first met.

"There's no magic hearing aid. I can't hear anything you say. The only way I know what you want to tell me is if I'm looking at your face. I read lips. When you have something to tell me you need to make me aware that you intend to speak. Especially if my back is turned to you."

He didn't bother hiding the fact that he was put off by the nuisance.

Gotcha. He shoved his gloved hands into his pockets. *I'll get the hang of it.*

It was going to be a long day.

I glanced at Barlow and caught him watching us. I shivered in spite of myself. He shouldn't even be here. But then, this case had just taken a turn for the worse. A single, random act of violence was one thing, but an encore performance down to the last detail made everyone in law enforcement nervous. Especially when it smacked of a past investigation, one still unsolved and marring Metro's record.

There was work to do. What-ifs weren't my concern right now, this latest victim was. I turned to my new partner. His attention was riveted to the victim. I wished I could read his mind.

Whatever Barlow's motivation for teaming me up with this guy, I was reasonably sure I had gotten the short end of the stick.

Dr. Ammon, the M.E., agreed to push Miss Wells to the front of the autopsy line considering it was possible that we had a serial killer, one who may have lain dormant for four years, at work.

Patterson and I left the crime scene shortly after the body and headed to the lab to view the preliminary procedure. Since we had arrived at the scene in different vehicles, we left it that way.

We suited up, gloves, shoe covers and gown, before entering the exam room.

Dr. Ammon, a man of Middle-Eastern decent, stood about three inches shorter than me. Not a large man by any stretch of the imagination. Fifty or fifty-five. Wore a shiny gold band on his left ring finger. Pictures of half a dozen kids graced his desk.

The thick glasses he wore indicated he was likely blind as a bat without them. He was known for his close attention to detail. Ammon didn't miss anything. I was glad he was the one on call today.

Extensive sexual assault, he noted aloud for the purposes of the audio tape. I didn't hear him, of course, but I read the words on his lips. *I call it assault because the activity was so savage,* he clarified with a glance over his glasses at me.

Dr. Ammon shoved his glasses up the bridge of his nose as he studied the victim's ankles. *The ligature marks appear the same size and depth as on the previous victim, indicating a similar material was used for restraint. Perhaps a nylon cord.* I appreciated that he always looked at me when he spoke. Not everyone thought to do that, forcing me to remind them.

"No semen this time?" I asked. I was hoping the

perp had made a mistake this go-round. If this victim turned out as clean as Reba Harrison, this case would only get more frustrating.

Ammon glanced at his assistant who was peering into a microscope at specimens. The assistant said something, but I could only see his profile so I missed it entirely. My gaze shifted back to Ammon who shook his head. *No semen as of yet.*

Damn.

I noticed Patterson looking away as Ammon thoroughly examined the victim's pubic area. Maybe the guy had a conscience after all, or at least limits on his comfort zone. Even I felt like an interloper as that part of the examination proceeded. I felt sorry for the victim. No matter that she was dead, this business was humiliating.

The M.E. lifted a number of hairs and placed them on a slide. Anticipation surged past my softer emotions. All we needed was one break. One piece of evidence we could use to nail the bastard, assuming we figured out who he was. That sounds dumb, but there's nothing worse than catching a perp, knowing in your gut he's the one and not being able to prove it in a court of law.

Ammon moved to the table where his assistant worked and slipped the slide into another microscope.

I surveyed the victim's body once more. She looked different under the harsh lights of the lab. The marbling of her cold skin gave her a blue-gray hue. She'd definitely taken good care of herself. Worked out daily, I'd bet. The breasts were store-bought. An incision beneath each one gave away her secret. She had probably taken out all the stops to make her dream of fame and fortune happen.

My gaze shifted up to my partner, who stood on the other side of the examining table. He shook his head and looked at me. *Another starlet bites the dust.*

God, I hated those kinds of labels. The case from four years ago had been called the Starlet Murders. I hoped like hell that if we discovered these two recent murders were committed by the same perp, we would change that.

Patterson's head turned toward the M.E., alerting me that the doc was saying something.

…got lucky. I have a couple of hairs that don't belong with this body.

But they could be someone else's. Not necessarily the perp's. That possibility hampered the enthusiasm I wanted so much to feel.

"She could have picked them up at the scene or during an encounter of some sort prior to her final one with the perp," I proposed.

Ammon shrugged. *Possibly, but there's always a chance one or both could belong to the killer or killers, considering they don't match. I have hair samples from three different individuals here.*

What a lucky break that would be.

When Ammon had finished looking for fingerprints, hairs, trace fibers, etc., on the victim's skin, I was ready to go. I had no desire to witness the inhuman mutilation of the body. Certainly I understood that the procedure was necessary, but I still didn't care to stand around and watch.

Patterson sauntered out alongside me. If he'd been the least bit squeamish about any of the procedures, other than the genitalia exam, he'd kept it to himself. He had nothing on me there. I could hang with the best of them. I was the only one in my class at the forensics academy who hadn't thrown up the first time watching an autopsy.

When I reached my Jetta, Patterson hesitated before moving on to his own vehicle, a big shiny red SUV. Figures.

Barlow talked to me this morning, he said, looking straight at me as he did so.

I told myself to hear him out before I jumped to any conclusions. "Oh, yeah?"

Patterson nodded. *He wants this partnership to work out.* He shrugged nonchalantly. *I just wanted you to know I plan to do my part.*

How sporting of him.

"That's great, Patterson. Why don't we get on down to the office and we can both do our part."

He looked uncertain as to whether my comment was positive or not. But only for a couple of seconds. *See you there.* Then he sauntered on over to his big, macho-man SUV and climbed aboard. I had two brothers who drove vehicles very similar to that. Gas hogs.

I slid behind the wheel of my conservative, ultra-efficient Jetta and headed for Metro.

I didn't want Barlow running interference between Patterson and me. We needed to work out this relationship on our own. On my terms, of course. I planned to keep that part to myself.

I considered Patterson's actions at the scene and then in the lab. He hadn't said a hell of a lot about the case. Just that one remark about having a serial killer on our hands. If he was half as good a cop as Barlow thought he was, he'd surely formed a number of conclusions. Just as I had.

But he'd kept them to himself.

Maybe that was partly my fault. I hadn't mentioned any of my thoughts thus far. I suppose I couldn't blame him for doing the same thing.

As soon as the stench of death had cleared from my senses, I would make an effort and invite him out to lunch. It was Sunday, might as well make the most of it. Break the ice so to speak.

But first we had to see what we could find on Mallory Wells and look for any connection, if one existed, between her and Reba Harrison. We could start at her place of residence.

Verifying the similarities between this murder and the ones four years ago wasn't necessary, I could already see that we either had a copycat on our hands or an old killer was back in business.

Someone in Nashville was killing young women who were chasing after the stars, literally and figuratively. Reba Harrison had been a known groupie for at least two country music stars, but she was also a singer herself.

If there was a connection we hadn't discovered yet between Reba Harrison and Mallory Wells, that link could lead us to the killer.

But it would never be that easy.

Nothing ever was.

Chapter 3

Being nice is definitely overrated.

If I'd ever thought otherwise, I knew differently now.

Ray Patterson might be younger than me, with less seniority in the Homicide Division, but that didn't stop him from bucking to be the boss. Or from being nosy as hell.

The chief seems awfully protective of you. You think it's because of your hearing impairment?

See what I mean?

"He's concerned about all his detectives," I countered, a subtle warning of *don't go there* in my tone. "That's his job. He knows our strengths and weaknesses. That's how he decides who would be best on what case when it comes to something like this."

Like the Starlet Murders, you mean, he suggested.

There he went, using that old moniker. I mean, maybe it's because I'm a woman, but I just didn't like it. In my opinion the case should be called the Jealous Male Scumbag Murders.

Thank God the food arrived. Kept me from saying something Barlow would probably make me regret. I imagine Patterson took my grunt for a positive response since he didn't pursue the subject further.

The deli-style restaurant was one of my favorites in town. A quaint little sandwich shop near Metro. Between the police force and other city workers, the place never hurt for business. Since most grabbed their sandwiches on the run, dining in was never a problem and could always be counted on for a relaxing environment, especially on a Sunday afternoon.

My thoughts drifted back to the case. Mallory Wells's home had revealed the same as Reba Harrison's—nothing. Typical single, white, working-female abodes. The murders definitely hadn't happened in either place.

I read the file on the Reba Harrison murder and some of the reports from the Starlet cases.

I wasn't surprised. A good cop would want to be prepared whether he landed a case or not. It paid to stay up to speed on the goings-on in the city, especially those in your division.

"What'd you think?" I took a bite of my turkey sub and chewed as he considered what he wanted to say.

Twenty-seven. College drop-out. Had her heart set on a career in country music.

That told me what he'd read but it didn't answer my question. "Reba was good," I countered. "Just a few days before her murder she'd been invited to sing at the Wild Horse." That was a big step in a new performer's career—maybe my new partner wasn't aware of that. Reba Harrison hadn't even gotten a CD on the market and already her talent was gaining some momentum.

Patterson nodded. *In more ways than one. Had herself an affair with Chase Taylor. Apparently it was no secret, although his wife claimed she had no idea the two had been involved. Adultery is a pretty good motive for murder.*

"Since the sexual assault continued after the murder, that pretty much discounts Taylor's wife," I argued. "And Taylor had an airtight alibi." He'd been on stage at the Grand Ole Opry at the time. A few thousand people had been watching. The affair between him and Harrison had happened ages ago and wasn't relevant, in my opinion.

Patterson swallowed a mouthful of ham on rye, then said, *He could have paid someone to do it. Someone who took things a little farther than he'd been paid for.*

"That's a possibility. That avenue has been under investigation." I shrugged. "But the dynamics of that murder have changed now. Unless, of course, we can find a similar connection between Mr. Chase Taylor and our latest victim." Not to mention we had to keep in the back of our minds that we had a four-year-old unsolved serial investigation that mirrored almost exactly our two current cases.

Unless his hired killer decided to have some more fun on the side for no extra charge.

It wasn't that his suggestion was completely impossible, it was simply highly unlikely.

"It's our job to find out what happened," I said, as much of an agreement as he was going to get out of me on that one. We would definitely check out every avenue. Leave no rock unturned, as the old saying goes. "It's possible that our killer remembers the Starlet cases and hoped to disguise his killings that way, shift our focus. That's why we can't assume anything at this point."

Something about the way he looked at me then riled my temper but I kept my mouth shut. No point making something of it. He was likely curious about the deaf woman. It wouldn't be the first time I'd gotten one of those looks. I knew exactly what it meant.

Weren't you once engaged to Heath Woods?

Boy, I hadn't seen that one coming, even this close. I blinked, startled. My personal life, past or present, was none of his business. That he had the brass balls to ask surprised me.

I mean, he clarified, obviously sensing my discomfort, *he's in the business. Would he be a source of inside information we could tap?*

Did he really think I hadn't thought of that? Please.

If you don't feel comfortable talking to him, Patterson suggested, *I'll be glad to do it.*

No way. If anyone talked to Heath it would be me.

"He's away on some secret vacation," I said pointedly. "None of his people can get in touch with him. Believe me, I've made life difficult enough for them. He can't be reached. I'll be the first person they call when he's found."

Patterson shrugged. *Oh.*

I studied my new partner a moment, decided that at least he was beginning to share his thoughts. I suddenly wondered if there was a woman in his life. He was certainly cute enough. Thick brown hair cut short for easy care, and because it looked damned good that way. Matching brown eyes. I realized then that I actually knew very little about him.

"What's the story with you?" I found myself asking. I hadn't actually meant to, but the question was on the table. There was no taking it back.

This time he was the one taken aback by the direction of the conversation. *What do you mean?*

Like he didn't know.

"You have a girlfriend? Engaged?" I shrugged. "Any family in the area?" Might as well get the whole story while I was at it.

I don't have a significant other, and I don't like mixing my personal life with the job.

His closed expression along with the stern line of his jaw told me he'd made the statement quite sharply.

Before I got all ticked off again, I reminded myself that my prying into his business would likely keep him wary of digging into mine. He would be scared to death I'd ask him something else. So, my snoopy question had, in a roundabout way, served my purposes, as well. And, jeez, he was the one who'd started it.

"We should get back to the office and start that digging expedition." I gathered my leftovers and stood. "I'll see you there."

After making a drop at the trash receptacle I headed for the door. As I settled into my Jetta, Patterson made his exit. He didn't look my way, just walked straight over to his big red SUV and climbed in.

Although I couldn't lay my finger on the problem, something about Patterson didn't sit as it should with me. He didn't mind saying right up front that he had a problem with a female partner, nor did he hesitate to ask me about my ex-fiancé. But when I asked a straightforward question about his marital status, he balked. Hmmm. Interesting. What was my new partner hiding? A messy divorce? A tawdry affair? A work-related situation? That could explain his reasons for not wanting to work with a woman.

It looked as if I might have a little extra digging to do. After all, one couldn't go into a relationship of any kind without all the facts.

The victim, Mallory Wells, had changed a number of things about herself, besides her cup size, after coming to Nashville. Her real name was Margaret Anita Wellersby. In addition to changing her name, she'd had her nose done and breast augmentation at the suggestion of a music video producer with whom she'd had a brief relationship. It was still unclear what she'd done in the way of repayment for the costly surgical procedures, since her financial resources had been somewhat limited.

My best guess was that the producer and the cosmetic surgeon had a racket going on. The surgeon worked cheaper than usual, but had lots of extra business thrown his way by the producer. The producer got his kickback in the way of sexual favors from the prospective patients. Or maybe both men enjoyed the perks of their alliance.

Sick, huh?

The producer, Rex Lane, and the surgeon, Xavier Santos, were now at the top of my super-short suspect list. Especially since Reba Harrison had been an extra in a music video by Rex Lane's company, Lucky Lane Productions. That particular aspect of Miss Harrison's past hadn't been significant until now.

I can track down the surgeon, Patterson offered. *I know the places his type likes to hang out.*

Another curiosity-arousing statement. Patterson didn't look like the country-club type. "I'll take the producer." No problem. They both had to be questioned.

Patterson gave me a nod and left my cubicle.

While we're on the subject of cubicles, I should mention that the term is probably not the right one to use. I don't have any walls around my desk. Mostly I have my space. About a yard of beige carpet all the way around my beige metal desk. There's a chair, also metal but embellished with a little fake leather, sitting in front of it for interviewing folks or conferencing with one's partner.

I was somewhat protective of my space. The day the desk had been pointed out to me I'd taken steps to make it mine. Framed family photos and a mug turned pencil holder were my only personal items on top of the desk. The mug had been given to me by the kids in my last class as a teacher. In an effort to clearly delineate the boundaries of my space, I'd brought in a six-by-eight burgundy rug to go beneath my desk. Needless to say, no one else had marked their territory in such a way. Coffee stains and the like were about all that surrounded the other detectives' desks, even the other two that belonged to females.

Oh, well, I'd always been different. Why change now?

I downed the last of my coffee, grimaced, and grabbed my purse. Sometimes I carried my gun in my purse, but only when I couldn't wear my shoulder holster. I preferred the latter. The .9-millimeter made my purse weigh a ton.

However, wearing the shoulder holster sort of dictated my wardrobe. It usually meant I would need to wear a jacket to hide it. Not a problem, because jackets were okay with me. Today I wore navy slacks—my favorite color—and a soft baby-blue blouse with a navy jacket, short cropped with no pockets and a cool zipper instead of buttons. The shoes were sensible pumps with two-inch heels. No one would vote me the best-dressed woman in Nashville, but I looked reasonably snazzy for a cop.

The drive to Franklin didn't take that long. Mr. Rex Lane lived in one of the more glamorous residential neighborhoods of Franklin. So did a lot of stars. Franklin and Brentwood were the two most popular areas outside Nashville. The commute was short and the houses were huge with masterfully landscaped lots. Though Patterson and I were supposed to be a team, time was of the essence here. Splitting up was the most efficient way to do the job.

I stopped at the gate and pressed the intercom button. I felt sure Mr. Lane wouldn't like having unannounced company on a Sunday afternoon, but I didn't want to give him an opportunity to be away when I showed up at his door.

I laid my hand on the speaker to feel the vibration when and if someone answered. Worked like a charm.

After moving my hand, I said, "Detective Merrilee Walters, Metro Homicide, to see Mr. Rex Lane." I quickly placed my hand back on the front of the speaker and waited. I didn't get an audible response but the gates began a slow swing inward. I took that as a "come on in" sign.

When the gates yawned open fully, I let off the brake, allowing the Jetta to roll forward. The driveway sprawled out before me, a good half mile long. As gorgeous as the landscape was, it didn't hold a candle to the circular parking patio in front of the house. A large fountain amid the seeming acres of cobblestone lent an old-world flair.

"Big bucks," I muttered. This guy was making some

major money in the video business. My ex had always said that these guys made almost as much money as the performers themselves. Definitely beat out the songwriters, he'd complained. Though Heath appeared to be doing pretty well these days. I'd noticed that one of his new songs, performed by a seasoned veteran, had topped all the charts.

Good for him, I mused. Maybe he'd choke on all the money he was probably making. No hard feelings.

As I got out of my car, the front door opened and the man himself, Rex Lane that is, stepped out onto the granite landing that stood at the top of about a dozen matching steps. Wide, luxurious steps. No expense had been spared in making this Italianate-style home an awe-inspiring mansion.

Detective Walters, what brings you to my home on a Sunday afternoon? he asked with a polite smile.

Well-washed jeans, a comfortable striped buttondown shirt and leather Birkenstocks dressed the man who looked around thirty when the background I'd pulled up indicated he would turn forty this year. Maybe the good doctor had done his partner in crime a few favors.

Back up, Merri, I told myself. I hadn't proven the two were partners in anything just yet.

"I have a few questions for you regarding one of your clients," I said as I climbed the elegant steps.

This client has a name, I presume, he said as I took the final step, bringing me up alongside him on the wide landing gracing the front of the mansion.

"Had," I corrected. "She's dead."

That got his attention, just as I'd intended.

The expression on his face shifted from annoyed to startled. *Come in, Detective.*

He opened the door and gestured for me to enter before him. As I did I couldn't help but notice his—or the decorator's—exquisite taste followed through to the interior. Marble-floored entry. Soaring ceilings. Beautiful artwork and tapestries. Marvelous antique pieces made up the furnishings.

I could almost smell the money.

Lots and lots of the stuff.

He said something I missed as he turned to lead the way to wherever he wanted to do this. I followed, kept an eye on his profile in case he said something else, despite my desire to admire the decorating.

When he led me into a parlor, he asked, *Would you like something to drink, Detective?*

"No, thank you."

He indicated the sofa and I sat. He settled into a leather chair directly across from me.

How can I help you?

That he didn't prod some more for the client's name alerted me to his nervousness and the possibility that he already knew.

"I'm sure you remember a client who came to you a few months ago named Mallory Wells." This was a statement, not a question. I didn't want to give him an easy out. I wanted him to worry about just how much I knew.

He took his time answering. Most of that time he used to arrange his expression into a thoroughly unreadable one. But he didn't accomplish that before I picked up on surprise and then a moment of horror that wilted into remorse. He hadn't known she was dead. He felt sick at the idea.

Both of those things helped lower his ranking on my suspect scale.

But I didn't mention that to him. Let him sweat.

Yes. He moistened his lips. His posture grew considerably more rigid. *I knew her quite well, as a matter of fact.*

"It's my understanding the two of you were involved in an intimate relationship," I said bluntly. Now this is a tactic known in cop world, or in poker, as bluffing. You take rumor and innuendo, or maybe a wild guess, and formulate a theory. In other words, you lie. Sometimes it worked, sometimes it didn't.

He blinked. *I wouldn't call our relationship intimate,* he hedged.

This time it worked.

"What would you call it?" I pressed. I wanted to ask him the most personal questions while the shock was still new.

It was intense but mostly about business.

"But you knew her in the biblical sense." Another statement of presumed fact that would amp up his discomfort.

We slept together once, he insisted without meeting my eyes. *That was the only time.*

So far so good. That he admitted having had sex with her surprised me. I wondered if he assumed I had evidence to back up my assessment. Apparently. "Did you part on bad terms?" I stayed clear of specific adjectives on this point. I didn't want to lead him, I just wanted to prompt him.

He gave a halfhearted shrug. *I suppose you could say that. She wanted more than I could give her.*

I found Mr. Lane's honesty refreshing. He was either totally innocent or completely stupid.

"Love?" I suggested.

He shook his head. *Nothing like that. She wanted to be a star.* He rubbed at his eyes with his thumb and forefinger before meeting my gaze once more. *That wasn't going to happen. She was a nice girl and I liked her, but she wasn't star material.*

The worst kind of heartache. In my experience with the entertainment business, a guy could break a girl's heart and she would get over it, but having him doubt her ability to become a star, well, that was a whole other epic struggle.

"How did she take it?"

Not well. She egged my Bentley.

Poor guy. I resisted the urge to roll my eyes.

Then she spread rumors about me to my friends.

"Rumors?" My curiosity piqued again. This could be significant. Maybe she got involved with the wrong people in an effort to get back at Lane.

That I was gay. He made one of those faces that said he was mortified and very nearly mortally wounded. *I can't believe she would do that. We may have had only one night but she had to know.*

That her final hours had been spent engaged in violent sex flitted through my mind. A scorned man might very well see that as the perfect revenge.

"When did you last see her, Mr. Lane?" I purposely made my voice accusing. I wanted him to squirm some more.

He shifted in his chair. Excellent.

Let me see. Another shift of position. *Perhaps two weeks ago. There was a party.* He waved a hand. *You know the type, where everyone who's anyone makes an appearance.*

Yeah, I knew the type. I'd been to a couple myself. Before. But that was another story. Another life. Definitely not anything I wanted to dwell on today.

Mallory had too much to drink, as usual, he went on. *She completely embarrassed herself.*

"Who was she with at this party?" That information could be very useful. Could give me a contact who'd had more recent dealings with the victim.

His brow furrowed in concentration. *Jones.* He scrubbed his hand over his chin. *The new guy making all the circuits. I haven't had the pleasure of working with him. TriStar got him.*

Rafe Jones. Young. Gorgeous. A little wild, according to the gossip rags. A rising star, according to country-music gurus. He had that controversial country-rap style down to a personal style that appeared to suit his sexy persona.

TriStar was another music video company in Nashville. The biggest, actually. A new company that had breezed into town three years ago and knocked the old-timers out of the top spot. Most likely made a few enemies in the process.

"Can you think of any reason someone would want to kill Miss Wells?"

He thought about my question for a time then shook his head. *Not really. She could be cloying but she wasn't a bad girl. And it wasn't that she lacked talent, she simply didn't have that star quality. The club circuit was the best she could ever hope for.*

"Like Reba Harrison?"

This question startled him all over again.

"She was one of your clients, as well," I went on. "Did the two of you have a physical relationship?"

No. Strictly business. She hadn't been my client in almost a year. And you're wrong—she had real talent.

That might be true but he was not telling me everything. The way he kept his eyes averted and allowed his hands to fidget told the tale.

"She had been invited to play the Wild Horse."

Yes, I know. He met my gaze briefly. *Her death was quite a shame.*

I found it surprising that he would know her agenda if they'd no longer had a business relationship. "You keep up with who's playing at the Wild Horse?"

He looked surprised at the question but quickly recovered. *Detective Walters, I keep up with everything related to this business. It's what I do.*

Okay, I guess his answer wasn't as surprising as I'd thought.

I stood and thrust out my hand. He got to his feet almost awkwardly and took it. The brief exchange revealed a sweaty palm and a shaky grip.

"Please let me know if you remember anything else that might be useful to this investigation." I took a card from my shoulder bag and passed it to him. "No matter how seemingly insignificant. You never know what will make or break a case."

He saw me to the door. I stopped there, frowned in concentration a moment then said, "By the way, do you know of any reason someone would be out to make you look bad?"

His face paled. *Certainly not.*

"With two murders victims linked to Lucky Lane Productions, it looks like being on your client list is hazardous to a girl's health."

I left, closed the door behind me. I wanted him to think about what I said…stew over it. I could imagine him leaning against the massive wood door and trying to pull himself back together.

Maybe he was innocent, and personally I leaned in that direction, but he was nervous. A one-night stand with a client who got herself murdered didn't make him guilty, but something about the case made him edgy.

My guess was he knew something he wasn't telling.

That seemed to be the theme for the day.

Secrets.

I didn't like secrets.

The trip back to Nashville turned interesting as I neared my neighborhood. I'd noticed the car following me a few miles back. Several unnecessary turns had confirmed that the vehicle was, indeed, on my tail.

So I did what any fired-up cop would do: I performed a little swoop and swap.

I floored the accelerator. Took two hard turns and whipped into a hidden driveway on a street I knew as well as I knew my own. I was out of the car before it stopped rocking and rushed over to watch from the overgrown shrubbery at the curb.

The sedan, four-door, gray, plain and ugly, slowed to a stop and the driver, male, thirty-five maybe, surveyed the neighborhood without getting out of his vehicle.

I eased down the shrubbery row until I reached the rear of his vehicle and then I dashed across the sidewalk and hovered near the trunk. He hadn't turned off the engine but he had shifted into Park. I'd seen his back-up lights flash as the gear shift passed through Reverse on its way to Park and I could feel the heat coming from the tail pipe, indicating the engine was still running.

Adrenaline fired through my veins as I risked a peek over the top of the trunk. He'd taken out his cell phone to make a call.

Distracted. Perfect.

I rounded the end of the vehicle and watched him in the driver's-side mirror as I moved toward the door in a low crouch.

Three seconds later I stood, my weapon aimed at his head through the window.

"Get out!" I roared.

He looked up at the gun then at me. Pallor slid over his face. I liked knowing I could make a man go white as a sheet.

Without a word, he closed the phone, tossed it onto the passenger seat and reached for the door handle.

"Keep your right hand where I can see it," I ordered. He'd used his right hand when tossing the phone. That was the one I needed to watch.

I backed off a step as he opened the door with his left hand, his right held up in a sign of surrender, and got out. If the bland, featureless car hadn't been a dead giveaway the cheap suit he wore would have.

Cop.

"Why are you following me?" I had my ideas but I wanted to hear it straight from the horse's mouth.

He started to reach into his jacket but I shook my head and waved the gun for emphasis.

Chief Barlow ordered me to. If his crestfallen expression were any indication, he didn't look forward to telling his superior that he had been made.

The anticipation I'd felt seconds ago morphed into fury. I reached into his jacket and felt for a wallet. He didn't resist. What I found was a badge, just as I suspected.

Officer Waylon Jamison. Murfreesboro.

What the hell?

"Since when does Nashville's Chief of Homicide

have any jurisdiction over Murfreesboro cops?" I shoved his badge at him and put my weapon away.

Now I was really mad. If Barlow was lucky I wouldn't be able to find him until I'd cooled off. First he sticks me with a partner who doesn't like female cops. Then he hires some out-of-town cop to watch me.

I just transferred to Nashville, he explained. *Barlow gave me this assignment because I was new.* He glanced nervously at the ground. *This operation was supposed to be a secret. I hope this doesn't affect my new assignment.*

How could I not feel sorry for the guy?

I planted my hands on my hips. "I won't tell anyone if you don't." I was a sucker, I admit it.

But I… He looked unsure what to say.

I held up a hand for him to listen. "I won't mention that I know you're following me on one condition."

He looked like a puppy anticipating a treat. *Name it.*

"I realize you have to follow orders," I said up front. "Just make sure you stay out of my way and don't tell Barlow anything without checking with me first."

He looked uncertain for all of two seconds then he said, *Deal.*

That, I decided, was the best revenge. Turning the tables. As long as Barlow didn't know I'd made Jamison, he wouldn't be dragging someone else into the scenario. I had Jamison by the short hairs. He didn't want to look bad to his new boss, making him, in reality, mine to rule.

And Barlow never had to know.

Chapter 4

When you grow up in a large Southern family there is one thing that follows you from the cradle to the grave. Family dinners.

The chosen night had changed from time to time over the years, to accommodate schedules, but the tradition remained the same. My mom did all the cooking, Sarah and I set the table, and the other three daughters-in-law did whatever Mom told them. Meanwhile, the men in the family, my four brothers and my dad, watched the news or a ball game.

I often wondered if this tradition was part of the reason Southern women had, for generations, cooked with lard, a seriously concentrated form of animal fat, and lots and lots of salt. Pump up the cholesterol and blood pressure levels and a woman didn't have to worry about living with their thoughtless men that long.

Not that my mother did that. She was a health nut to the core. Walked three miles every day with my dad in tow. Walters men would live forever. Good thing they had strong willed women who tolerated the family-dinner crap but not much else.

Truth was I loved all the men in my family, even when they were swizzling beer and yelling at the television set as if the referee could hear them via sheer determination alone. Sports were like a religion around here.

Sarah reached to settle the final glass into place, then frowned. She bracketed her protruding belly with her hands and grimaced.

"You okay?"

She nodded. *I think so. Just a Braxton-Hicks contraction. They come and go.*

I managed a wan smile. "Maybe you should sit down for a while. I can finish here."

Sarah waved me off, as I knew she would. *Don't be silly. I'm fine.*

A few minutes later a platter of baked chicken and rice, steaming bowls of fat-free green beans and steamed carrots graced the empty space between the place settings for eleven at the table for twelve. Even my youngest brother, Max was married. I staunchly ignored that last empty chair.

Since Sarah was on the verge of giving birth, the pressure was off me for a while. My mom had something else to obsess about besides my ongoing single status. And, thank God, the blind-date dinners had ceased, at least temporarily. Oh, yes, Southern mothers weren't above having some single guy or gal over for dinner in an attempt to prompt a marriage. Poor Max had endured his share of those during his final year as a bachelor.

Have you noticed there's a kind of theme going on here with the Walters kids' names? All *M*'s. Martin, Michael, Marshall, Max and Merri. My mother must have been going through some sort of odd Sesame Street phase during her late twenties. Or maybe it was the fact that she'd had five children in six years. I suppose it was a miracle we'd gotten names at all.

When the water goblets were filled and a bottle of wine positioned at each end of the table, we were good to go. The herd hustled into the dining room. It didn't take much imagination to summon the memory of the sounds that accompanied the Walters clan settling in around the long table for dinner.

I missed those pleasant sounds. A pang of wistfulness broadsided me.

Okay, shake it off, Merri.

I get emotional like that sometimes. Can't help myself. But it passes quickly. Besides, my mother's famous for her baked chicken and rice. The herbs and spices smelled heavenly. The food would distract me as soon as I'd had a chance to dig in.

What's going on with the Starlet Murders?

This from my brother Martin, the cop. He was a

good cop but he'd never had any interest in homicide. That he used the nomenclature from the old investigation annoyed me unreasonably. Despite the speculation in the press, no one at Metro had mentioned the connection.

"Not much to know yet," I admitted. And it was true. We didn't have any real leads and not the first damned clue. "I'm hoping we'll know more after the latest victim's autopsy is complete." I remembered the hairs the M.E. had found on the second victim that morning. A single hair would be better than nothing. "And, just so you know," I said matter-of-factly, "there has been no official connection between this case and the murders four years ago."

Martin smirked. *Like we don't see that one coming.*

I refused to rise to the bait, and, thankfully, the family focused on eating for a while. Whenever the conversation ventured into what I was up to at work, trouble would follow. Trouble for me. Tossing out the term *autopsy* at the dinner table had, I hoped, averted that course.

I hear you went undercover as a street walker the other night, Marshall said eventually.

Here it came. Talk of the autopsy had gained me a little time but not much. The horrified look on my mother's face had me flashing a look that said "Gee, thanks" at my brother.

"It was an operation to draw out a suspected cop-killer. A witness agreed to be bait and I was her protection for the event."

My explanation didn't help.

That's very dangerous, little girl.

How did I explain to my father that I'm not a little girl anymore? It was a good thing he hadn't seen me in the hooker get-up.

Since I knew it wouldn't do any good to argue my ability to take care of myself I didn't bother.

Have they caught the guy yet? Martin inquired, a direct challenge in his eyes. He wanted my folks to know exactly what I'd been up to. *The killer you were trying to bait, I mean?*

I wanted to slug him.

I should have forced myself to think before I spoke, but my irritation overrode my few more-sensible brain cells. "Actually, they may not catch him at all. I wounded him so he could be dead already. Who knows if they'll ever find the body."

You shot a man? The disbelief widening my mother's eyes was no doubt reflected in her voice.

Might as well get it over with—this was where the conversation had been heading since my knuckle-headed brother asked the first question about my work. "Only because he shot at me first."

Half the people at the table started talking at once. I tried to keep up, but let's face it, I could only read lips so fast. And it was impossible to read the words of two or more talking at once. I didn't even try. Let them hash it out. I was hungry. I intended to eat.

As I lifted a forkful of rice to my mouth Sarah covertly winked at me and lifted a forkful of rice to her own mouth. At least I had one person on my side. I could always count on Sarah. She'd been my best friend long before she'd become my sister-in-law.

We ate while the others argued about what was best for me. Eventually their bellies lured their attention back to their plates and the conversation died an overdue death.

I glanced at Sarah to flash her a conspirator grin but my grin slipped when I saw her grimace again. Another Braxton-Hicks? Maybe that baby couldn't wait to join this rowdy group. I wondered if he or she would be on my side. I could use a little more support.

The dinner topic stayed clear of me and my work for the rest of the meal. Thank God.

As usual when the feasting was done, the men retired to the den to watch the news and talk about how they'd eaten far too much. And the women cleared the table. For all my complaining I really didn't mind. I loved our family dinners—all but the part where everyone got into my business, anyway. Otherwise I wouldn't trade my family for anything.

They were the best, if overprotective and misguided.

Just like my boss. Barlow was far too much like my family where protecting me was concerned. I appreciated that he cared about my safety, but I needed to do my job. I loved it. It's who I am now.

Still, somehow I just couldn't quench that burning need to be with him, the shimmer of heat I felt when I thought of him. It happened every darned time. But that relationship couldn't be. Not now, with him the chief.

How could I jeopardize my new career? I knew the rules. I couldn't see any way to get around that.

Sarah rinsed the dishes, handing the plates to me one by one and I loaded them into the dishwasher. Kathy, Carla and Nancy took care of the other cleaning while my mom choreographed the routine as if none of us had ever done this before. She loved having daughters to boss around.

A plate shattered in the sink. My gaze swung from the broken pieces to Sarah, who now clutched her belly. Her eyes met mine and she said, *I think this is the real thing.*

Things got a little crazy from there. Michael rushed Sarah to the hospital. My mom and I drove over to their Brentwood home and picked up Sarah's already-packed bag. The rest of the family headed to the hospital to wait out the arrival of the first Walters grandchild.

I drove to the hospital as quickly as I dared considering a drizzling rain had started to fall. Just enough to require windshield wipers but not quite a sufficient amount to keep them from squeaking across the glass. Really annoying. Hearing the sound wasn't necessary. I could see the way the wipers dragged against the glass.

Mom knew how difficult it was for me to see her face at night with only the dash lights for illumination so neither of us spoke, yet the anticipation was palpable.

We both loved Sarah dearly and wanted only the best for her. A safe delivery and a healthy baby.

I dropped my mom off at the front of the hospital so she could get on in there. I knew she was dying to join the others. The parking garage wasn't that crowded, so finding a spot didn't take long.

Snagging the bag from the back seat, I slung the strap over my right shoulder and locked my Jetta. I considered the level on which I'd parked, two, and decided the quickest route to my destination would be to take the stairs to level four and use the pedestrian cross ramp. Sarah would be on the third floor. A new wave of anticipation washed over me.

I was going to be an aunt!

Being an aunt was a big responsibility. I needed to think about that and make sure I didn't forget anything important. There would be birthday parties, special Christmas traditions like going to visit Santa at the mall, oh, and shopping. Lots and lots of shopping.

And then there was school. I would personally interview all the kid's teachers to ensure he or she got the best. I gnawed my lower lip at that thought. Maybe I'd better not do that. I remember how badly I'd hated those kinds of parents. The ones who made teachers feel like they were lesser forms of life or incompetent at the very least.

I struck that task off my list.

Goosebumps abruptly rushed over my skin, issuing a silent warning.

I stalled. Slowly turned around.

A couple of dozen or so cars were scattered around the semidark garage. There was room for at least a hundred more. I studied the shadows, watched for the slightest variation in shading. Allowed my senses to soak up the vibes. The unpleasant but familiar smell of gasoline and oil filtered through my nostrils.

When I'd surveyed the garage as thoroughly as possible I decided maybe I'd overreacted. I was hyped about the baby. My perceptive wires must have gotten crossed.

Moving briskly, my right hand resting on the butt of my weapon beneath my jacket, I headed for the stairwell.

The sensation of being watched wouldn't relent.

At the door to the stairwell I hesitated, turned around again and slowly scanned the garage.

Nothing.

And yet there was something…or someone there.

I was almost certain.

I entered the stairwell and took the stairs to the next floor up, then the next. Glancing over my shoulder now and again, I marched across the pedestrian cross ramp as quickly as I could without breaking into a run. Then I had to find an elevator or another stairwell inside the hospital. I wanted to get to the third floor, to Sarah and the others. That was part of my hurry. The other part, as badly as I hated to admit it, was that I had gotten spooked in that garage.

Then I remembered. Jamison. Barlow had him watching me.

As I entered the hospital I felt heat rush to my cheeks. What an idiot I was. Officer Jamison had probably followed me to the garage. The worst part was the idea that he likely recognized that I was spooked.

What a doofus.

On the third floor the whole family, except Michael, loitered in the waiting room. Apparently there were no other imminent deliveries since we had the place to ourselves. Good thing, too. The room wasn't that large and since Sarah's parents had arrived, as well, we were quite a crowd.

At some point the men took a fresh-air break. The wives appeared intent on flipping through all the magazines. Except for Mom. She paced the room, wringing her hands like the worrywart she was.

I pushed to my feet and fell into stride next to her. "I think we should go for coffee."

She looked at me, her eyes filled with that worry she was famous for. At first I thought she would decline but then she nodded.

I glanced around the room. "Anyone else like coffee? Or a cola?"

Heads shook, each waiting for my visual confirmation. I appreciated the effort to make my life easier. Just further proof of what a great, however nosy, family I have.

Mom didn't say anything as we took the elevator down to the first floor. We wound our way through the maze of lobbies, admin offices and gift shops on the ground level until we found the cafeteria. You'd think they would make it easy to find. Maybe they figured if you couldn't eat or get coffee you wouldn't hang around as long.

After we'd paid for our coffee and Mom had added creamer, I headed for the exit.

Mom put her hand on my arm and I turned to face her.

Let's stay down here a while.

Surprised that she would want to risk missing a single second of the historical event playing out upstairs, I nodded and followed her to a table.

She slipped the top off her cup and stared into it for a long while. I wondered if she couldn't decide whether she'd added enough cream or not. My mother was not one to be at a loss for words.

When her gaze finally came to rest on mine, she opened that same old can of worms. *You know how much we worry about you, Merri.*

Yeah, so did everyone else in my life. When would they learn that I had to get on with my life in my own way?

"Mom, I—"

Just let me finish.

The one thing the Walters children were particularly good at was shutting up when told to do so, whether directly or indirectly. Not one of my siblings had ever talked back to our parents. It simply wasn't tolerated.

But I think we've all accepted that this is what you want to do with your life. She sipped her coffee, considered the flavor and appeared to be satisfied. There were things I wanted to say, but I would let her have her say first.

Martin hears rumors about you, she said.

Great. Just what I needed. My brother going to my parents and detailing my professional exploits.

The word is you're a very good detective.

Startled, I searched her eyes. "Really?"

She smiled. *You know you are. We didn't need rumors to confirm it.*

Wow. Why hadn't they said this to me before?

Personally I would have been much happier if you'd stuck with the profiling rather than the higher-risk position you chose. But I can't say that I was surprised. I knew you would never be happy sorting the details. You need the interaction with people. I think you crave the anticipation of tracking down the bad guys.

I was thirty years old and I had no idea that my mother knew me so well. Frankly, I was stunned.

I want you to know that for all our bluster, we do respect what you do. She stared at her coffee another moment before meeting my eyes again. *We just worry. Don't expect us ever to stop doing that.*

I placed my hand over hers. "I love you, Mom. I love all of you and I wouldn't want you to change for anything."

Good thing, she retorted. *Because we won't.*

We chatted and laughed a while longer, even managed to finish the coffee before our curiosity forced us back to the third floor.

It was almost dawn before little Sasha Michelle

Walters made her debut. She was beautiful. Gorgeous pink skin and her daddy's blondish red hair. Ten fingers and ten toes. Eight pounds and twenty inches long.

Perfect.

Sarah looked beautiful. She absolutely glowed. The nurses had given up on keeping the number of visitors in her room down to three. There wasn't a square of floor space that wasn't occupied by an adoring family member.

I couldn't imagine where my brother had gotten the roses. He must have called one of the flower-shop owners at home, but the room was filled with dozens and dozens of roses. Red, white, yellow...even pink for his new daughter.

When my turn to hold the baby came around, my chest swelled with pride. She was so precious. And just like that it was as if she had always been a part of our family. As I passed her to Nancy, I couldn't help noticing the way Martin looked at her. They wanted to start a family, as well. This would only make them want it more.

As I watched my loved ones make a fuss over the new baby I found myself wondering if I would ever have children. Not that I was in any hurry. My career had just gotten started. Besides, there really wasn't a man in my life. Some rogue brain cell immediately contested by flashing a picture of Barlow in my head.

I crossed my arms over my chest and tried to dispel the lingering feel of the baby's weight there. How could holding a baby make one yearn to have one of their own? It was silly.

If things had been different Heath and I would probably have had one by now. But things hadn't been different. And that was definitely okay with me. I loved my new career. Was happy with my life. Wasn't I?

Enough. Yes, I was very happy. What I did made a difference. A husband and children could come later. My gaze drifted back to Sarah and the baby that was finally back in her arms. As little girls we had dreamed of this day...of when we would marry and have babies.

As if I had somehow summoned him with my foolish musings, Barlow appeared in the doorway. I blinked to be sure I wasn't imagining him.

Nope.

My heart leaped before I could remind myself not to overreact. How had he heard about the baby?

Our eyes met and for a second I saw raw emotion in those eyes. Yearning...hunger. And then they were gone, a fleeting mist of sweetness that made me ache. The seriousness that followed warned me he wasn't here about the birth.

I made my way over to Sarah and kissed her forehead. "Great job, Sarah. She's amazing."

Her eyes glistening with emotion she gifted me with a shaky smile. *She is, isn't she?*

I nodded. "Listen, I have to go now."

Sarah glanced at Barlow then back at me. *I know.*

Barlow shook hands and passed along his congratulations before apologizing for dragging me away. I hesitated at the door and watched my family. I would remember this moment for the rest of my life.

My life didn't have to be perfect. I didn't need the fairy tale. I had my family…and that was all that mattered, at least for now.

At the elevator I started to ask Barlow to bring me up to speed but he turned to me and spoke before I could. *We have a third victim.*

The warmth of all that had happened that evening seeped out of me. Another one? This soon?

"The same MO?" I shuddered inside as I considered what that entailed.

He nodded. *Exactly.*

"What about Patterson?"

He's there already. You couldn't be reached immediately. But it didn't take me long to figure out where you were.

The elevator doors opened and we stepped inside. "I had to turn off my cell phone in here." There wasn't any reason to explain. He would know that. Still, I felt guilty that I hadn't been available. I also didn't like that Patterson was on the scene before me, but I doubted this would be the last time that would happen. I should get over it.

"I'm in the parking garage," I told Barlow as I belatedly remembered to depress the button for the fourth floor. He'd selected the lobby since he was probably parked out front in the emergency lane.

He gave me the location of the crime scene and tagged on, *I'll see you there.* He reached out as if to touch my arm, then lowered his hand.

I thought there was more he wanted to say, but he

left it at that. When the elevator doors opened, he exited on the lobby level. As the doors paused before closing I watched him walk away. Even the way he moved beckoned to me on a purely feminine level, no matter the situation. I shook my head and sighed. Why didn't he say what was on his mind? Or was it all in my head?

The doors glided closed and I rode back up to the fourth floor, where the pedestrian ramp would take me back to the garage. I thought about the address Barlow had given me. Another upscale neighborhood. How was it that three murders could take place in areas that surely had community watches and responsible residents? Why hadn't someone somewhere seen anything?

It just didn't make sense.

Unless the perp knew the areas well enough to know how and when to act.

Did that mean he was a resident?

Like Rex Lane? Though he lived in Franklin he socialized with the folks in the neighborhoods where all three of these murders had taken place. I had sensed that he was keeping something from me. I didn't know exactly what. But something.

I didn't know the identity of the latest victim or her story, but I would…soon.

These women deserved justice.

When the elevator bumped to a stop and the doors slid open I walked quickly to where I'd parked my Jetta. I jumped in, snapped my seat belt into place and roared out of the parking slot, driving as fast as I dared down to the exit. Once on the street I floored the accelerator.

My destination was only fifteen minutes away, unless I ran into unforeseen traffic, which was highly unlikely at this early hour. Still, I pushed my Jetta, the rush of adrenaline dissolving my inhibitions. I told myself it had nothing to do with the idea that Patterson was already at the scene.

But I wasn't exactly sure I wasn't lying to myself.

Headlights bobbed in my rearview mirror as I made the next turn. Jamison? Maybe. I'd been in such a hurry when I roared out of the garage I hadn't noticed if I'd been followed from there.

It seriously irritated me that Barlow would do that behind my back. I wanted so badly to call him on it, but then he'd just call in someone new to take Jamison's place. Who knew, the next guy might be too good to catch and then I wouldn't be able to make a single move without Barlow knowing it. Nope, it was far better for me to keep that piece of knowledge to myself.

Whatever. I didn't have time to worry about that right now.

I had another homicide victim.

It was my job to find her killer and make him pay.

Chapter 5

The houses along the street were still dark. No one in the high-end neighborhood had any idea a murder victim had been found within its boundaries.

Crime-scene tape cordoned off the area where the body had been discovered by a man out for his pre-dawn run. Patterson was interviewing him in his SUV rather than one of the squad cars. Keeping the guy calm and feeling as comfortable as possible would facilitate his recall of details. Sometimes it was the seemingly insignificant stuff that mattered the most and got overlooked the easiest.

Crime-scene technicians were combing the area using high-powered flashlights and a fast and steady grid pattern to ensure every square foot of the landscape was covered. The process would be repeated in the daylight to ensure nothing was missed.

The M.E. had arrived already, but, like me, he stayed back while the techs completed their work. Everyone appeared to have landed at the scene well ahead of me. Just another annoying note.

I thought of my darling little niece and decided I should cut myself some slack. I couldn't possibly regret being there for her birth. Patterson's getting here first didn't matter.

Then there was the frustrating little detail that Barlow was here yet again. Was he worried we would bumble this investigation? Or was it that protective thing again? Nothing I accomplished appeared to set him at ease as to my ability to take care of myself.

Clarence Johnson very well could decide to come after me, which was probably Barlow's point in keeping me under surveillance, but at least there was no way he could get to Shameka. And that was the most important issue here. I understood what I was getting into when I signed on for the job. She was a civilian.

I suddenly felt guilty for not having stopped by to see Shameka that morning. Barlow's unexpected appearance with news of this latest murder had preempted anything else that should have crossed my mind. I'd have to check in on her later today.

Since Johnson's body hadn't been discovered and he hadn't checked himself into a hospital I had to assume he'd lived through being shot.

Too bad.

I looked around this crime scene. The dumping site was only twenty-five or thirty yards beyond a relatively large intersection. Stone pillars welcomed residents to River Creek. Beyond the stone pillars on either side of the street a triangular section of land had been groomed to perfection. Leyland cypress, hollies and varying sizes of boxwoods were surrounded by brand-new spring annuals blooming with color. I'd driven by dozens of times, never once thinking that I might be standing here doing this one day.

The well-designed landscape made for an inviting picture as drivers and pedestrians alike passed the entrance to the upscale development. But this morning something ugly marred the quiet beauty of one of Nashville's prominent neighborhoods. Murder. The naked body sprawled behind the towering stone pillar left a jarring statement on the fragility of life no matter where one lived.

As the techs wrapped up their work I tugged on shoe covers and latex gloves and ventured beyond the yellow tape. The breeze kicked up, almost jerking the tape out of my hand as I lifted it to duck underneath.

I shivered, wishing I had worn a windbreaker. The birthing adventure had happened too fast for me to think of something as trivial as protection from a sudden dip in the temperature. As late as mid-May the Nashville climate could abruptly shift to unseasonably cold as easily as it could to unexpectedly warm. I'd seen snowstorms in April. It wasn't typical but it happened.

Purple and pink streaks of light had started to penetrate the predawn gloom. I felt sad for the young woman lying on the cold, damp ground. She hadn't realized when she got out of bed yesterday that it would be her last day on Earth anymore than she'd had the faintest idea that a brutal murder as well as an equally brutal autopsy would be included in that final day of life.

We take life for granted far too often.

I banished the depressing thoughts and focused on the scene. No tire marks had been discovered on the pavement to indicate a speedy getaway. Our killer hadn't been in any hurry, probably had felt comfortable with the situation. No footprints were visible in the thickly sodded layer of grass that covered the ground. Though the rain had left the grass wet, it hadn't helped in providing clues. In fact, it might very well have done the opposite by washing away any trace evidence on the body.

I crouched down next to the victim and studied her. Painfully young. I winced at the idea that she might even be under twenty-one. Very slim, almost anorexic. Damn. No breast augmentation here, I noticed, squinting to be sure. The M.E. would determine if surgical procedures not readily visible had been done in this case.

The same bruising on the wrists and ankles and, of course, the throat. I ached at the delicateness of her slim arms. She hadn't stood a chance against the brute strength of this killer. Or killers, I amended. There might very well be more than one involved.

The M.E. had found two different hair samples on the last victim.

Outrage battered against my chest. We had to stop this bastard or bastards. He'd killed three women in the space of ten days, the last two barely forty-eight hours apart.

But how could we stop him if we didn't have any evidence?

Someone crouched down beside me and I instinctively flashed my light in his or her face to for identification purposes. Patterson held his hand in front of his eyes to block the harsh brightness.

"Sorry," I muttered as I lowered the light's beam enough to keep it out of his face but to allow some amount of illumination for my lip-reading needs. Actually, I really wasn't sorry. And that was bad because he was my partner. I had to get past my dislike for the guy...whether he deserved it or not.

Patricia Ryland, he said. *Twenty years old. She came to Nashville six months ago from Nebraska.*

"Damn." I shook my head. Too young to die, especially like this.

Patterson tapped me on the shoulder to get my attention again. *The runner knew her.* Patterson hitched his thumb in the direction of the stone pillar. *Puked his guts out over there.*

Great. Crime-scene contamination. "Could he tell you anything significant about her?"

Patterson grinned. *You bet. She's been working with a music video producer. Can you guess who?*

I'll be damned. "Rex Lane." Now, why wasn't I surprised?

Patterson nodded. *He'd recommended she get a boob job if she wanted to be in one of his upcoming videos. Apparently there were financial issues. Miss Ryland had been living in this neighborhood with a friend of hers from her hometown, Delia Decker.*

I'd heard that name before. I concentrated hard to dredge up the necessary memory. A shot of caffeine would be good right now. Decker. Some kind of talk show host if I remembered right.

I thought we might pay her a visit next, Patterson suggested. *She has a midnight talk show on one of the local radio stations called "The Night Owl."*

Bingo. That's where I'd heard Delia Decker. She was pretty good. The show offered relationship advice to callers. Maybe I should start listening in.

According to our runner, Patterson went on, *Miss Decker sometimes stays the night at the station when she feels too tired to drive home. I checked, she's not home. We could catch her at the station.*

I clicked off my flashlight as the first rays of daylight crowded out the night little by little until I could see fairly well. The M.E. looked restless standing near his van cradling a cup of coffee.

There was nothing else Patricia could tell me. Whatever else she had to say would have to be interpreted by Dr. Ammon. I hoped there would be something…anything that might help us nail this killer.

"Tracking down Miss Decker sounds like the best

step to take next," I agreed. "You got the address of that radio station?"

Patterson nodded. *Twenty minutes from here.* He named the place.

I recognized the location. "I could drop my car by the station and we could go together if you like." I couldn't believe I was doing this, but I had to make a show of good faith at some point. Might as well be now. Besides I hadn't had any sleep—driving any distance might be hazardous to my health. And Metro was on our way.

You would have thought I'd given Patterson a raise; he actually smiled. *Sure,* he said. Then his expression turned solemn. *I really prefer driving.*

He should have shut up at "Sure." "Pig," I muttered under my breath. If he heard me he didn't let on.

Some guys just didn't get it. No wonder he was single. What woman in her right mind would want a boyfriend or husband who thought the female species was inferior somehow?

I didn't talk to Barlow before we left. There really wasn't any reason to and the last thing I wanted was for Patterson to pick up on the tension vibrating between Barlow and me.

Funny. If there wasn't any reason to talk to him…why did I always look for an explanation for why I shouldn't or didn't? Come to think of it, I spent a lot of time trying to assess the minutest detail of our relationship. Problem was we didn't exactly have a relationship…we had a thing. Whatever that meant.

As I slid behind the wheel, I saw him watching me. I was too far away to see his expression, but that didn't matter. I knew the look by heart.

WKRZ was one of Nashville's most popular radio stations. Krazy for Kountry was their motto. Country-music stars often popped in for impromptu interviews and the contests were wildly popular. WKRZ constantly gave away money to ninth callers or the one who had the answer to the day's trivia question. Delia Decker's "Night Owl" talk show was another of the station's success stories. Occasionally, if I couldn't sleep, I would turn on the television to catch some talk show. I didn't get anything from the music, unless it was an old tune I remembered from my hearing days. But I enjoyed reading the banter between the talk show hosts and their guests. I remembered listening to "Night Owl" a few times back when I could hear.

In three years I hadn't really thought about how much I missed music…until now. This case had reminded me of all I'd lost.

I got out of Patterson's big, beefy SUV and kicked aside the depressing thoughts that appeared determined to loiter in my head.

Since the station wasn't officially open for business at this hour, we flashed our badges and one of the two guards stationed in the lobby showed us up to the third floor where the broadcasting studios were located.

There's a private lounge for the night folks, the guard explained. *Miss Decker uses it pretty often.*

On the third floor, down a long corridor past two studios, the guard indicated the final door on the left. *She might still be asleep*, he offered.

"I'll go in." If Miss Decker had partially undressed to get comfortable, having a man walk in probably wouldn't be something she would appreciate.

Patterson said to the guard, *You got any coffee around here?*

I could have used a cup myself but I needed to talk to Miss Decker first. Every minute wasted allowed a case to go colder. Too many bodies were piling up. I didn't want to give this scumbag any additional slack.

I knocked on the door, said, "Miss Decker, are you awake?" Then I went on inside, felt for the light switch and flipped it to the on position.

A woman about my age sat up and blinked repeatedly. *Is the building on fire?*

"I don't think so. Do you hear any alarms?" I didn't, but then that didn't mean anything.

She hesitated, then shook her head. *Guess not. Who are you?*

Delia Decker combed her fingers through her long black hair and then attempted to straighten her clothes. She'd tossed aside a chenille throw. The chaise lounge made for a decent bed, I supposed. A couple of other chairs were stationed around the room as well as a small, dorm-size refrigerator, a microwave, a sink and a coffeemaker.

I pulled my credentials from my purse and showed

it to her. "I'm Detective Merri Walters from Metro Homicide."

Her gaze jerked from the badge to me. *Homicide?*

I nodded. "I need to ask you a few questions."

She looked confused. *Wait. Does this mean someone I know has been murdered?* Denial punctuated by fear claimed her face as her still-groggy brain answered her own question.

"Miss Decker, I'm sorry to have to tell you this but your roommate, Patricia Ryland, is dead."

Her eyes welled with tears. *Patricia? Who in the world would want to hurt Patricia? Are you sure? She just moved here and—*

"We made a positive ID. I'm sorry." Metro had developed a new system for matching photos taken by the forensic techs to those in the DMV database. As long as a victim had a valid Tennessee license and hadn't made major changes to their appearance, the ID was a fairly simple procedure. In this case the victim had an arrest record. Nothing serious, just a public drunkenness charge, but the record made for an additional means of verifying her identity. The runner had actually ID'd Miss Ryland, but the DMV and criminal-records match had confirmed that ID.

It took a few minutes for Miss Decker to compose herself after hearing the news. Apparently she and the victim had known each other back in Nebraska. Both had dreamed of becoming stars, Delia in radio and Patricia in acting or modeling.

She worked so hard. Delia sat back, pulled the chenille throw up around her as if she were cold. *She wouldn't eat for fear of gaining weight. Attended every class she could find in acting. She modeled on and off for several of the department stores at the malls. But that was the best she could manage until…*

She closed her eyes while she gathered her composure once more. I didn't push. I understood how difficult this must be for her. But I needed anything she could give me.

"Until," I prompted when her eyes opened once more.

Until she met Mr. Lane. He said she had just the look he needed for an upcoming music video. She got all excited. At first, she qualified.

"What quelled her excitement?" I could feel my investigator's antennae standing at attention. That Rex Lane was involved with yet another victim couldn't be coincidence.

Mr. Lane insisted breast augmentation was necessary to give her the curves she needed. She didn't have the six thousand dollars to do it. So he offered her a deal.

When Delia fell silent I knew I was on the verge of a major lead. Something in the air, the thickening tension combined with the atmosphere of resignation.

If she appeared in two of his personal ventures he would pay for the surgery that would allow her to take part in the big mainstream music video project she needed to kick-start her career.

Tension rifled through me. Personal ventures… damn Rex Lane. I knew exactly what that meant.

"Porn videos," I said for her when she hesitated to go into the subject.

That's my impression. Patricia sort of clammed up after that, like she was ashamed to discuss it.

Sweet little Nebraska girl, of course she was ashamed. I wanted to kill Rex Lane.

I told her she should stay away from Lane. That she didn't have to get her first big break that way. But she wouldn't listen.

"Do you know who she was supposed to see yesterday? Did she have an appointment with Mr. Lane?"

She shook her head. *She's been very secretive since she told me about Lane's offer. I don't know who she's been seeing or even where she's worked lately.*

My every emotion diverted toward absolute fury. "Miss Decker, I'd like to take a look at Patricia's things when it's convenient for you. But be aware that the more time we allow to lapse the less likely we are to catch this guy."

I understand. I'll help any way I can. She swiped the tears from her face.

I gave Miss Decker my card and assured her I would be in touch with her later today. I asked her to keep any details related to Patricia and her death quiet for now. Then I tracked down my partner.

"I need you to take me back to my car." I should never have come here with him. Now I was stuck riding with him and I needed to do this alone.

Did you learn anything? he asked as we made our way to the elevator. Employees of the station were beginning to filter in now. *You were in there a hell of a long time,* he nudged when I didn't readily respond.

I stabbed the button for the lobby level. "She'll talk further with us this afternoon. Right now I have something personal to take care of."

Okay, so it was a lie. I needed to see Lane alone. I had things to say that I didn't want any witnesses to.

Patterson waved his hand in front of my face. Annoyed, I glared at him. "What?"

I don't mind driving you. That way once you're finished we can get on with this investigation. We do have a murder case to solve, you know. By the way, I verified Rafe Jones's alibi. It's airtight. He didn't murder Mallory Wells, at least not according to the twenty other people who were partying with him that night. He crossed his arms over his chest. *So, where are we going?*

He's your partner, I reminded myself. He would have to know all this sooner or later.

Fine. The doors opened to the lobby. "We're going to see Rex Lane."

I thought you already talked to him.

"I did, but now I'm going to talk to him again."

Patterson hesitated at the main entrance, blocking my way. *Maybe you should start at the beginning and fill me in on everything Miss Decker said.*

"There's no time, Patterson, now let's go."

He didn't like it but he relented. Maybe I would learn to like him after all.

The city of Nashville had roused by the time we hit the highway headed to Franklin. Traffic wasn't as heavy as it would be in another hour but it still slowed us down a bit. I tried not to fidget, but I just couldn't help it. I couldn't remember ever being this angry. I wasn't even sure I could conduct this interrogation properly.

"Listen to me, Patterson."

He glanced my way then refocused on the traffic.

"Decker said that our latest victim was involved with Rex Lane's production company. Apparently he had recommended she get breast augmentation from his pal, Dr. Barbie-Maker."

From the corner of my eye I saw Patterson's lips quirk at my reference to the surgeon.

"She couldn't afford it so Lane offered her an opportunity to make some quick cash to spring for the surgery."

Patterson braked for the exit and our gazes met briefly. In that moment I saw realization in his eyes. He didn't have to say a word, he felt the same way I did. Disgusted.

"Decker doesn't know if she went through with it, but my guess is that she did, considering she clammed up and stopped telling her friend anything about her business."

I thought about all I knew, however little that was, and decided we needed to scare the hell out of Lane. Right now he had no idea we were on to him. Unless he was the killer, and I still wasn't convinced of that, he wouldn't yet know another of *his* girls was dead.

The element of surprise, I hoped, was on our side.

And there was always the possibility that a serial

killer from four years ago had started to feel the hunger again. But why? Why now? And what the hell did it have to do with Lane and Santos?

Patterson tapped me on the arm and I turned to look at him.

Do you think Lane killed them?

Reluctantly, I shook my head. "But he is connected to this somehow. I'm as certain of that as I can be without his signed confession."

Neither of us spoke again until we reached the gate to Lane's property. Rich jerk. Did he really think he could lie to me and get away with it?

Well, he would soon know that I wasn't playing around.

Patterson pressed the call button, then identified himself and me. Five seconds later the gates moved slowly inward to allow our entrance.

I watched the awe play across Patterson's face as he drove up to the house. Just like before, the fountain was the showstopper.

"Isn't fair, is it?"

He glanced at me. *No.*

Scumbags like Lane could live like this and innocent girls like Patricia Ryland lay dead and naked with nothing. Well, there was nothing I could do to bring her back to life but I could damn sure make the man who might be her killer or her killer's accomplice miserable as hell.

Starting right now.

My partner parked his SUV and turned to me.

"Give me five minutes before you come in," I told him. "There's something I have to do."

Chapter 6

Rex Lane answered his ornate door wearing a silk robe and matching lounge pants. His feet were bare. And if his tousled hair was any indication, he'd just rolled out of bed. I wondered why he didn't have a houseman or butler. He could, from all accounts, afford one.

Detective Walters. Annoyance visibly deepened on his otherwise unlined face. *What're you doing here at this time of the morning?*

My first, and overwhelming I might add, instinct was to slug him but then I'd only get into trouble and I didn't need any more professional drama. Barlow was just looking for a chance to stick me back in forensics or profiling. I liked it out in the trenches. How else would I meet lowlifes like Lane here?

"We need to talk, Mr. Lane," I said with all the cold, clinical accusation I could infuse into my tone—at least I hoped it came out that way.

The uncertainty that crept into his expression assured me I'd hit my intended mark.

Of course. He stood back, opened the door wider. *Would you care for coffee?*

I didn't answer immediately. I wanted the door shut between us and Patterson, who I knew would be watching from his SUV. I stepped inside and once the door closed I went toe to toe with my rumpled host.

"Mr. Lane, you are in some deep trouble and there isn't a thing anyone else on the planet can do to help you…except me." I pressed closer as he attempted to back up. "You tell me the truth this minute and maybe, just maybe, I can help you."

He blinked a couple of times, visibly struggled to maintain his polite composure. *I'm not sure what you're insinuating, Detective. Are you certain you're all right? Perhaps I should call your superior.*

I smiled, made sure he wouldn't find it in the least bit pleasant. Judging by his mounting uneasiness he didn't. "I'm fine, Mr. Lane, but your client, Miss Patricia Ryland, is dead."

There was no way he faked the stark fear and utter surprise I saw in his eyes upon hearing the news. I hated to give the guy any credit whatsoever but I had to call it as I saw it.

I feel badly for Miss Ryland but I don't understand what that has to do with me.

"I know about your little sideline business, Mr. Lane," I pushed. "I know how you tried to use her desire to become an actress to your benefit."

He swallowed with monumental effort. *I should call my attorney.* He backed into the elegant table gracing the center of his lavish entry hall. The vase of flowers shook but didn't fall over.

I didn't let up, just kept pressing him with my accusing gaze. "Call your lawyer, Mr. Lane—maybe you'd better call two because it's going to take some fancy footwork to keep you out of prison…or worse. I'd hate to think what would happen to a man like you in prison."

I…I didn't have anything to do with this… I only know what you've told me and what I've seen on the news.

Two more minutes, that's all I needed. He was worried. I could break him. I could feel him weakening under the pressure.

"I may be crazy, but I believe you," I said, and that wasn't far from the truth. "But my partner out there," I hitched my thumb toward the door, "he thinks you're guilty as hell. I asked him to give me five minutes to try and cut a deal with you. That's the best I can do. He'll be in here any second and then there won't be anything I can do to help you, Mr. Lane. You need to make your decision quickly if you want to avoid how ugly this might get."

The desperation in his eyes sent victory roaring through me. But the appearance of another man on the staircase above us ruined the moment.

Rex, you've said enough.

Lane spun toward the man sauntering down the wide, curving stairs.

Well, well, the gang was all here. I'd only seen the DMV photo of Xavier Santos but I would wager my Jetta that this was the good doctor. I wouldn't be surprised if he carried around a couple of breast implants in his pockets to use as conversation pieces.

Xavier Santos, he said as he moved up alongside his friend. *Perhaps you could explain your gestapo tactics, Detective, before our lawyer arrives. If your excuse is credible I might be able to persuade him not to press charges of harassment. Otherwise—* he shrugged *—I'm certain you will quite regret your charge into my friend's home.*

Mr. Rex Lane looked mortified for about five seconds then he appeared to regain his voice. *I've told you all I know, Detective. Just because I know the victim doesn't make me guilty of anything. I certainly don't appreciate the innuendo.*

It wasn't lost on me that Dr. Santos was also dressed in silk lounge pants. The main difference was that he hadn't bothered with a robe. Instead, he stood before me with bare chest and bare feet. I felt reasonably certain he was quite proud of his physique considering the way his chest puffed out as I surveyed his tall frame.

But, at the same time, I understood perfectly that whether or not I found him physically attractive in no way concerned the man. I found it ironic that two men who preferred their own sex would be involved with the making of heterosexual pornography. Then again, I hadn't actually seen any of the illegal videos.

When both Santos and Lane abruptly looked beyond me at the door I knew the bell had rung. Patterson no doubt. My five minutes were up.

Lane excused himself to go answer the door.

How polite, I mused.

...should check your sources before you jump to conclusions, Detective Walters.

I'd missed the first couple of words but I got what Santos meant.

"I always follow my instincts, Doctor," I let him know. "They've never let me down before."

The man had black, black hair and eyes so blue they were almost electric. Startlingly so.

There's a first time for everything, Detective. You should never overestimate your capabilities.

As if to prove his point he turned his profile to me as he continued speaking.

He knew.

Surprise, anger hot on its heels, rushed through me. How could he know?

As the other two men approached, Santos's gaze swung back to mine and triumph gleamed there.

How the hell...?

I eased back a step to allow for seeing all three men at the same time. As I did I was disturbed by the look of disbelief on Patterson's face.

Detective Patterson. Santos extended his hand. *Have you met Rex Lane?*

The three shook hands and exchanged the usual pleasantries while I was still trying to come to terms with Patterson's unexpected reaction to Santos. The last time my partner and I had talked he had gone to check on the surgeon, who'd performed victim number two's breast augmentation. I hadn't had a chance to ask him about it. Was he simply surprised to see the man here, with suspect number one?

Or was this why he'd offered to follow up on the doctor—because he knew Santos?

I shook off that whole line of thinking. Patterson would get the benefit of the doubt from me until we were alone and I could interrogate—I mean, ask him—about it. I definitely wasn't going to jump the gun without giving him a chance to come clean.

The lawyer arrived post haste and both Patterson and I were instructed not to talk to his clients again without his being present.

We left with our tails tucked between our legs, so to speak. The last thing a detective wanted was a suspect lawyering up.

When we arrived back at Metro, Patterson didn't get out immediately. I followed his lead. I had a feeling he knew that I knew something was amiss.

So ask, he said. He'd turned his face to me but his eyes remained averted. *I don't want this hanging between us.*

"You know, Patterson," I began, using his name and forcing him to meet my gaze before I would continue, "I don't care what your sexual preference is. That's your business. But I do care whether or not you get your job done. When we talked about the doctor, you didn't mention that you knew him. In my book, that's the same thing as lying. I need a partner I can depend on."

This is exactly why I transferred. He looked directly at me now. *I don't want questions about my personal life to interfere with my job here.*

"There are laws against that, Patterson. Like I said, I don't have any problem with what you do on your own time, but the—"

We had an encounter. He propped his elbow on the steering wheel and rubbed his forehead. *While I was still at the Forensics Academy a bunch of us went out. It happened one time. I had no idea I'd see him here. I didn't know where he was from or even that he was a plastic surgeon. When I heard his name in connection to our case, I panicked. And I didn't know for sure until I saw him face to face.*

"Can you work this case?" I had to know. "If not, we'll think of some way to get you moved onto something else. Your personal life doesn't have to be part of it. I can talk to Barlow."

I think having gone through my hearing loss made me particularly sensitive to the problems others faced. As different as our situations were, both were profoundly life-altering.

I can do this, Walters. Just give me a chance. I won't screw up again. I swear. There's nothing between me and Santos. I can still be objective about him.

Was it really possible to have that kind of encounter with someone and still be objective? Ever? But then, was it fair to Patterson not to give him the benefit of the doubt? What could I do? If Metro hadn't given me a chance, where would I be?

"No need to swear, Patterson. We're partners. Just remember that whenever you have something you need to tell me. I don't like finding out like I just did."

Relief sagged his tense posture. *Thanks, Walters, I owe you. I won't keep you in the dark about anything else.*

I reached for the door handle to get out but a new thought waylaid me. "Hey." I turned back to my recently humbled partner. "So what was all the crap about not wanting to work with a woman?" Patterson, of all people, should be the last person caught casting stones.

He shrugged sheepishly. *I was afraid you'd figure out my secret. Women usually spot the difference first.*

Though I couldn't claim to have nailed his secret, I had known from day one that he was hiding something. Well, at least I didn't have to wonder about that anymore.

Satisfied with his answer, I climbed out of the SUV and headed across the street. I needed to call the hospital and check on Shameka. I dragged out my cell phone, glanced at the display. Ten o'clock. Too late for breakfast. Too early for lunch.

As I punched in the necessary numbers I glanced right then left. That same eerie sensation of being watched rushed over my skin, sending chill bumps tumbling over each other. I paused once I reached the other side of the street and surveyed the area while I got an update on Shameka's condition. Continuing to improve, just what I wanted to know.

The few cars parked along the curb were empty. The sun had popped out nice and bright, drying the last of the rain from the grass and trees. Most of the office buildings were closed for Sunday. Maybe the watcher was just my imagination. I was tired. Still, I couldn't shake the feeling. Jamison? Maybe. But his sedate sedan should have been easy to spot. Come to think of it, I hadn't spotted his vehicle in a while. Maybe he'd changed to another in an attempt to throw me off.

Patterson waited by the side entrance. I wondered if he was actually being polite or just wanted to make sure one last time that I really meant to keep his secret.

We're good, right?

Just as I suspected. The guy probably didn't have a polite bone in his body.

"Yeah, yeah, Patterson, we're good."

He nodded and gestured for me to precede him.

When we reached the homicide bull pen I told him, "I want to talk to Holderfield a minute and then I'll catch up with you. We should take a look at the room Ryland called home at Delia Decker's house."

Patterson nodded his agreement. *I'll see if we have an update from the medical examiner.*

We went our separate ways. I found Holderfield at his desk. I had known he would be there. Since his wife had passed away he never stayed home. I couldn't blame him. You couldn't spend a lifetime with a mate and then just go on with your life as if they'd never existed after they were gone.

From the looks of things I wouldn't have to worry about that particular problem.

"Any thing new on Clarence Johnson?"

He looked up as I settled into the standard-issue chair in front of his desk. He peered at me over his reading glasses.

Haven't found him yet. Maybe he's dead. Those hazel eyes twinkled with the smile that tilted his lips.

"I couldn't be that lucky."

We've got his parents' home staked out and his girlfriend has turned informant on him to beat a prostitution charge.

"How do guys like that get girlfriends?" I couldn't see it. What was wrong with these women?

Drugs, my dear Merri. Some folks will do anything for drugs. And among his many hats, Johnson also wears a drug-dealer cap.

That was true. "Let me know if you find him." I got up.

Will do. Holderfield bowed his head once more over the report he'd been studying.

I found Patterson at my desk. He was on the phone. When he noticed me he started to get up, I motioned for him to keep his seat. I dropped my purse onto my desk and reached for the messages left there.

Patterson's call was likely about the case but in the

event it wasn't, I kept my gaze away from his face. I didn't want him to think I was eavesdropping.

Maybe I had time to call and check on Sarah and Sasha.

Warmth filled my chest when I thought of my precious little niece. That I'd had to go to the scene of a homicide right after her birth made the morning bittersweet. Life could be so fleeting…and yet so incredibly awe-inspiring. I felt myself smiling as I thought of those tiny fingers and toes and those pudgy little cheeks.

A tap on my shoulder dragged me back to the here and now.

Barlow.

That tingly sensation I could never contain shivered across my every nerve ending. Heat followed hot on the heels of every last tingle spreading along my nerve endings.

We're going to lunch, he said without preamble.

I glanced at my partner who was still on the phone but whose attention had shifted to me. He waved me off as if I needed his permission. I fumed. What was wrong with the men around me? Did Barlow think he could waltz up and demand I go to lunch with him anytime he wanted just because he was the boss? Well, maybe. I glared at Patterson, who looked confused. I sure as hell didn't need him facilitating Barlow's high-handedness.

I grabbed my purse and stalked out of Homicide. I didn't wait for Barlow to lead the way. I knew where he parked his car.

No matter that I wanted to demand to know what this was about, I refused to look at him until I reached his car. He'd traded his conservative sedan for a sportier high-end model since being named Chief of Homicide. Some would call it a chick magnet, but I knew Barlow. He wouldn't have gone to the trouble. A woman either liked him or she didn't.

Unfortunately I was cursed with the former. I liked him. A lot. But he was the boss now and there was nothing I could do about that. I knew the rules. So did he. The chief didn't fraternize with the detectives on that level.

I had met Steven Barlow twelve months ago. As I considered our first official introduction, he rounded the hood and opened my door. He knew the gentlemanly show wasn't necessary but he always did it anyway. His shoulder grazed mine and another of those fiery sensations washed over my skin. Had he felt the same thing?

"Thank you." I slid into the seat, carefully avoiding eye contact. I knew that would get under his skin. That was my intent.

We'd kissed once, at the end of our first case together. The chemistry had been mind-boggling. For me. I'd thought we both wanted to pursue those feelings, but then Barlow had been named Chief of Homicide and…nothing. In those twelve months, fraternizing, by definition, had crossed my mind many times. I would like to fraternize with him in my bed, in his bed, in this car. I surveyed the luxurious leather interior. But he would only use that very event, which he wanted every bit as badly as I did, to usher me out of Homicide. For my own protection. He had never, *never* agreed with my doing field work. I had to admit that a tiny part of me was flattered that he cared so much. But the woman in me who wanted to kick the butts of criminals just couldn't let anything else get in the way of my career.

He settled behind the wheel and started the car.

"Why are we going to lunch?"

I watched his profile, enjoying it far too much as usual, until he paused at a red light and faced me long enough to respond. *We need to talk in private.*

I knew exactly what that meant. As you may have already noticed, there's this ongoing curse in my life. People like to tell me what's best for me. Most of the time I can ignore what I don't want to hear. But as I considered Barlow's flinty profile I worried that this might not be one of those times. Maybe Lane's lawyer had called in a complaint. I decided to stick with my decision not to confront Barlow about Officer Jamison. At least, not right now. If I was in trouble, it was best I kept my humble side in view.

Besides, if he found out I'd made Jamison he'd just send someone else to take his place. The next guy might be harder to spot. Speaking of my tail, I needed to touch base with Jamison…just to make sure it was him I kept feeling watching me. Had to be, I decided.

There was always the chance it was Clarence John-son but that would be pretty stupid considering the police were conducting a massive manhunt just for him and he'd been wounded. If I were him, I'd be lying way, way under any sort of radar and praying God would have pity on my wicked soul.

I remembered this place, I realized fifteen minutes later. Frank's Place. Hot dogs were his specialty. I shuddered just a little when I thought of how grimy the joint had been the last time I rendezvoused here with Barlow. But, I had to admit, the hot dogs were pretty damned good. All one had to do was get past the first impression.

As part of our ongoing "friends" relationship, Barlow had taken me out to dinner several times in the past year, all before I reported back to duty after training. He had taken me to some classy restaurants, including Alexander's. Bottom line, if he was bringing me here he wanted absolute privacy. No one we knew would eat here.

Hot dogs and colas in hand we took a table in the farthest corner of the dining room. The tile looked as chipped and dingy as ever. The tables fared no better.

Barlow consumed half of his hot dog before he opened the dialogue. *Johnson still hasn't been found. I want you staying close to Patterson when you're on duty. I'll have a unit watching your house at night.*

I felt proud of myself for not rolling my eyes or laughing outright and saying "tell me something I don't know." As I suspected, he didn't mention Jamison.

"I can take care of myself." I stuffed another bite of hot dog into my mouth, chewed and swallowed. "But I understand you need your reassurances."

You won't get an argument from me. But this is different. I would insist on protection for any one of my detectives. He didn't meet my eyes.

I wished I could disprove his assertion just to make a point but I had no examples to list and, knowing Barlow, he probably would. The problem was, this thing between us made it too personal. I wasn't sure how we were ever going to handle that. It was like we were stuck in this paralyzing zone. We couldn't move forward and neither of us was willing to go back...or let go completely.

I told myself not to look at him exactly the way I was at that very moment...but I couldn't resist. That he hadn't shaved this morning was very uncharacteristic, but I liked the way it looked on him. Super sexy. The expensively tailored suit was navy, my favorite color, and the white shirt looked as crisp as if he'd only put it on minutes ago rather than hours, as I knew to be the case.

You know how I feel, Merri. He wiped his hands with his napkin and then sat back to study me as I had studied him. *We've been dancing around this attraction for months. Do you have any suggestions on how we proceed?*

I stared at him, mouth open. He'd finally confessed what I'd pretty much known all along. I knew what he wanted. He wanted me to say I would transfer to another division or step down from being a detective to clear the way for moving forward with a personal relationship. Had he held back all this time in hopes that

I'd surrender first? I couldn't do it. As much as I wanted him…as much as I cared about him, he couldn't ask me to make this kind of choice.

"That's harsh, Steven." I rarely used his first name. Sticking with the surname was like an extra degree of separation…of protection for my heart. I'd had my heart broken once. I was in no hurry to go there again. "You're putting this gorilla on my back and that's not fair." I held my breath to prevent the feelings that wanted to engulf me. I couldn't let that happen. My eyes burned with the emotional struggle. Dammit. I would not let this meeting go there.

He closed his eyes and exhaled mightily. *You're right,* he admitted as he allowed his gaze to meet mine once more. He clasped his hands in front of him and let me see precisely how he felt. The intensity of the emotions played out on his handsome face and in those caring eyes. It took everything I had to resist reaching out to him.

I don't know how much longer I can watch you put yourself in harm's way. If anything were to happen to you. I thought I could do this…but I don't know.

He turned away but not before I saw how close to breaking down he was himself. I felt confused and exhilarated at the same time. I'd hoped his feelings went as deep as my own, but the constraints we worked under…

His gaze rested on mine once more. *When this investigation is over we need to take a step back and think long and hard about our priorities.* One wide hand closed over mine and my heart fluttered, causing me to lose my breath. *I can't keep pretending I can get on with my life without you.*

My throat tightened, felt so dry I couldn't possibly swallow. For the first time in ages I desperately wished I could hear the sound of his voice....

"Sounds reasonable," I managed past the huge lump in my throat. "I don't like pretending, either. I..." Fear constricted my ability to speak. What did I tell him? That I loved him? That I wanted to make love with him...here...now?

But would doing that make a difference? What could we do? The only thing I was entirely certain of, I suddenly realized, was that I absolutely could not go through the rest of my life not knowing...always wondering what might have been. I had to see this through to whatever end.

Neutral territory?

"Agreed." Getting out of town, way out of town, would be the only way to put aside any distractions related to work.

He squeezed my hand before letting go and something passed between us...something that felt very much like a forever kind of thing.

My cell phone vibrated. Apparently Barlow's rang, as well. We answered simultaneously.

Patterson. His words poured across the screen making my pulse skip. *M.E.'s office. Meet me. ASAP.*

That could mean only one thing.

Evidence.

Chapter 7

Dr. Ammon waited in the examination room near the autopsy table. The latest victim, Patricia Ryland, still lay on the table. The full autopsy had not been completed yet, since her body appeared as intact as when it had arrived. No obvious dissection.

I had to admit, I was glad whatever we were going to discuss wouldn't involve delving beyond the preliminary. I prided myself on being able to stomach the autopsy from start to finish, but I was no glutton for punishment. Just give me the abbreviated version any time.

Patterson had already arrived but apparently the meeting had not started. I appreciated that he'd waited for me.

"Did the hair samples you took from the body of

victim number two match up with something you found…here?" I inclined my head toward the autopsy table.

Ammon nodded. *Scalp hairs from two different individuals besides the victim. Although there are no matches in any of our databases, the two extraneous hairs taken from Miss Ryland's body are exact matches to the two extraneous ones taken from Miss Wells's body.*

Anticipation stirred. We didn't have an ID, but at least we had a lead that connected the two murders beyond the details of the MO.

"So our perp is getting sloppy?" He—or they—hadn't left any evidence behind on Reba Harrison. Maybe killing so close together had caused him to make a mistake.

Patterson looked as impatient as I felt as we waited for Ammon to decide how to relay his thoughts.

The M.E. rubbed his hands together. *Perhaps he is getting sloppy. Perhaps the hairs do not even belong to the killer or killers. But I have solved the mystery of why we haven't found any trace evidence, other than the hair, of course.* He paused. *The killer washes their bodies very thoroughly. Every crevice. I suspected this was the case with the first victim, but I couldn't be sure until I had a comparison situation.*

In other words, another body.

"Is this some sort of ritual?" I wanted evidence that pointed to Dr. Santos, not ruled him out. He didn't exactly look or act like the ritual type. But then, looks and behavior could be deceiving.

I don't believe so. He attempted to throw me off by using a different cleanser each time. He was very careful. Typical skin cleansers were used on the skin, while feminine cleansers were utilized where needed. He didn't want me to recognize what he'd done.

He could have used what was available from each victim's home, Patterson said.

Crime-scene techs had gone over the homes of the first two victims. The process was being repeated at this victim's house right now. But I already knew what they would find. Nothing—except maybe cleansing products that matched those used on the victims.

That's possible, Ammon allowed. *If we had samples from the homes of the victims, we could do a comparison.*

I supposed that would at least confirm another detail of the MO.

I've seen this before, Ammon said knowingly.

He didn't have to say more. I knew what he meant. The Starlet Murders of four years ago. The perp had cleansed his victims in a ritual-like manner. And not a speck of evidence had been found from a single one of the crime scenes.

He was definitely back. The question was, why had he suddenly started to leave trace evidence?

Ammon and Patterson continued to talk but I was hung up on how we would ever catch this guy when two of Metro's best detectives hadn't been able to last time. Even the Federal Bureau of Investigations had consulted on the case and they'd been baffled, as well.

No evidence, no mistakes. Nothing but a string of murders all committed in exactly the same manner.

Some shrinks believed that all serial killers wanted to be caught in order to receive the glory for their deeds. Not this one. Which told me something important about him: he wasn't finished having fun yet.

We had three dead bodies this go-round and not a lick of evidence. If his course ran the same as last time, we would have three more before he was through.

What we needed was motivation.

We actually had several connections between the women. All longed to be in the country-music business. All worshipped the current stars of the industry. And all three had done business, on one level or the other, with Rex Lane. And let us not forget that two had seen his friend, or lover as the case might be, for cosmetic surgery procedures. Patricia Ryland just hadn't lived long enough to get hers done.

That was the one difference between these murders and those of four years ago. None of the victims had been tied to Lane or Santos back then. I had checked.

Was the connection mere coincidence? I didn't think so.

When we left the morgue, Patterson stopped on the sidewalk outside. I took the opportunity to draw some fresh air into my lungs. The chemical smells related to death were repulsive.

We should check out the place where Ryland lived.

He wouldn't get an argument from me. Making that impromptu call on Rex Lane this morning had overridden all else. And then I'd gotten dragged off to hot-dog heaven with Barlow. Which was good, I supposed. At least we had a plan now. The delay in going to the home of Miss Ryland actually worked in our favor. The crime-scene techs didn't like us to show up before they got most of their business done. As with the other two victims, it was doubtful the home was involved in any way, but it would be considered a secondary scene until that assessment had been confirmed.

I decided to ride with Patterson again. I could pick up my car later. The decision had nothing to do with my being worried about Clarence Johnson sneaking up on me. It was just more convenient. Gave me and Patterson a chance to chat. To bond. Partners were supposed to do that.

We rode in silence for a bit, then I asked, "Do you think Xavier Santos is capable of cold-blooded murder?"

Patterson regarded my question for a time before looking at me and saying, *I don't know.*

I decided then that his lengthy consideration had more to do with protecting his reputation than with analyzing the suspect.

At a four-way stop, he turned to me again. *The encounter was brief and basically anonymous. But it was intense, if that helps any.*

He searched my face for several seconds before proceeding through the intersection. I knew what he was looking for. Any sign of how I judged him now that I had heard that snippet of information. The admission hadn't been easy. I could understand that.

"On my first case," I began, not really sure why I was doing this, maybe for the whole bonding thing...whatever, "I got involved to a degree with one of the bad guys. A man who killed because it was his job. From what I understood, he was not only good at it, but he enjoyed it." My insides quivered just a little when I thought of Mason Conrad. I hated that I still felt something for him. The man I really wanted to be with was Barlow... How could I have any sort of feelings for another man?

Patterson glanced my way, surprise occupying the planes of his face.

I shrugged. "I'm human. I was attracted to him and it just happened. I didn't see the killer side of him...I only saw the man. At the time I needed someone to reach out to, and he was handy."

Mason Conrad had gotten a short sentence at a minimum-security facility for spilling his guts on his colleagues. He'd saved my life, so I couldn't complain that he'd gotten off lightly.

Mason Conrad. I hugged my arms around my middle. My one detour into the danger zone where my love life was concerned. When I thought of him and Barlow in the same thread of reflection I felt confused and completely out of my element. So I avoided that pesky situation most of the time. Why was I having so much trouble with that lately?

Patterson parked in front of Delia Decker's town house and he said to me, *He wasn't just intense—he was brutal.*

He didn't have to explain who he meant. Santos.

If I had to label him, I'd call him a masochist. Patterson's gaze bored heavily into mine. *He enjoyed the pain when I gave tit for tat.*

With those words echoing in my brain, I went inside the town house to see if the techs had made any discoveries. I wasn't holding my breath, but I could hope.

The lead tech shook his head at me when I stopped at the door of the bedroom that had been used by our newest victim.

I left Patterson to go over the nonexistent details with the tech while I went in search of Delia Decker. Her car had been out front so I knew she was there.

She had escaped to the rear patio outside her galley-style kitchen. A small water fountain and a table with four chairs took up most of the flagstoned space. Lots of green plants and a Siamese cat who immediately wound around my legs finished the picture. Miss Decker sat at the table staring into what looked like a cup of coffee.

"Miss Decker."

She looked up. *Yes?*

"We'll be through here very soon. I'm really sorry for the inconvenience."

She stared back down at her cup, said something I didn't get.

I pulled out the chair next to her and sat down. "Miss Decker, you'll have to look at me when you speak."

She did look at me but she frowned as if she couldn't imagine why I would make such a request.

"I'm deaf. I need to read your lips to know what you're saying."

The shock in her eyes was something I had grown accustomed to over the past three years. She blinked it away and did what everyone I say this to does. *I'm sorry…I…had no idea.*

Well, of course she hadn't had any idea. It's kind of like when someone tells you that they've lost a loved one, you automatically say you're sorry even when you didn't know them and certainly didn't have any reason to apologize for something you had absolutely nothing to do with. It just sounded nice…made you feel better about doing or saying whatever you did to prompt their telling you the sad news.

Speaking of knowing things, I wondered how Santos had picked up on my deafness. How had he known that about me? Metro was very careful not to release any info about my situation to the media. I muscled the question aside and focused on Delia Decker.

"You were saying," I prompted, otherwise she would next ask what had happened to cause my deafness. Had I always been this way? I knew the drill. It rarely changed.

She slumped with resignation. *I just don't understand how this happened. Who would want to kill Patricia? She didn't have anything anyone would want to steal. She didn't know anyone's deep, dark secrets. She hadn't witnessed any crimes. There just isn't any reasonable explanation.*

She was looking for reason in an unreasonable act.

"We don't know the killer's motivation yet."

Do you have any suspects? Anything I could tell her parents to give them hope that whoever did this will be brought to justice?

"I'm sorry but I can't discuss that information with you."

She didn't look happy about that.

"But you can help us by telling us anything else you've remembered about her interactions with others in the past few weeks."

I wondered if she would answer when seconds expanded into minutes.

I told you everything I know already. I don't think she has dated anyone in particular since coming to Nashville. She chased after the usual pack of stars. But she wasn't a groupie. Not like you think anyway. She adored the stars but she didn't throw herself at them like some of the girls who come here looking for fame do. She was a good girl when she came here.

I placed my hand on hers. "We'll do everything we can to nail this creep, Miss Decker. This has been a big shock to you. When you've had time to come to terms with it to some extent, you call me if you remember anything at all. Or if you have any questions." I'd told her this before but I needed to make sure it penetrated the haze of denial and disbelief.

My cell phone vibrated. I excused myself and went in search of a private place to take the call.

Barlow.

I wasn't sure I wanted to talk to him again this soon,

but I couldn't exactly ignore the call. It was more than likely about the case.

"Walters."

I watched the message move across the screen. *Return to division ASAP. Emergency press conference.*

I snagged Patterson and ushered him toward the door. "Press conference," I explained.

He looked about as happy as I did.

How could we conduct a press conference?

We didn't know squat.

Chief Kent, the Chief of Detectives at Metro, and Chief Barlow started the press conference. Patterson and I stood behind them like obedient soldiers.

It constantly amazed me how much a politician could make out of nothing at all. Chief Kent had the press eating out of his hand. Talk about spinning straw into gold.

Since the press had already gotten wind of the repeating MO of the murders and the similarity to the Starlet Murders of four years ago, Kent gave it to them like it was. Or at least a well-washed version of what it was. We had reason to believe the Starlet killer or a copycat was back in business.

He answered every question without actually providing any significant information at all. I was impressed.

Patterson nudged me. I frowned at him.

One of the reporters just asked you a question.

My attention snapped back to the throng of reporters. He could have told me which one.

Barlow said something into the microphone at the podium. If I read it right, he said, *Would you repeat the question please?*

Great save. I'd have to thank him later.

The female reporter pushed to the front of the crowd. *Detective Walters, as a woman, what is your take on the kind of person who would commit such heinous murders?*

I knew the standard answer for questions like this: We're still considering all aspects of the case—any comment I made at this time would be premature.

I knew it and yet I couldn't bring myself to pass along that pile of rubbish. I had definite thoughts on the killer. Sharing them in an acceptable fashion that wouldn't get me called on the carpet was the hard part.

As I moved up to the podium I could feel both Barlow's and Kent's eyes on me. I'm certain Kent was hoping I wouldn't undo everything he'd done to keep this press conference on the straight and narrow. Public hysteria was not something he wanted to see, nor did I.

"The person who committed these murders," I said, my voice stronger than I would have imagined—not that I could hear it but I always felt the quivers when it wasn't, "is a self-centered, pathetic slug merely passing himself off as a man. He's afraid of his own shadow and obviously has something to hide about his performance since he doesn't allow anyone to live after he's finished."

I was deaf…totally and utterly so…and still I recognized that the room had fallen so absolutely silent a hearing person would have been aware of a pin dropping a dozen yards away. That and the flabbergasted expressions on the reporters' faces. Who knew it would take so little to blow them all away?

Chief Kent resumed control of the press conference and I slunk back to my position next to Detective Patterson.

The moment hands started to come together in applause I was out of there. Patterson was right on my heels.

I wasn't about to hang around and get called to Kent's office.

Honestly, I don't know what made me say those things.

Temporary insanity?

Or maybe I just couldn't get the idea of what that scumbag had done to those women out of my head long enough to think rationally. I reminded myself that this case might actually involve scumbags, plural. Just further proof of what I'd said. The first go-round he'd appeared to work alone; this time he obviously required an accomplice. Otherwise why would the same hair fibers be found on each victim? Hair from two different individuals? Two killers was my estimation, unless, of course, the hairs had been planted. But for what reason?

As I entered the homicide bull pen, every detective in the house—and there were only five because it was late on Monday evening—stood and applauded.

I glanced at Patterson, who looked worried and

rightly so. He said, *If I were you I'd be out of here before the brass get free of those media sharks.*

I spotted Barlow coming through the door. "Too late," I muttered. I did a lot of that these days, mostly at myself.

Barlow pointed to me and then to his office.

You want me to go with you?

That my new partner would offer to share the heat with me altered my perception of him so totally that I scarcely recognized how I felt.

"I'll be fine, but thanks."

I pivoted on my heel and strode determinedly toward Barlow's office. I'd said what I said. There was no taking it back. I doubted it would be the last time I would overstep my bounds or otherwise say something wholly unauthorized.

And guess what? I would do it again.

Barlow stood in the middle of his office, his hands propped on his hips. He looked furious. No, strike that. He looked madder than hell.

"You wanted to see me?" Might as well play innocent. Aiming for pity was my only hope if I read him right. To avoid eye contact I surveyed the family photo of him and his two sisters that sat proudly on his desk. Two younger sisters. I was pretty sure that's where Barlow had honed his overprotective tendencies. The framed, crudely drawn picture of stick people flying kites next to that was a gift from his four-year-old niece.

In my peripheral vision I noticed that he'd crossed

his arms over his chest. Might as well get this over with. I looked up at him and the fury on his face made me want to take a step back. To my credit, I held my ground.

Sit down, Detective Walters.

Hmm. Detective Walters. There definitely wasn't a friendly chat on the agenda.

When I'd taken a seat he glared down at me. *You understand that the killer is more than likely watching every move we make related to this case?*

I cocked an eyebrow, refused to answer what surely was a rhetorical question.

Your actions in that press conference could very well make you his next target. His stoic expression slipped ever so slightly.

"Isn't that the point?" I argued. "Getting him in our line of sight? Luring him out into the light of day?"

A vein throbbed in Barlow's forehead. I was reasonably certain I had never seen him this angry.

This is not a game, Walters. This is life and death. Yours and possibly other women's. What if your slap in the face prompts him to kill again, sooner than he would have?

I suddenly felt sick to my stomach. I hadn't thought of that. Truth was, I hadn't thought at all. I'd acted on visceral instinct.

I'd made a mistake.

"You're right. That was a mistake." Damn. I really had screwed up. The thought that my actions might cause someone else to lose her life...

Go home, Walters. Get some sleep and come back

here tomorrow with a clear head. Otherwise I'll have no choice but to put someone else on this case.

I stood. Would have walked out with my tail between my legs but something made me look back. The depth of distress etched across the familiar lines and angles of his face made my chest heavy with regret. I hadn't considered things from this point of view.

"I will be more careful."

He nodded.

I didn't talk to Patterson on my way out. I didn't talk to anyone. I needed to go home and lick my wounds. Self-inflicted wounds. I'd taken an unnecessary risk…and hurt the man I cared about more than I wanted to admit.

Patterson hustled up alongside me as I reached the parking area. *I'll take you to pick up your car.*

I whacked myself on the forehead with the heel of my hand. I'd completely forgotten about leaving my car at the morgue.

"Thanks." Man, I definitely wasn't firing on all cylinders.

You okay?

I nodded. "I'll live."

When we'd settled into the front seat of his SUV he held my gaze a moment before starting the vehicle. *You said what we all wanted to say.*

And that's what I had done. With no care as to the consequences. Just like Barlow said.

Maybe I did belong in profiling or on a crime-scene tech team. A good detective had to have self control.

Today I had proven to the world how very little I had.

* * *

On the way home I stopped by the hospital to check on my niece and her mommy. I also popped into Shameka's room, as well. All were doing well. Shameka was complaining about wanting to go home. But I'd seen the fear in her eyes when I admitted that we hadn't found Johnson yet.

God, I hated killers.

I closed my eyes and sank lower in the tub of frothy bubbles. I didn't take a bubble bath often—mostly I didn't have the patience—but tonight I needed pampering. I needed to totally relax and clear my head of all the garbage crowding out my good sense.

Tomorrow I would do better. I would focus on the investigation with a rational mindset. Dig more deeply into the Starlet Murders of four years ago and pray I'd find something someone missed.

More digging was needed on Lane and Santos as well. And we needed to determine if the women had any other associates, boyfriends or peers in common.

We needed to get samples of cleansers to Dr. Ammon from each victim's residence. That would tell us if the killer had been in the victim's home.

More than anything I'd like to get a hair sample from my two main suspects. Hell would freeze over sooner. I would need a warrant and I didn't have sufficient evidence to get one.

Technically I wasn't even supposed to talk to Lane again without his attorney present. But I would take any chance I got to question him. He was cocky all right but not nearly as cocky as his friend Santos. The two had something to hide, I felt certain. All I had to do was prove it.

But how did they tie into the old case? Lane just didn't strike me as the serial-killer type. But what about Santos? Maybe he was the one four years ago. He could have gotten sloppy this time—or lazy—and started hunting among his own patients. But he seemed too smart for that.

I felt suddenly cold despite the hot water. A creepy feeling flitted down my spine. The same feeling I'd been getting the past couple of days whenever I was alone. As if someone was here, in my home, watching and listening to me. I told myself to relax and forget that idea. It was probably my imagination. I was exhausted.

I tried to push it away but it didn't work. No matter how I tried I just couldn't relax. I had to get up. Had to check it out.

I pushed up from the water, grabbed my gun, which was on the table near the tub, then wrapped a towel around my dripping body.

Paranoia at home was not acceptable. I should be asleep by now, not worrying about whether or not someone had sneaked into my house.

Besides, I had my own personal shadow.

Jamison was likely sitting right outside my house at this very moment. Not counting the patrol unit Barlow had admitted to assigning to my house.

With my weapon in my right hand, I grabbed the

bathroom doorknob and gave it a twist. No one waited for me on the other side. Room by room I went through the whole house. Nothing. No one. Just my overworked imagination. I pulled the plug in the tub, brushed my teeth and trudged off to bed.

I plopped onto it without even bothering with a nightshirt or drying my hair. The towel would just have to do.

When I started to reach over to turn off the light on my bedside table a folded piece of paper caught my eye.

I tensed. Knew unquestionably that this was not something I had left on my pillow.

Instead of grabbing the paper and unfolding it as I wanted to do, I scrambled out of bed and went in search of latex gloves. There were always extras in my jacket pockets. The drycleaners complained all the time that I left them in my pockets.

Gloves stretched over my hands, I sat down on the edge of my bed and picked up the twice-folded paper. I opened it up and read the words written there.

You think you're so smart, Detective Walters. I'm going to have to teach you a lesson. See how easy it would be.
A Pathetic Slug

Chapter 8

We have three victims, ladies and gentlemen. Three murdered using the same, down to the last precise detail, MO as one who eluded us four years ago. A repeat killer...a serial killer.

I only half listened as Metro's staff shrink droned on about who and what we were dealing with. This was the same shrink who had worked the Starlet case before. The two detectives from that case were now officially assigned to support Patterson and me.

Every homicide detective in the division was present for the morning's briefing, as was the Chief of Detectives, the Chief of Police, Barlow and the mayor.

Feelings of sexual inadequacy often drive predators of this type...the motive dwells deep within his psyche.

Maybe so, but I'd been soaking in my tub last night

when this particular predator had slipped beneath surveillance's radar and into my house. Barlow had confirmed that a patrol unit still watched my house at night.
He hadn't fessed up to Jamison yet, but that wasn't surprising. He wanted an ace up his sleeve. Well, so did I.
What Barlow didn't know wouldn't hurt him.

Judging by the note the perp had left me, personally
I didn't think he felt inadequate at all. Pretty darned
cocky if you ask me.

Just another scumbag who got off on hurting women.

*…though these murders seem irrational they make
complete sense to the killer. Preliminary conclusions
would indicate that this offender is a sociopath. He
tends to be self-centered, manipulative and emotionally shallow and devoid of empathy and remorse.*

Finally, something we agreed upon.

*The psychosexual pathology that drives this kind of
killer is generally ingrained early in life and grows
stronger as they mature into adults. Many have suffered
from one or more types of abuse, sexual, psychologi-
cal or physical. Their only escape from that horrific
world is fantasy. At some point, ladies and gentlemen,
fantasies evolve into action and a serial killer is born.*

I glanced down at the profile that had been passed
out at the beginning of the meeting. I hadn't needed it.
I had already formed a rough profile in my mind. How
did the killer gain access to the victim? Unknown, possibly through associates. Considering what the killer
had done to the victims and the fact that he'd tried to
cover his tracks, he was in no hurry to get caught. That

he was organized and killed close to home—this part was assumed since he appeared relaxed enough in the environment to dump his victims—showed he preferred to stay in his comfort zone. He took no physical trophies from the victims, but the personal effects of all three were still missing. The tiaras were his idea of marking his victims, his signature. Or maybe just a sick sense of humor considering all three of the victims had had stars in their eyes. Just like four years ago.

Not every aspect of the current cases matched the previous investigation. This time the victims lived in upscale neighborhoods. Last time they'd come from all over the city. But the MO was too similar to discount.

…*restraining the victims is significant,* the psychiatrist was saying now, *and is perhaps indicative of his inability to physically hold his own with the victims without the aid of bondage. The restraint of his victims equals power. He revels in his power.*

I shuddered at the idea that he could have stood outside my bathroom door…could have listened to my sighs and moans as I relaxed in my hot bath.

According to the crime-scene techs he hadn't left the first print or any other evidence except the note, and it was typed and printed from a run-of-the-mill inkjet printer. The only thing unique about it was the weight of the paper, high cotton content, very expensive. Tracking down the retail source of the paper would be time-consuming, but it was all we had. I hadn't expected that much. Our killer was far too careful. What I found most disturbing, however, was that no evidence of forced entry or lock-picking had been discovered on any of my doors or windows. It was as if he'd had a key or could walk through walls. A locksmith had been at my house first thing this morning to install new locks as well as heavy-duty dead bolts.

His having a key was impossible, I know...but still, it gave me the willies.

How could he just waltz in like that? As if he owned the place. And without anyone noticing.

I pushed the troubling thoughts aside and focused my attention back on the group of speakers at the front of the conference room. The mayor had launched into his usual pep talk. For a politician he should vary his monologue a little when it came to talking to the troops. It was beginning to sound a little dated and a whole lot generic. I tried to avoid the employment of adjectives like *boring* and such for him since I liked him, but this was bad.

Chief Barlow took the floor next and acknowledged Patterson and me as the primaries on the case. He emphasized the need for a quick resolution to the case. If this was indeed the same perp as the Starlet Murders, he might very well stop after victim number six...which meant three more women might die and we still might not be any closer to catching him.

Another worrisome feeling shivered over my skin.

I had reacted on emotion and I'd gotten the killer's full attention with my statement at that press conference. He'd reacted. It was kind of like the dog-chasing-the-car scenario. What did I do with his attention now that I'd captured it?

Getting killed wasn't something I'd intended to go out of my way to do, despite what Barlow thought.

When the meeting started to break up Patterson tapped me on the shoulder. *You up for lunch?*

I perked up immediately. It was kind of nice having a partner with less seniority. "Are you buying?"

Why not? You took me to lunch last time, remember?

I had. I'd almost forgotten about that.

My gaze collided with Barlow's and I read the message in his eyes as clearly as if he'd made the statement out loud for all to hear.

My office. Now.

"Give me a minute," I said to Patterson.

I said hello to a number of the other detectives as I pushed through the crowd. I imagined most were wondering how I'd landed this high-profile case. I had the least seniority in the division, except for Patterson, and then there was the issue of my being deaf.

If they really thought about it they would know that I'd only ended up on the case by chance. I'd been the detective on call when the first victim had been found. Who knew then that this would turn into a multiple-offender status? And there was always that little point that Barlow wanted me off the Clarence Johnson case. He'd unknowingly taken me out of the frying pan only to drop me right smack into the hottest flames of the fire.

Oh, well, I kind of liked the hot seat when it came to cases. It never got boring.

I realized that chance wasn't my only reason for still

being on this case. As Barlow himself had said, I'm particularly good at zoning out all else and focusing on the details. I don't hear all the hype related to victims or ongoing cases. I concentrate on the facts.

There had to be some sort of perk for losing one of my senses and that, so far, appeared to be it.

I was about five steps behind Barlow all the way to his office. That was definitely okay—I liked the view. He didn't turn around and speak to me until we were both inside with the door closed. This was becoming a habit. I wasn't sure I liked it even if I did like the man. Maybe a little too much. Okay, maybe a lot too much.

Just so there is no misunderstanding as to my stand on the situation, I told Chief Kent I would prefer to take you off this case.

"No!" I bracketed my waist with my hands and prepared for battle. What the hell was he doing? He'd been the one to assign me to this case. My leftover feelings of guilt about how my actions had affected him disappeared. "No way! This is my case. The killer and I have connected. No one else—"

He held up his hands to halt my tirade. *You don't have to argue the point. Chief Kent nixed the idea.*

If I hadn't been so fire-spitting mad I would have let out a victory whoop. I felt reasonably certain Barlow wouldn't take it very well. Not that I really cared just now. How could he do this to me? Was he purposely trying to undermine my confidence with my peers and superiors alike? His determination to take me off any case that got hairy was a huge red flag, in my opinion—

Merri Walters isn't capable of handling herself in a tense situation. For him to talk to me about his concerns was one thing, but to go to his Chief of Detectives.... That crossed a line, in my opinion. I didn't appreciate it at all.

It was a miracle Patterson hadn't requested a partner change considering the mixed signals Barlow gave about me. Maybe my new partner only hung in there with me because he was worried I'd use his secret against him. He needn't have been. No way would I do that.

This isn't about whether I believe you're capable of the job, Barlow said, obviously reading my mind. He did that rather well.

Yeah, right, raced to the tip of my tongue but I kept my mouth shut. He didn't believe I was capable of taking care of myself or we wouldn't even be having this conversation.

Last night made this investigation personal for you. That changed the dynamics considerably. Made you, as well as the others assigned to work with you, vulnerable. Though my hands are tied, I hope you understand my position is about protecting the integrity of the investigation as well as the investigators. Including you.

"I understand perfectly." Everything he'd said made a certain sense, but I also knew him. This was not the first time he had done this—purposely looked for an excuse to take me off a case. Enough was enough. I had a right to the same treatment as all the other detectives.

I skirted his desk, walked straight into his personal space and said what was on my mind. After all, he'd made his position clear, didn't I have the same right? "Like your position on the Hammond case? And the Clarence Johnson case?" Fury boiled up inside me so fast I shook with it. How dare he keep doing this to me! I'd proven myself time and time again. I deserved his respect, not his blown-out-of-proportion concern.

The Hammond case was different. You were an untrained civilian. Chiefs Kent and Adcock took advantage of your naiveté and ambitiousness.

Wrong answer.

"But I got the job done, didn't I? I can't spend the rest of my life hiding from the Clarence Johnsons of the world or the Luther Hammonds just because I'm deaf. I am who I am—you might as well get used to that. When all your tactics fail what're you going to do, fire me? There are laws that protect people in my position."

He looked away. Even I knew that one had been a low blow but he'd pushed me too far.

Merri.

He looked into my eyes and an ache went through me. How had we let this happen…allowed our hearts to hope knowing all along we couldn't go there?

You've tied my hands. I can't stop this thing and you're caught right in the middle. He delivered a warning to you, personally, with a patrol unit right outside your home. He was in and out like smoke. We have no evidence. We have no idea who he is. The only thing we know for sure is that he is smarter than we'd like. He proved that four years ago. He took both my hands in his, and my pulse rate rocketed into high gear. He searched my eyes for what he wanted to see. *He's completely comfortable taking risks. His intelligence and bravado make him extremely dangerous. I don't want you to end up on a slab at the morgue.*

He closed his eyes a moment before going on and in those few seconds I fully understood just how much he cared for me. God, I wanted to tell him I felt the same way. Wanted to throw my arms around him and hold him close, to feel those powerful arms around me.

But I couldn't…not just yet.

I thought about this killer's victims and how I'd looked at each one laid out on a cold, hard slab at the morgue. Maybe Barlow was right. Maybe this time I was in over my head. It was one thing to know your enemy, but another altogether to be totally in the dark.

Blind as well as deaf.

That summed up my current position on this case a little too well. As much as I wanted to nail Lane and Santos for these murders, every instinct warned me that this was way bigger than those two.

I had to see this through.

"I'm a homicide detective, in case you hadn't noticed," I said, careful not to use his name and to keep the emotional quiver out of my voice. I pulled my hands free of his and took a step back. "My job is dangerous. I do not want you or anyone else to attempt to make my job easier. I expect to do the same work as

every other detective in this division. No exceptions."
I drew in a deep breath for courage and said the rest.
"I would sincerely appreciate it if you would stop interfering to an extent that feels inappropriate, as if
you're singling me out. It isn't fair."

For the first time since Steven Barlow and I had
shared that kiss all those months ago, I felt his complete withdrawal. Uncertainty hit me like a rock. This
was what I'd needed to say to him for a long time. I
wanted to do my job just like everyone else. He, of all
people, should understand that. Yet, he didn't. I saw a
finality in his eyes that…terrified me.

The tension closed in around me so tightly I could
hardly breathe before he spoke again. Fear that I'd
made the biggest mistake of my life snugged like a
noose around my neck.

Thank you, Detective, that's all.

And just like that we were done. That mask of control he wore so well had fallen firmly back into place.

I walked out of his office with my stomach dragging
on the floor. I'd almost made it back to the bull pen
when I encountered my partner.

I thought you'd gotten lost on me. He pushed away
from the wall, slung his jacket over his shoulder. *You
ready?*

Lunch. Oddly, I'd lost my appetite.

"Maybe I'll just get something from the lounge
later."

Patterson studied me a moment then shrugged. *I
said I was paying.* He grinned. *If you want to choose*

the place, that's okay by me. I have to say, though, you're a cheap date.

I wanted to urge him to go on and have a break somewhere nice without me, but a part of me wanted to burrow into this case. That was the quickest way to make everything else go away. Dive into work. So I took advantage of my partner's willingness and off we went.

After picking up sandwiches and drinks, I led the way to the small briefing room. We'd already set up a timeline there. Basically we'd created a map of the killer's steps in chronological order beginning with the first victim, Reba Harrison. Estimated time of death, location of body, means of discovery, and anything else we knew about her relevant to her manner of death and the known events leading up to that final moment had been diagrammed around an eight-by-ten photo of her.

Mallory Wells was next and then Patricia Ryland. As the later two victims were added, additional notes and lines connected them to victim number one. Known associates in common and anything else that linked one to the other.

Each of the women had been young and beautiful with big dreams and one common weakness: desperation to make their futures happen.

The other detectives on the case were doing their own research. Looking for connections between these murders and the Starlet case. Digging through mountains of additional research on most anyone the victims were closely associated with. A lot of work and so little time.

We've cleared any boyfriends, Patterson said as he sat down at the conference table. *No known family squabbles. No known drug problems. Other than being starstruck, these ladies were pretty low-key.*

He was right. Not a single one of these women could be called high-risk targets for any reason other than their dreams of becoming celebrities and their preoccupation with those who already were.

"What about Rex Lane?" I asked. I propped a hip on the corner of the table. "You said his friend Santos could be brutal. What's your impression of Lane?"

Patterson rubbed his chin. *He's not the aggressor in the relationship.*

"Which relationship?" Being blunt was necessary, people were dying here. "With Santos or with the women?"

Santos. He arrowed me a pointed look. *It could very well be a different story with the women. Lane could still be trying to convince himself that he isn't who he is.*

"Do you think it was Lane or Santos who came into my house?" My money was on Santos, if it was either. I didn't like him. But deep down I was pretty sure it was someone else…a killer who had spent four years in hibernation. What had awakened him?

Patterson lifted one shoulder in a noncommittal gesture. *Maybe. But you know we don't have any proof these guys are even involved. We're speculating entirely here. And there's no connection whatsoever between these two and the murders from four years ago.*

I stared at the haunting board. "Strange, isn't it? If it is Santos, why would a gay man brutally rape and murder a woman?"

When I turned back to Patterson, he said, *The shrink said the perp wasn't likely to be gay. More likely he's bisexual.*

I wondered if his reminding me of that was in defense of his sexual preference. I wished I could make him understand that he didn't have to defend himself to me. "I think what he actually said," I challenged, "is that the *unsub* wasn't likely gay."

The Feds used terms like *unsub* for *unknown subject.* We cops, we just use *perp* for perpetrator or killer or shooter. Why make things complicated?

"You know," I contemplated aloud, "we won't be able to nail this guy without some evidence." I didn't know why I bothered making the comment. Patterson knew that as well as I did. That's why the top brass, including the mayor, were getting so antsy. Folks in Nashville couldn't keep dying with no visible progression by the police. Especially considering this appeared to be an encore performance of the Starlet murders.

The mayor had made his feelings clear. He wanted us to come up with a suspect to nail. One way or another.

The families have been interviewed, Patterson commented. *Friends. Co-workers. Anyone who knew them. We've gotten nowhere.*

"Don't remind me," I grumbled.

The only links we have are the business and Lucky Lane Productions.

And that just didn't make sense since neither was related to the Starlet case.

"I say we start going down Mr. Lane's client list, past and present. Someone may have seen or heard something that will connect him to activity like this. What we need is to show a pattern. Then we'd have something to go on. Maybe get a search warrant and see if we can find even a single item that belonged to one of the women in his home or his place of business. Get a strand of his hair or a sheet of paper from his printer." I shook my head resignedly. "There has to be a way to find something on him, enough to make him talk. Maybe verify he either is or has been involved in making porn. He's all we've got. And, who knows, maybe we'll find a link between him and whoever killed those six women four years ago." Maybe the Starlet killer had been roused back to activity by something Lane or Santos had done.

And let's not overlook Santos. His client list might very well shed some light on his activities.

That was, sadly, about the only route we had to choose.

"How do you propose we do this?" I didn't qualify the question with anything like "within the law" or "legally." He knew the rules. We could bend 'em but we couldn't break 'em. Not when a mere technicality can negate even the most compelling evidence.

All we needed were the client lists.

But without a court order that might not be an easy feat. And a court order would take time. We didn't have time. More important, we didn't want to alert the enemy to our ultimate goal…pinning multiple homicides on them.

Let's start with Google.

Realization of Patterson's intent dawned. "Both probably have Web sites. And anyone who's chatted about one or both on the Net will be easy to track down."

Two minutes later we were skimming names on Santos's website. His site contained a page of "praise," complete with names. Though I couldn't be sure until I'd looked them up, I would bet they were mostly locals.

Lucky Lane Productions showed clips from various music videos, complete with extensive casts.

We printed the names, cross-referenced with DMV and compiled a list of most recent addresses.

"Which one do you want?" I was champing at the bit to get my hands on Lane again. I suspected he wasn't the cold-blooded one in this couple but he would break the easiest. I could handle Santos, as well. It might not be such a bad idea to drop in on him anyway.

I can take Santos.

I wondered if Patterson actually wanted to go after Santos or if he'd made that decision to protect me. I swear, Barlow had made me paranoid.

With my list in hand, I suggested, "We should touch base with each other every hour." We did have more detectives for support but they had their hands full canvassing the areas around the dumping sites and sorting through all that research. If the perp was watching the process, and he probably was, he would recognize just how desperate we were. That might pump up his cockiness, hopefully encouraging his sloppiness.

When there were no leads to speak of and no real evidence, going back over and over the compiled data, the crime scene and the testimony of witnesses or friends and family of the victims could unearth evidence we'd previously missed.

My intent when I settled into my car was to go straight to the address on the top of my list, but I just couldn't get Lane off my mind. I knew with the right prodding he would talk. I needed an opportunity with him. Alone.

So I drove to Lucky Lane Productions and I waited. I didn't have to wait long. His six-figure Jaguar rolled out of the underground garage and I followed him, careful to keep my distance. He drove around, seemingly in circles for half an hour and I'd started to feel as I'd wasted my time when he finally pulled to the side of the street. I parked, as well.

None of the shops lining this particular street gave me pause. Boutiques, shoe stores and the like. What was he doing? Shopping?

He emerged from his car and looked around. Instinctively I slid lower in my seat, but I knew I was parked far enough away not to garner his attention. He walked straight over to the pay phone and made a call.

I bolted into action, grabbed my binoculars from the

glove box. This guy had dozens of phones back at the office and a cell phone in his pocket. The only reason he would make a call from a phone booth was to ensure it wasn't traced back to him.

It's me.

Judging by the frustration on his face the person he'd called hadn't expected or wanted to hear from him.

I don't care. This is out of control. We have to do something…tell someone.

He let his head drop back as he listened. Apparently not happy with the response his head shot up and he flung his free arm outward. *Don't you get it! This isn't a game. I got another note last night. He's going to destroy us.*

Anticipation soared through my veins. I could barely breathe.

Oh, yeah, that's a perfect answer. I'm sure your plan will work ingeniously if we don't end up dead first. He slammed the phone back into its cradle and stormed to his car.

He had to be talking to Santos. My heart was pounding. There was a third party involved. Lane was scared.

As if abruptly sensing my presence, Lane stalled when he reached for the door of his Jag. He looked around, taking his time, scrutinizing each vehicle parked close by.

I slid even lower in my seat. Held my breath.

I didn't breathe again until he'd gotten into his car and driven away. I followed just to make sure he went back to the office.

Any doubts that I'd had as to Lane's part in this were now gone. He was a puppet. I couldn't be sure if the puppet master was Santos or someone else…the unknown element from a killing spree four years past.

But I had every intention of finding out.

I drove across Nashville to the west side and began with the address at the top of my list.

This lady had starred in several music videos as an extra or backup singer, all produced by Lucky Lane Productions. She was one of the few who'd managed to make a dent in her fantasies. She hadn't been on the threshold of topping any charts with a hit single, but, hey, success is relative. Reba Harrison had been on the verge of doing the same.

The community wasn't gated but it was well-kept and seriously upscale. Nestled in the shadow of Vanderbilt University's hallowed halls, the community's diverse mixture of architectural styles was awe-inspiring.

I hoped I would find her at home. A phone call from a cop would put her on alert. I wanted her surprise fresh when I questioned her.

When the front door opened I decided maybe this was going to be a better day after all.

She looked as gorgeous in real life as she did in her photos. She had that classic beauty that never really went out of style. Like Elizabeth Taylor.

"Laura Sares?"

She scrutinized me from head to toe and back, making me wish I'd gone for the emerald suit this morning. Instead I'd taken the easy way out and grabbed something from the safe side of my closet, navy slacks and jacket, my standard uniform.

When Ms. Sares had completed her assessment of my wardrobe she briefly attempted to place my face, or so it appeared. "Yes?"

I flashed my credentials. "I'm Detective Merri Walters from Metro Homicide. I need to ask you a few questions if you have a moment."

She looked surprised, then maybe a little frightened, but the most intense reaction was the one that settled on her face last, and the one I'd least expected. Laura Sares looked resigned to her fate. Why would talking to me instill that kind of reaction?

Unless she had something to hide.

She visibly shored up her courage by drawing in a deep breath and then gestured for me to come inside.

Once we'd settled on opposite sides of the cocktail table, I got to the point. "When was the last time you worked for Lucky Lane Productions?"

She shook her head, said something like she knew this would come back to haunt her. Reading her words was difficult with her head moving side to side so swiftly.

"In what way, Ms. Sares?" Anticipation stirred in my empty tummy. Patterson and I had completely forgotten about the sandwiches we'd bought. Probably just as well.

Rex Lane isn't everything he appears to be, she said, her chin held high, her eyes determined now. *I knew when Reba Harrison got murdered it was about him.*

Anticipation sent my heart into a gallop. "Why don't you start at the beginning and tell me everything you know about Mr. Lane."

Chapter 9

Ah-ha! Gotcha.

I settled behind the wheel of my Jetta and wiggled my fingers at Officer Jamison. He reluctantly waved back. His modest gray sedan sat across the street about halfway up the block from Laura Sares's home.

So, he was still watching me. I thought so.

When this was over, Barlow and I were going to have a really, really long talk—assuming we were still speaking to each other. This working relationship was way out of bounds. He had to see that. He was too sharp not to. I'd gone as far as I dared to point that out earlier today. Why in the world did he insist on being so all-fired overprotective?

One possible answer to that question paralyzed me.

Steven Barlow was the Chief of Homicide. He'd

spent years and years as a homicide detective before that. No one I knew was more dedicated to his work or more savvy on the job. Why would he go to such extremes to watch over me as if I were made of glass or unreliable? Of course he cared about the health and welfare of all his detectives, but as I had pointed out to him the last time we talked, being a homicide detective was risky business. All who chose the profession understood that from the outset.

His behavior wasn't rational. Unless…

Was it possible that Barlow's feelings went far deeper than I suspected?

My heart fluttered wildly at the idea.

Wait. He'd been protective of me on the Hammond case when he'd scarcely known me. But, I had been a civilian. It was his duty to protect civilians.

I moistened my lips and slowly, carefully turned the idea over in my head as the sun glinted in through the windows of my car. The cool, soggy morning had turned into a beautiful day, I purposely noted in an attempt to ground my runaway thoughts in reality.

It had only been three years since I'd had my heart broken completely in two. I'd spent the time since bracing myself for the possibility that a long-term relationship might not be in the cards for me anymore. Who wanted a wife who couldn't hear? I know that sounds harsh but I have to face facts here, no matter how I wanted to pretend I could do anything. There were certain drawbacks associated with my condition.

I closed my eyes and worked toward pushing the

GET FREE BOOKS and a FREE GIFT WHEN YOU PLAY THE...

Luck7

Just scratch off the silver box with a coin. Then check below to see the gifts you get!

SLOT MACHINE GAME!

YES! I have scratched off the silver box. Please send me the 2 free Silhouette Bombshell™ books and gift for which I qualify. I understand I am under no obligation to purchase any books, as explained on the back of this card.

300 SDL D732   **200 SDL EE2H**

| |
| |

FIR3T NAME   LAST NAME

ADDRESS

APT.#   CITY

STATE/PROV.   ZIP/POSTAL CODE

7	7	7	**Worth TWO FREE BOOKS plus a BONUS Mystery Gift!**
🍒	🍒	🍒	**Worth TWO FREE BOOKS!**
♣	♣	♣	**Worth ONE FREE BOOK!**
🔔	🔔	🍒	**TRY AGAIN!**

www.eHarlequin.com

(S-B-12/05)

DETACH AND MAIL CARD TODAY!

The Silhouette Reader Service™ — Here's how it works:

Accepting your 2 free books and gift places you under no obligation to buy anything. You may keep the books and gift and return the shipping statement marked "cancel." If you do not cancel, about a month later we'll send you 4 additional books and bill you just $3.99 each in the U.S., or $4.47 each in Canada, plus 25¢ shipping & handling per book and applicable taxes if any.* That's the complete price and — compared to cover prices of $4.99 each in the U.S. and $5.99 each in Canada — it's quite a bargain! You may cancel at any time, but if you choose to continue, every month we'll send you 4 more books, which you may either purchase at the discount price or return to us and cancel your subscription.

*Terms and prices subject to change without notice. Sales tax applicable in N.Y. Canadian residents will be charged applicable provincial taxes and GST. Credit or debit balances in a customer's account(s) may be offset by any other outstanding balance owed by or to the customer.

crazy notion of Barlow being in love with me out of my head. Admittedly, it wasn't the first time I'd considered it recently, especially with the way he'd touched me in his office. But I had to focus.

I had to concentrate on the case. Barlow and I could sort this out later…as promised. Another zing of anticipation made my foolish heart skip a beat.

God, I was hopeless.

A few minutes later with my head back on straight, I started my car and snapped my seat belt into place. I had two more names and addresses on my list. If what I'd just learned from Laura Sares was true, and I believed it was, I would be seeing Mr. Rex Lane again very soon, with or without his attorney's approval. He might not be a killer, but he knew something pertinent to this case.

As I turned around in Ms. Sares's driveway I checked in my rearview mirror to see if Jamison intended to follow. I frowned. He was already gone. I had to laugh. He was like a ghost, popping up at the oddest times and then seemingly invisible at others. Maybe I needed to take surveillance lessons from the boys in Murfreesboro. They apparently weren't nearly as inept as I'd first thought.

The second former Rex Lane client on my list, Jana Wiley, had moved away and left no forwarding address. I could track her down later if need be, but for now I moved on the final name.

Katie Jo Campbell lived in a modest apartment building between Nashville proper and Brentwood. Sixth floor, front side of the building.

Since entering the building had been as simple as walking right through the door, Miss Campbell received no warning of my arrival until I'd knocked on her door. That was the way I liked it.

"Good afternoon, Miss Campbell. I'm Detective Merri Walters." God, I loved saying that. I showed the woman my credentials and pushed onward before she had a chance to form a response of her own. "I need to ask you a few questions, ma'am."

When Katie Jo Campbell recovered from her initial shock she graciously invited me inside. She had a cozy place, shabby-chic style. Kind of like my own, only I felt reasonably certain hers had been a decorating scheme from the outset, not just the wear and tear of time. The slipcovered sofa and chairs and eclectic selection of prints on the walls suited her. She wore faded soft jeans and a pullover sweater that looked as comfortable as the woman appeared to feel in her own skin.

I admired that. So many women never found that place, that elusive spot that was uniquely their own. I was pretty sure I'd found mine, maybe for the first time in my life. As much as I'd enjoyed teaching I hadn't felt as at home with myself as I do now, in spite of the hearing loss. Life could be strange.

I'm not sure how I can help you, Detective, Katie Jo said, her confusion gaining momentum with fear tagging along. *Should I be concerned?*

Generally when a person asked this question they wanted some reassurance that she or he wasn't in trouble even when they knew they'd done nothing wrong. It was an automatic defense mechanism.

"No, ma'am, you have no reason to be concerned. I'm here about your brief association with a music video producer, Rex Lane."

She frowned. *That ended nearly a year ago.*

"Yes, we're aware of that. However, my questions are relative to that time frame."

Katie Jo looked like a smart lady. I hoped she, like Laura Sares, had looked beyond the surface when she'd been dealing with Lane. And maybe that she'd been privy to the talk, gossip actually, between his other clients and/or associates.

She shrugged. *Okay. Have a seat.* She indicated the sofa as she climbed into one of the overstuffed chairs, tucking her feet under her.

I perched on the sofa and took out my pad and pen. "I'd like any impressions you got of Mr. Lane, professionally and personally, during the time that you worked with him. Anything at all, don't worry about significance."

She thought about that for a minute. *We didn't work together that long. I finally realized that keeping steady gigs on the club circuit was better for me. Like everybody else in the business I'd had visions of grandeur in the beginning.* She shrugged. *I guess I just saw the light before I hit bottom.*

"Is that what you do today?" I knew it was, but I didn't want her to realize that I'd checked out her background to the extent possible in a few minutes' time. Most people took that as a sign that they were suspects.

She nodded. *I'm happy with it. Pays the bills and gives me a chance to work on my first love.*

I inclined my head. "What's your first love?"

Songwriting. I don't know if I'll ever write anything saleable but I enjoy it and that's what counts. Money can't buy happiness.

This lady really had herself together, or so it seemed.

Time to get the conversation back on track. "So what were your impressions of Mr. Lane?"

You want the truth? She didn't wait for me to say one way or the other. *He's a class-A jerk. He wouldn't be where he is now if he hadn't had help.*

That's what I wanted to hear. "What kind of help?"

I got all this secondhand, mind you, she qualified. *But, the rumor was he had this silent partner who helped him get Lucky Lane Productions off the ground about five years ago. Before that he had been floundering with one flop product after the other.*

So far the same story I'd gotten from Laura Sares. What I found so frustrating was that I hadn't heard anything about this in any of my research on Rex Lane. There wasn't a single mention of any partner at all. Whoever his silent partner had been, he'd been invisible, as well. The timeline both women mentioned matched up. It was five years ago that Lucky Lane Productions evolved into one of the movers and shakers in the industry.

The way I heard it, Katie Jo went on, *fame and fortune wasn't enough for Lane. He started another business on the side.* She shifted in her chair, started to look uncomfortable. *The new business produced videos you won't be seeing on VH1.*

"Porn," I interjected.

She nodded. *I know that part is fact because he tried to blackmail me into doing one for him, but I refused. He swore if I didn't, any real future my career had in this town would be over. I guess that's when I realized I wasn't cut out for the sacrifices related to fame. I haven't looked back since and, considering the news lately, I'm damned glad.*

"After you walked away, did he approach you again?"

No. I never heard from him again. But I did hear rumors about a breakup between him and his silent partner. Apparently the other man was extremely upset about Mr. Lane's illegal venture.

"And you're certain you never heard the name of this silent partner."

She shook her head. *Sorry. I wish I had.*

"Where did you hear about the breakup?"

From another singer I met while working on one of the music videos.

This was the single most important piece of information I'd come here for.

Reba Harrison, she said. *She told me it got pretty nasty. Whoever the silent partner was, she seemed to know him. Apparently he, the silent partner I mean,* she clarified, *just disappeared after that falling out with Lane.*

I punched in Patterson's cell number, got him as the indicator for the second ring flashed. "Meet me back at the office." I didn't wait for his response. I dropped my phone back into my pocket and paid attention to my driving. Driving in Nashville can be hazardous if you're not on your toes.

Had what Reba Harrison learned about Lane's silent partner gotten her killed? If so, why murder the others? Certainly Patricia Ryland was too new in town to have known any dirt on Lane.

Or maybe Reba had actually known the silent partner, as Katie Jo suggested. Maybe that's what had cost her life.

I had to know the answer. From the moment Laura Sares had told me Reba Harrison had spilled that secret to her I had known that it somehow related to her murder.

I knew what Barlow would have to say: If that's the case, then how is that piece of information relative to the other two murdered women?

Maybe it wasn't. But my gut said it was. Somehow, this was part of the motivation.

It didn't make sense yet, but it would.

By the time I reached Metro's headquarters I was itching with mounting anticipation. This was the big break we'd been looking for. I didn't care if Barlow or Kent thought so or not. I intended to see this all the way through. That's how convinced I felt. Somehow, whatever had set off this killing spree was intrinsically tied to Lane and Santos. The question was, how?

I knew the instant I got off the elevator on my home floor that something wasn't right.

Too quiet. Not quiet as in a lack of sound, but a lack of activity…like entering an empty tomb.

My cell phone vibrated as I wandered slowly down the corridor toward the bull pen. I fished it out of my pocket in case it was Patterson and looked at the read-out.

Barlow.

Frowning, I pressed the talk button and said, "Walters."

No hello, no where are you, just straight to the point. *I need both you and Patterson back here now.*

I stared at the words on the small display screen and wondered what the hell could be up now. "I'm here," I told him. "Patterson should be here any minute."

Barlow wanted us both in his office. After the call ended I didn't immediately put the phone back in my pocket. I stared at it as if it held the answers to what was going on with him. Surely I wasn't in trouble again. I couldn't think of anything I'd done *today* that broke any rules.

From the corner of my eye I saw the elevator doors slide open and I turned back in that direction.

What's up? Barlow tried to reach me but I was in a dead zone.

A burst of hysterical laughter popped out of my mouth before I could stop it. I wanted to say: Get used to it, Patterson, we work in a dead zone. After all, this is Homicide.

I shrugged. "Dunno. But I've got a new lead on Rex Lane." I glanced toward Barlow's office at the other end of the corridor. "I guess it'll have to wait."

That was the thing about high-profile cases. You couldn't get a damned thing done for all the meetings the brass called.

I guess we should face the music and get that over with, Patterson said.

"Yeah."

When we arrived in the reception area, Barlow's secretary told us to go on in. *They're waiting for you,* she added.

Another knot twisted in my stomach. Who were *they?*

Patterson opened the door but allowed me to enter first. His momma had trained him right. I was sure glad he hadn't turned out to be the macho jerk I'd first thought he was.

Barlow, Chief Kent and another gentleman waited for us. I didn't know the other guy, but the tailored suit, shiny shoes, meticulous haircut and arrogant expression spelled Fed. All three men stood as we entered.

Detective Walters, Detective Patterson, Chief Kent said, *this is Special Agent William Stratton of the local Bureau office.*

Stratton shook hands with each of us in turn. He looked to be about thirty-five or -six. Blond hair, blue eyes, nice tan. Not particularly handsome, but not bad-looking.

When we'd all taken seats, Chief Kent brought Patterson and me up to speed. Barlow didn't add anything, nor did he meet my gaze. I found that particularly disturbing.

We're very pleased that the Bureau has decided to lend a hand into our investigation since we have every reason to believe these murders are related to the Starlet case, Kent said.

I wasn't sure whether to be excited or worried. Help would be great but I'd heard nightmare stories about the Feds coming in and taking over a case. According to Barlow, the Feds had royally screwed up on the Hammond case. That hadn't appeared to happen four years ago with the Starlet case but then I hadn't been there.

"In what capacity will you be helping out, Agent Stratton?" I piped up. I didn't see any reason to beat around the bush. Might as well say what was on my mind.

Thank you for asking, Detective Walters. He smiled widely. Looked a little practiced to me. Definitely not genuine. *The way the Bureau sees our role is in an advisory capacity.* He glanced at Barlow. *Chief Barlow believes you have the investigation under control without our having to get involved in a hands-on manner. But, in cases like this, we feel our presence can be reassuring.*

Okay, hold up. What was the deal here? In that fraction of a second, maybe two, where Stratton shifted his attention to Barlow there was this thing…and it definitely was not a good thing.

I hadn't seen Stratton's eyes, but I'd definitely seen his profile harden. And Barlow, well, suffice to say, his look at the guy was nothing short of lethal.

Hmmm. I sensed a history there.

In other words, Patterson offered, drawing me back to the conversation, *we just keep doing what we're doing and we can let you know if we need any assistance.*

We will be sitting in on briefings and press conferences, Stratton's gaze strayed to me as he said that last part, *but, basically, yes, you just keep doing what you've been doing.*

Patterson looked at me. I looked at him.

He shrugged and said, *I guess I've heard enough, how 'bout you?*

"Definitely." I stood, my partner did the same. "Thank you, Agent Stratton. We'll be sure to keep you informed."

And just like that my very first briefing with a federal agent came to a slightly inelegant end.

If anyone said anything after we'd turned to leave, I, of course, didn't hear it and Patterson didn't acknowledge it so I assumed we were clear to go.

Once the door was closed behind us, I gave Patterson a high five. "You're the man, partner."

I didn't see any point wasting our time once we knew the rules of his game.

A smile stretched my lips wide. Today had turned out to be one of firsts. My first real partner and I had officially bonded to the maximum. I had a good feeling about this relationship. At least this was one in my life that appeared poised to work.

For the next three hours Patterson and I delved into

Rex Lane's background. We'd done this already but we'd had nothing specific to look for. Now we did. Seemingly irrelevant details were easily overlooked when one didn't know to view them as possible red flags. Whether or not he'd had any financial support in getting his business off the ground hadn't been significant before. And how on earth did any of it tie into a serial killer who'd gotten away?

See what I mean about going over the same place or information more than once? You never know what will be important.

The material we'd collected from various sources— the Internet, the newspapers and a number of government offices like Tax and Probate and the Hall of Records—was spread over the long table in the smaller of the two conference rooms on the floor. This was also where we had the timeline reflecting the victim's final days and hours of life.

"We're onto something here, Patterson." I surveyed the list I'd made. At the very top was the one crucial piece of information that made all the difference in the world.

Walt Kennard.

He had been Rex Lane's silent partner.

Walt had also been the godfather of the first murder victim, Reba Harrison. Major red flag.

Five years ago, according to a single article tucked away in the business section of one of the smaller newspapers, Kennard had invested heavily in Lucky Lane Productions. It was the only media information we could find related to the business merger. However, a lien had been recorded at the courthouse against the business. Kennard had been named as the lien holder. The lien had been released, paid in full less than one year ago. Nearly two million dollars. That payment allowed Lane to wash his hands of his partner's involvement with Lucky Lane Productions. Oversight had been specified in the lien. No lien, no fingers in the pie.

I couldn't see Rex Lane being happy with someone else telling him what to do.

But it got better.

There was no record of Walt Kennard in the past fourteen months. His homes, and he had several, stood empty. His financial accounts were serviced by an attorney who didn't have a clue where Walt Kennard might be. The attorney insisted that a missing persons report had been filed just over one year ago with the authorities in Knoxville, Kennard's main place of residence, but no indication of foul play had been discovered. Mr. Kennard had simply vanished. He'd told his attorney he intended to take an extended vacation and was never heard from again. Two different private investigators had found nothing to indicate Rex Lane was involved in Kennard's disappearance.

I made a mental note to call the Knoxville office about the missing person case. Maybe someone would remember something about it.

Fast forward a few months and Reba Harrison forms a working relationship with Lane. Kennard's lawyer claimed he knew nothing about that. We'd managed to get him on the horn during all this, as well.

He might not know anything, but I did.

Reba Harrison had been singing since she was a kid. According to Laura Sares and Katie Jo Campbell, she'd been a little on the reserved side when it came to putting herself out there. Both women found it odd that Reba appeared to be more interested in what Rex Lane was up to businesswise than in her career. Katie Jo went so far as to say that Reba's invitation to perform at the Wild Horse had been an accident. Not that the woman hadn't been talented enough, but she just wasn't bucking for that kind of move. She'd spent a lot of time hanging around Lane's territory and going to his posh private parties. An agent heard her perform at a local club and set up the offer to perform at the Wild Horse in an attempt to lure her in as a client.

Neither Katie Jo nor Laura had any idea what had happened between Lane and Reba. She'd participated in the one video as far as the two knew and nothing more, at least on a professional basis.

It's pretty circumstantial, Patterson pointed out. *Mostly hearsay and theorizing. This gives us motive for Reba Harrison's murder, but what about the others? Why kill the other two if they didn't know anything? And that still doesn't explain the connection to the Starlet Murders.*

I couldn't deny any of those charges. I wanted so badly to say our killer was just a copycat. I wanted to be able to point to inconsistencies in the MO. But there were none. Admittedly, that could be chalked up to the expo that was done about a year ago. A local author had written a book on the Starlet Murders using inside information from a detective who had since been kicked off the force. So it wasn't like we had any hidden details that could prove our killer a copycat. We could only speculate.

"Assuming this has nothing to do with Starlet, maybe the other two murders were ploys to throw us off. To make Reba's murder look like part of a serial killer's work—just exactly what happened." I let go a mighty breath as that epiphany struck. Our killer could be diverting attention by copying the exact MO of another killer. That put Santos right back at the top of my suspect list. "I think we should go to Barlow with this."

This could give us some leverage where a search warrant or wiretap is concerned.

Either one or both would be great.

"Let's do it then." I got up, shuffled the pertinent papers into a manageable stack.

I still think Santos is involved the deepest, Patterson said as we headed to Barlow's office.

My partner's instincts on the doctor hadn't panned out the way mine on Lane had. He'd found nothing that impacted the case other than the fact that Santos had performed some cosmetic surgery for one of the victims. Santos and Lane had a few other clients in common but those were all still alive. It would take more digging to find the dirt on Santos, though my gut told me he just might be the puppet master.

I hesitated at the entrance to the reception area outside Barlow's office and leveled a confident gaze on my partner. "We won't quit until we can prove exactly what happened."

It was after six before I called it a day.

Barlow hadn't been nearly as impressed as Patterson and I. He played devil's advocate, especially with the idea that the murders couldn't be separated. If Lane murdered Harrison because of her missing godfather, then why would he repeat the act two other times? Once more I'd thrown out the possibility that the last two murders were decoys, intended to toss suspicion toward the still-unsolved Starlet murder case. Barlow hadn't bought it completely. Still, in the end, he agreed that we should move forward with additional surveillance on Lane, as well as maybe a tap on his phone to see who he was talking to.

Now all we had to do was convince a judge.

That Barlow had suggested we not inform Agent Stratton until we confirmed our theories surprised me and only reinforced the idea that there was a history between the two.

My cell phone vibrated. Braking for a light, I dragged it from my pocket and checked the name of the caller.

Mom.

A jolt of adrenaline went through me at the thought that maybe something had happened with Sarah or the baby.

"Hey." I held my breath as I waited for her response to fill the display screen.

Sarah and the baby got to go home this afternoon. Just thought you'd want to know.

We chatted for a while and then I ended the call. It was difficult for me to carry on a lengthy conversation while driving. I gave myself a mental kick for not realizing that it would be time for Sarah and Sasha to go home. I hadn't even made it back to take the baby and new mother a gift.

What kind of aunt was I going to make? Evidently not a particularly thoughtful one.

I took the next turn and headed for the nearest shopping area. Hillsboro Village. Lots of trendy shops and a really cool mall. The Village was Nashville's answer to NYC's SoHo. I had gifts to buy. I could drop them off at Mike and Sarah's and then go home and crash. I was physically exhausted and emotionally drained. I could use a long, hot bath and some thinking time.

I shuddered when I thought of a killer coming into my house while I did just that.

I refused to let fear paralyze me. Patterson and I were on the precipice of busting this case wide open. Every instinct told me we were close. I couldn't wait to make Rex Lane and Xavier Santos pay for their part in all this, including possibly sneaking into my house, though I wasn't sure either of them was smart enough to have accomplished that feat. I supposed they could have paid someone skilled in the art of stealth and illegal entry.

On a Tuesday night the mall wasn't too crowded. I parked in the lot on the east end. If I remembered correctly the store I had in mind was on that end. My stomach rumbled, reminding me that I should start thinking about what I would do for dinner.

The Baby Store was right where I thought it would be. As I lingered down the decorative aisles my thoughts went back to Barlow. I wanted to ask him about the Fed, Stratton. I wondered again if Barlow's feelings for me were as complicated as I was beginning to believe they were. My pulse fluttered at the idea. I reminded myself that the whole concept was an exercise in futility.

That relationship couldn't happen…or could it? There had to be a way…

Stop obsessing, I ordered.

A cuddly pink bear caught my attention. And then I was lost. My arms were full of soft toys and precious pink and yellow outfits by the time I reached the checkout counter.

I sat my purse on the counter as the cashier tallied my purchases and dug around for my debit card. I felt my phone vibrate again. I checked the display. Mom. What now? I answered it. Promised to pick up a yellow bunny for her. How had she guessed I would be at this particular store? Mother's intuition? I snagged the bunny and plopped it on the pile.

The cashier announced my total. I set my phone aside and passed her the debit card. I remembered to write the total in my check register. I'd made the mistake of opting to do it later too many times…overdraft fees were no fun.

Loaded down with packages, I headed through the mall toward the exit where I'd parked my car, hoping this would make up for my not getting back by the hospital.

I was about halfway to my destination when harsh fingers manacled around my upper arm.

I twisted to see who'd walked up behind me, but something poked into my ribs. I recognized it instantly. Gun.

Too many people to risk trying to break free, not to mention I'd probably end up dead if I did. Instead, I let him usher me into a side corridor.

At a door marked Maintenance Personnel Only, he leaned past me, into my line of sight, and opened it.

Clarence Johnson.

Though he wore a gray hooded sweatshirt, with the hood pulled up over his head, I recognized him instantly.

No way was I letting this scumbag drag me through that door.

I released my packages at the same instant that my elbow slammed into his gut.

He bent double.

I ran like hell.

Straight into the maintenance area. Any other direction was out of the question. The stark white corridor had offered no cover. Johnson was armed.

My weapon was in my purse, on the floor with my packages.

I took the stairs two at a time, moving down toward the basement level.

A spark against the metal railing alerted me to the fact that he'd fired at me at least once. I zigzagged as best I could, tried not to be an easy target.

Once I hit the basement level, sparse fluorescents and snaking pipes overhead combined with the huge electrical transformers and heating and cooling units taking up floor space made for very poor visuals. I didn't slow down. Could feel him too close for comfort.

I took a sharp right. Wished I had anything to use as a weapon.

My forward movement abruptly halted. I fell back against a hard chest. His fingers were knotted in my hair. I could feel his chest heaving. The running had cost him.

He whirled me around and shoved the weapon under my chin. *Fucking bitch,* he snarled, his lips curling in cruel hatred as he spat the words. *You helped that whore ruin my life. Now I'm gonna ruin yours.*

"You're an idiot, Johnson," I spouted back. Why not? He would probably kill me anyway. "You could have been halfway across the country and instead you're hanging around here going for revenge. You're dead already, bro, you just don't know it yet."

He shoved me to the floor and aimed his .38 at my head. *I'll see you in hell, bitch.*

Then something unexpected happened. Johnson got this strange look on his face and then he fell forward, right on top of me.

I scrambled to get out from under him. For a skinny guy he was darned heavy.

He'd have to kill me if he intended to rape me.

Something hard landed against my head.

What the...

The room spun and things went totally dark.

The room was black. My head throbbed. I groaned, tried to move. Where was I?

Johnson. Where the hell was he?

My working senses abruptly kicked into gear. I was lying on top of something...no...someone. I shuddered violently.

Stay calm. Think. Don't move and give yourself away.

The various odors hovering in the darkness with me started to penetrate my frustration. Sweat. Mine. Nope. The other...person.

One by one I stilled the hurricane of emotions and thoughts whirling inside me so I could pay closer attention.

And then I let the darkness speak to me.

I smelled the grease and some sort of cleaner. Tool storage maybe? There was a more organic odor as well...something I'd smelled before. I tested the air, inhaled deeply. Then I recognized it.

Blood.

I scrambled up and stumbled around the room. Hitting the wall, I felt around for a light switch. Couldn't locate one. Tension flowing through my muscles, I eased toward the center of the room. Stretched out my hands to make sure I didn't crash into anything.

One step forward, then another.

My right foot bumped against a firm object.

Adrenaline shot through my veins. The body…person I'd been lying on top of. He or she still hadn't moved.

The stench of blood was even stronger now. Or maybe it was my imagination.

"Calm down, Merri," I mumbled.

Slowly, keeping my balance while readying myself for battle, I crouched down far enough to touch the body.

I held my breath.

The fabric on the torso felt soft and worn. Thick. As I trailed my fingers upward I decided the person was male. My hand paused over his sternum.

No movement.

My breath caught. A layer of sweat formed on my skin. Reaching higher I touched the neck of the man's shirt. Followed it around.

Hood.

Clarence Johnson.

Had to be him.

But…what the hell had happened?

I examined his body as best I could without the aid of light and then I found the source of the blood. The back of his head. Sticky, cool. He'd been dead long enough for his body to cool significantly.

That meant I'd been unconscious for a while.

But who the hell had killed him?

I sat back on my haunches. And how had I ended up here...wherever the hell here was?

Chapter 10

Clarence Johnson was dead. That case was closed.

Shameka was back on her feet and at home. She'd insisted on going by the morgue to see for herself that Johnson was indeed dead.

I had a mild contusion, nothing serious. But I still had no idea who'd shoved me into that basement storeroom with Johnson. Not a storeroom exactly. A tool room for maintenance personnel. Same difference as far as I was concerned. Cluttered and smelly.

I'd apparently been in there just over an hour before I regained consciousness. By that time someone had discovered my bags and purse and called the cops.

Patterson had been the first to arrive. He'd called the paramedics and hovered over me like a mother hen until he was certain I was all right.

Once I'd been released by the hospital—the para-medics had insisted I have a CAT scan—I'd gone home and showered immediately. I couldn't live another minute with tainted blood clinging to my body.

After I'd had time to think about it, I'd wondered where the hell Jamison was when I needed him. If he was supposed to be watching me, why hadn't he been there? The idea that he'd killed Johnson and locked us in that room crossed my mind, but that wasn't feasible. Jamison might take out Johnson, but he certainly wouldn't have hurt me. Barlow would kill him.

The Metro patrol unit was parked outside my house, and, for once I was glad. Barlow had showed up at the hospital before I was released. I was thankful he hadn't made a scene. He'd been strangely quiet. Somehow that had felt worse than if he'd made a fuss about how I took too many chances. Like I could have foreseen that Johnson would show up at the mall. Apparently he'd been stalking me. Maybe that's why I'd felt someone watching me. All the more reason Jamison should have noted him skulking about. Maybe he wasn't half the cop Barlow thought he was. I definitely had a few questions for him.

The bags of goodies for my new little niece sat on the floor where I'd left them near the door when I came in. I was glad no one had taken them. But as badly as I wanted to make that delivery, it was late and I couldn't wait to lay my head against my pillow. Exhaustion was not nearly a strong enough appraisal of how I felt. I'd been running on adrenaline for the past few days. A good night's sleep was definitely in order.

Tomorrow, I promised myself, I would go by and see mother and daughter. Happiness bloomed in my chest at the thought of my good friend and this new beginning to her life. I couldn't help wondering which of my other sisters-in-law would be next in ushering forth the next generation of the Walters' clan.

After I'd showered I'd wrapped myself in a towel and switched on lights as I moved through the house, surveying each room as I did. Even checked the back door. I kept thinking how easily a killer had slipped past my locks, as well as the unit watching my house. On Friday a security system would be installed. I wasn't about to take any more chances. This wouldn't be the last time I would be making enemies in this business.

Considering how I spouted off to Barlow that this line of work was dangerous, I should put my money where my mouth was and take the precautions readily available to ensure my own safety.

Peeling off the towel, I passed through my bedroom without bothering with the light. Both doors had still been locked, the house was clear. I had to relax at some point, might as well be now. I deposited my weapon onto the dresser and rummaged around for a night shirt and panties. Seeing wasn't necessary. I'd long ago memorized every square inch of my room.

An old, familiar ache twisted through me. I hated when I did that. Always swore to myself that I wouldn't do it again. And truthfully I didn't exactly dwell on it but sometimes, like now, when it was late at night and I was alone, I would wonder...just a little.

Would I ever hold a child of my own?

I realized that the question was probably brought on by the recent arrival of my niece and then tonight's shopping. Or maybe by the close encounter with death. Heck, maybe a combination of all three.

Would anyone ever share my bed with me night after night?

Barlow's image elbowed its way into my mental anxieties and I had to admit that whenever I thought about the future he was always there. I couldn't imagine my life without him in it, even if he could be damned annoying.

He was right. When this was over...we had to get away to neutral territory and hash this out.

I shivered at the idea of really being alone with him. That one kiss hadn't been enough and had been far too long ago. We needed to give "us" a fair shot.

At moments like this, all alone in my room, I could admit that I craved him. I closed my eyes and imagined how he'd tasted that one time.

"Enough, Merri."

I opened my eyes and ran my fingers through my damp red mane. I didn't have the energy to bother with drying it. I needed sleep. Now.

I plopped onto the edge of the bed and fell over onto my pile of pillows with a satisfied sigh. It felt good to be home.

It wasn't until I flopped onto my back that I realized I wasn't alone in the bed.

I bolted up. Scrambled off the bed.

My heart rammed into my throat.

What the hell?

I lunged to the dresser and grabbed my .9-millimeter. With a bead on the bed, I backed to the door. My left hand slid over the wall until I'd hit the light switch. The glow from the overhead fixture illuminated the room and cast a spotlight onto my bed.

A long lump beneath my covers took about a tenth of a second to register in my brain.

Body.

Definitely.

I swallowed back the sour taste that instantly rose in my throat.

Shit.

Keeping my aim steady, I slowly moved in that direction.

Deep breaths. Stay cool. Ignore the pounding in my chest. When my knees bumped into the mattress, I stood stone still to the count of three. Keeping my grip on the weapon firm, I reached down with my left hand and snatched back the covers.

My breath deserted me.

Female.

Young.

Very dead.

The shiny silver and cut glass tiara and clownish makeup she wore grabbed my attention first. Then the ligature marks on her throat.

I drew the cover down lower.

Damn.

She was nude.

Same ligature marks on her wrists and ankles.

For the first time since beginning my fast-tracked career as a Metro homicide detective, I knew I was going to lose my lunch.

I rushed to the bathroom and let it go.

When I'd pulled myself together again. I rinsed, wiped my mouth with my gun still in my hand. The idea that the killer could still be in my house, hiding somewhere, exploded in my head.

My emotions churning wildly, I rushed around my bedroom. Yanked open the closet door, checked under the bed. I raced from room to room, checking behind, under and inside every possible hiding place.

I had to call this in.

I felt oddly woozy.

This was crazy. Was I going to faint now?

I glanced down at myself and belatedly remembered to go back to my room for my robe and lash it on.

The phone on my bedside table was the closest. I used it to call dispatch, then I went to the living room so I wouldn't risk contaminating the scene any more than I already had. Plus I didn't want to look at the body anymore.

It wasn't like it was the first body I'd seen, far from it. And it wasn't like I hadn't spent some time with one tonight already. But the fact that this one was in my bed put a whole other spin on the situation.

This was too personal.

I sat in a chair that faced the hall. Just sat there, staring until the cavalry arrived. One of the officers from the unit outside had come inside before that, but I didn't talk to him. I was unclear on exactly why. Nothing to say, I suppose.

Victim number four had just been discovered.

In my bed.

Barlow was suddenly there. Another note had been found. He offered it to me. My hand shook as I accepted it.

I stared at the note.

How the hell had he gotten into my house a second time without anyone noticing?

He'd had to get a little creative since my new locks weren't so easily manipulated. He'd broken a single pane of glass and unlocked the bedroom window.

And left me a gift.

This one could have been you...you're missing all the clues. I'm very disappointed in you, Detective.

My throat felt so dry I could hardly swallow.

Same paper. Same kind of printer. Same font.

I looked from Barlow to the note and back. "What is he trying to prove?" Deep down I knew, but I sure as hell didn't want to admit it.

That he's in control. That he's manipulating you. He's leading you—he wants you to follow.

The worry in Barlow's eyes made me ache to reach out to him. I hadn't felt this vulnerable since I'd first lost my hearing. Oddly, he looked every bit as vulnerable.

Yet another of those firsts I'd been experiencing lately hit me hard right between the eyes. I needed Barlow right now. He sat across the table from me in my kitchen. Not a single part of our bodies touched, only our gazes. But somehow it wasn't enough. I needed him to hold me.

Whatever Lane or Santos or whoever the hell was doing this was up to, it had made me realize in the last hour the difference between independence and detachment.

I'd spent the past three years disengaging from as many deeper emotions as possible in order to protect myself, I hadn't realized how far out of touch I'd gotten. Way too far. I needed to find my way back.

I rubbed at my eyes. Had to get on track here. Where was Patterson? He was my partner. He should be on the scene already.

I leveled my gaze on Barlow once more. "It's Lane and Santos. I know it. They're playing games with me." My teeth clenched in an effort to hold back the fury roaring inside me. I wanted…no…I *needed* to nail those scumbags.

One of the techs stuck his head in the door. *We got a positive ID on the vic.*

I watched the tech's face in anticipation of learning the young woman's name. She couldn't possibly be a day over twenty-five.

Gail Allen, the tech relayed.

I allowed the name to filter through my memory banks. A newspaper headline flashed across my mind, confirming that I had heard the name before.

Starstruck Fan's Dreams Come True.

Gail Allen had gotten a contract from one of the big labels. One of those success stories that kept young desperate hearts believing anything was possible. But Miss Allen had gotten more than just a contract. She'd bagged the celebrity she'd fantasized about.

She'd been seeing Heath Woods, songwriter to the stars.

My ex-fiancé.

"Jesus." I didn't even want to consider the unlikelihood of this kind of coincidence.

Barlow got up and moved across the room to talk to the crime scene tech while I remained seated, reeling from the announcement.

Had my foolish actions caused this? I should never have provoked these lowlifes. Now they were playing some kind of insane game with me.

Anger flamed stronger inside me. I couldn't let these guys keep killing…I had to stop them.

I stood. Tightened the sash on my robe. I waited for Barlow to finish his conversation with the tech. Just as he was about to turn back to me, his cell phone must have rung because he reached into his pocket and retrieved it. I watched his profile, tried to read his end of the conversation.

Where...condition...yes...thank you.

I couldn't make sense of the conversation since I missed so much with him looking away from me. The bottom dropped out of my stomach as I watched his movements when he closed the phone. He took a deep breath before tucking it away and then turned back to me. I'd watched him a thousand times and the way he moved always did strange things to my ability to think straight. I was especially vulnerable right now. That assessing blue gaze landed on mine and I saw the weariness and worry there and regret abruptly filled me. I didn't want him to worry so much about me.

Every chance he got he tried to protect me and I thumbed my nose at his attempts. Was I wearing down whatever feelings he had for me? Was Barlow my one last chance at having a real relationship?

Detective Patterson has been in an accident.

His words cut through the haze I'd slipped into like a machete. My heart bumped hard against my sternum. "Is he all right?" I held my breath. I so did not want this to be bad news. My new partner and I had just found our groove. We were a fit.

Yes. He's fine but he'll be spending the night at the hospital for observation.

I thought about the scene playing out in my bedroom. Then I thought of my partner. "I should go to the hospital. There's nothing I can do here right now."

I'll have one of the units take you. I'll stay on top of things here.

I started to argue about the transportation offer, but

he was right. I was in no emotional condition to drive myself. I would be crazy not to take advantage of the offer.

As I walked across the room, he stopped me with a hand on my arm. I turned to look at him and all the craziness and exhaustion abruptly diverted, funneling into something hot and fierce.

Be very, very careful, Merri. I can't lose you.

There was no mistaking what I saw in his eyes. Any doubts I'd had were shattered.

"I'll be careful, Steven."

And then he did the last thing I'd expected. He brushed a kiss across my forehead.

For several seconds I couldn't move…couldn't think.

And then another tech burst into the room and the moment passed.

With my bedroom off limits for now, I rifled through my laundry basket until I found a pair of jeans and T-shirt I could wear without offending anyone. I met the M.E. in my living room. He apologized for the intrusion into my home. I assured him it wasn't a problem and tried to muster a smile. My lips didn't quite make the transition, but it was the thought that counted, right?

Outside an Officer Nichols opened the passenger-side door of his cruiser. *I hear you've been through a helluva night, Detective Walters.*

"You could say that, Nichols." This time I did manage a smile. I slid into the seat and he closed the door. I had to close my eyes, just couldn't think anymore.

Nichols not only drove me to the hospital, he escorted me to the fifth floor where Patterson had been assigned a room. But that's as far as he went. He waited in the corridor while I went in. I was glad for that.

I winced when I saw Patterson's face. His left eye and cheek were bruised and swollen. His right hand was bandaged. "Damn, partner, you look like hell."

Thanks.

"What happened?" I asked as I crossed the room.

He flared his good hand. *Some jerk ran a red light, T-boned my SUV.*

"Oh, man."

His expression lapsed into one of resignation. *Looks like we'll be stuck using that rinky-dink car of yours.*

"Watch it." I propped on the side rail of the bed, clasped my hands around it. "I guess you heard about my unexpected bed partner."

He nodded. *I knew you and your ex had parted on bad terms, but, jeez, Walters, did you have to go this far?*

"Funny."

Same MO?

"Looks that way so far." I shook my head slowly from side to side. "It's them, Patterson. I just know it. Somehow all of this goes back to Lane and Santos. But there isn't a damned thing I can do. Barlow said the judge hasn't agreed to anything yet."

Patterson came out with a couple of hot curses. *Sorry,* he muttered.

The guys around the bull pen were always apologizing for swearing in front of me.

"Please, Patterson. After what I've been through to-night I can definitely survive a potty mouth."

He shook his head in obvious frustration. Not at me, at the restraints on our investigation. *How many women have to die before they let us conduct this investigation the way we need to? We don't have any physical evidence. Can't they see we need to follow up on whatever other avenues we discover? What the hell is wrong with these people?*

I placed my hand on his shoulder. "Whoa...calm down. I don't want the nurses to come running in here thinking you're having a heart attack or something."

He pressed his head deeper into his pillow. *This sucks. I should be out there helping you and they won't release me until tomorrow. Even then I'll likely be on leave a while.* He patted his left thigh. *Fractured tibia.*

"Sounds painful."

He nodded.

An idea began to take shape, splintering my attention. "You know, I don't see what difference a little off-the-record surveillance could make." I shrugged. "I mean, if I'm just watching. As long as I don't do anything or draw any attention to myself, what would the harm be? And maybe," I said before he could interrupt, "I'd see something helpful, then—"

Then what? Whatever you learn gets thrown out of court 'cause you didn't have the paper to back up your actions?

Darn it. He was right. I knew this. But that didn't mean I had to like it.

"Yeah, yeah, I know."

Keep pushing Barlow. He can make this happen. Maybe that request for a wire tap will come through.

I arched an eyebrow to show him my skepticism. "We are talking about Barlow. He's going to do this his way. There won't be any pressuring him into doing anything any differently. And if the judge hasn't gone along with our request by now, he probably isn't going to."

Patterson adopted his own skeptical look. *The guys think he's a hard-ass, but I think you've got more influence over Barlow than you know.*

"And I think you're fishing." With that said I launched into another first. I leaned down and kissed my partner on the forehead. "I'm glad you're all right. You've kind of grown on me."

I couldn't believe it. The man actually blushed.

You should get out of here. But you'd better keep me up to speed on what's going on.

I promised I would, punctuated it with a salute, then said, "See ya."

I paused at the door and looked back at him one more time. "I still believe it's Santos doing the killing, you know. Him and maybe a third party we don't know about yet."

Maybe he and Lane work as a team, he countered.

I thought about that. "That's possible, I guess. I'll talk to you tomorrow."

Before I could turn to go he said, *Remember, no going after the bad guys without backup.*

I waved off his worries and made my exit.

No way would I go after the bad guys alone. I'd learned my lesson on that strategy.

I didn't want to go after anyone until I had what I needed to ensure they paid for their crimes. But I just didn't see the problem with doing a little recon all by myself.

As long as I didn't get caught, there wouldn't be any harm done.

And I definitely didn't plan to get caught.

Chapter 11

Officer Nichols dropped me off at my door a little while later. Three other squad cars, the M.E.'s van and the vehicle utilized by the crime scene techs pretty much blocked the street near my house.

I felt Nichols watching me until I opened the front door and went inside.

Thankfully, I noticed that the living room was clear. I moved carefully toward the kitchen. Barlow and the M.E. were deep in conversation there. I knew the techs would still be in my bedroom.

Now or never.

I walked quickly back into the living room, grabbed my purse and weapon, and the keys from the table near the door and just walked out. I climbed into my car, started the engine, and backed out of my drive. The feat wasn't easy since I had to maneuver between a couple of official vehicles, but I managed without scraping the paint off anything.

On the street I had no choice but to power my window down and give the cops watching my house a reason for my departure. I doubted Barlow would be calling off this additional surveillance in my lifetime considering how things were going and how I continued to do exactly what he told me not to. Like now.

"I'm going to my parents' house for the night. I'd appreciate it if you guys kept an eye on things here after the others are gone."

The driver nodded. *Yes, ma'am.*

I drove away, hoping they wouldn't check my story with Barlow for at least another hour. I didn't really like lying but sometimes it was necessary.

I decided to check Santos's place first. Although Rex was the known connection, I still suspected Santos as the killer. He lived on the west side in one of the older but very ritzy neighborhoods. Lots of other doctors and even a few country music celebs lived there.

I parked up the street a ways and walked back to Santos's place. The houses on the street were spaced far apart and partially camouflaged by decades-old mature tree growth.

No lights came on in any of the houses as I walked briskly along the sidewalk. In my experience, if barking dogs woke them, people usually flipped on an exterior light to see what the trouble was.

The house belonging to Xavier Santos was a sprawl-

ing single-level home that sat back from the street a little farther than the others I'd passed. His lot was at the
end of the block with one side butting on to the woods
that bordered the neighborhood. The street turned
sharply away from his property and went on to inter-
sect with another. On the other side of the thick line of
trees was a public park.

This was the first time I'd been to his residence,
since Patterson had followed up on Santos.

I took a moment to think of all the security measures
Santos might have in place. Motion detectors. Dogs
that could come running out at the first sign of an in-
truder.

I tucked my weapon into my waistband at the small
of my back, allowed my shirt to conceal it. I'd never
appreciated my penchant for navy more than tonight.
My T-shirt was that color and the jeans were a little
faded but still dark enough to blend with the night.

My mission was simple. See if one or both men
were here and what they were up to. Surely if they'd
killed a woman tonight, not to mention shot Johnson,
there would be something out of the ordinary to see.
They could be celebrating…having a post-mortem discussion on what they or their hired help had done if I
was really lucky.

I wouldn't hold my breath waiting for either, but I
could hope. And this was all assuming the Starlet serial killer wasn't the perp in this case, which really
didn't make sense. In fact, none of it did. Why keep
killing? Using the MO of an old murder case made a

kind of sense, but what was the point of continuing the ruse? Did the two men believe they had to carry out six murders to make their plan realistic? Or was one of them the original Starlet killer?

"Just do it, Merri." I drew in a deep breath and took my first step onto Santos's property.

I stayed in the treeline on the wooded side. Moving slowly was necessary since I didn't want to have a head-on collision with a broad trunk. Taking the extra time was worth it. The dense trees would provide good camouflage and I was far less likely to encounter a dog in the woods. I wouldn't let myself think about snakes and the like.

This whole scenario had me suffering a moment of déjà vu. I'd done something similar to this a little over a year ago when I'd been working in the case archives. I'd gotten obsessed with an unsolved cold case and decided to try and solve it myself. I'd followed the killer into terrain very much like this.

My amateur sleuthing had gotten me into hot water with the local authorities, but I'd succeeded in nailing the killer. That's how I'd ended up in homicide.

That's also how my and Barlow's relationship began. In the dark, while watching the plot to hide a body unfold.

Santos's house was Mediterranean-style. Not so lush and lavish as Lane's but certainly elegant enough. The landscape leading up to the house was the usual: meticulously cut grass and well-maintained shrubs. The low wattage exterior lighting ensured the well-designed layout was visible even in the dark. Not exactly the optimum situation for me. Thankfully the lighting in the rear was concentrated around the house itself rather than the yard.

The back of the house was mostly brick and stone with a generous-size pool. The pool area and the terrace separating it from the house were well lit, but not much light shone beyond that. I took advantage of the shadows on the far side of the pool and moved closer.

The front of the house had been dark beyond its windows but the back was a different story. Most of the windows spilled light out onto the terrace. Movement inside jerked my full attention to what looked like a den or family room where a line of French doors created the exterior wall, allowing an unobstructed view out over the pool.

Wearing similar silk lounge pants as he'd had on the first time we'd met, Santos sauntered across the room, a stemmed glass of wine or some dark drink in his hand. As before, his chest was bare, as were his feet.

Adrenaline sent my instincts to the next level when Lane entered the room. He wore boxers and a chunky gold chain around his neck. His drink was in a tumbler rather than a stemmed glass but I couldn't be sure what it was.

"Well, well," I muttered, "the gang's all here."

I eased closer, positioning myself in a small copse of ornamental trees on the side of the pool farthest from the house. I could see the well-lit room clearly from there. The good lighting greatly facilitated my ability to observe what these two had to say to each other.

Lane sat his drink on a table and flung his arms upward as if in frustration. He shouted something at Santos but I missed most of it. I didn't miss, however, the furious expression on his face.

Santos had settled onto the overstuffed sofa. His expression was one of bored amusement. Man, I hated that cocky SOB.

You need to calm down, Rex. There is nothing we can do.

I frowned. Nothing they could do about what?

The cell phone in my pocket vibrated. I ignored it. No way was I taking my eyes off these two long enough to check it. Like I didn't know who it would be.

Lane stalled, his hands at his waist, his gaze now seemingly fixed on the water. *We shouldn't have killed her.*

My heart practically stopped. Oh...my...God.

Santos said, *We did what we had to do. Discussing it won't change anything. It's pointless.*

I had known they did it! Fury detonated inside me. Dammit. I wanted these two jerks to pay and I couldn't even use what I'd just read on their lips against them.

I thought of each of those dead women. Brutally abused and then strangled until they surrendered to the inevitable power these bastards had wielded over them. I had to find a way. Had to learn something that would help me make that happen. I would bet a year's salary that the two extraneous hairs the M.E. had found belonged to these two scumbags.

I will get you, I promised the two men arguing only a few feet away. I wouldn't give up until I proved what I now knew for a certainty.

What I was doing was totally illegal. I was trespassing. Securing evidence without authorization. I could lose my job. I could be sued.

But I didn't care.

I wanted these guys.

It wasn't right that women should die and men too smart to leave clues could get away with it. The law said I should just be patient, be dogged, hang in there until they screwed up and left me some evidence. But how many more women would die before that happened?

This way was better. Dammit.

All I had to do was make sure no one found out.

So I ignored my stinging conscience and did what I had to do.

Watched two killers disagree.

Four women had died in less than two weeks, three in as many days. I wanted the one I'd found in my bed to be the last. The idea that maybe my actions at the press conference had caused her death gnawed at me.

I needed to talk to Heath. So far police efforts to contact him had been unsuccessful. Where the hell was my ex?

I know she's on to us.

My full attention riveted to Lane and all other

thought had to be shoved to the back burner. I felt certain the *she* he referred to meant me.

Don't worry about her, Santos assured him. *She doesn't have anything on us.*

Fear trickled through me, but rage instantly replaced it.

I considered the timing and I decided these two might just have someone else working for them after all. I couldn't see Lane or Santos carrying out that hit at the mall tonight. Too high-profile. Too dicey. These guys weren't professionals and, quite honestly, whoever pulled that one had some experience. Besides, these dirtbags did their dirty business behind closed doors then dumped the results in the open to get their glory.

Not for much longer, buttwads.

We shouldn't have started this. Look what it's caused, Lane warned before grabbing his drink and downing it.

Santos sipped his wine. *You worry too much, Rex. Besides, it's out of our hands.*

But he knows who we are...what we did. Lane paced the room. *...knows what he'll do.*

What the hell did that mean?

Lane flung his empty glass against the far wall. *...should never have listened to you.*

I missed the first word or two he said because of the way he'd twisted around. But I could guess. He blamed Santos for getting him into this.

We have an agreement, Rex. Don't go getting ner-

vous on me now. I'm not going to throw everything away and neither are you.

I was right. Santos was the brutal one.

My fingers itched to make him pay.

I desperately needed one of them to say something that would give me a starting place for the evidence I needed. What did they do with the victims' personal belongings? Where was the murder weapon? It certainly seemed they used the same one every time. Some sort of cord that left no fibers behind.

If I could just find—

A hand came down hard over my mouth. Survival instinct kicked in, sending adrenaline searing through me. A strong arm jerked me back against a rock wall of muscle.

I struggled to free myself. Clawed at the arm with one hand and reached for my weapon with the other.

The grip loosened slightly, but before I could get away, powerful hands had hauled me around one-hundred-eighty degrees.

My gaze locked on my assailant's face.

Barlow.

Relief instantly drained away the fight-or-flight rush. Made me weak. But fury abruptly obliterated that short-lived sensation.

I jerked free of his hold, wanted to rant at him but didn't dare for fear the dirtbags I'd been watching would hear. I wasn't sure who I was more ticked off at, him for interfering or me for getting caught.

Barlow stepped a little farther to the right, still maintaining his cover but allowing a thin shaft of light that stretched this far to fall across his face.

What the hell do you think you're doing?

I glanced back at the house and the two men still arguing. I didn't want to miss what they were saying.

"Look." I glared at Barlow for a second, wasn't sure if he could see my face since I wasn't in the light at all. "I'm here. Lane has already made a statement related to one of the murders. I know nothing I learn can be used in a court of law, but I want to know the truth. So just get off my back and let me watch a while longer."

Incredibly, he didn't argue. He shifted back into the shadows with me and we watched in silence.

I refused to be distracted by the way his body moved up so close behind mine. But it was tough. He felt warm and strong and I wanted to lean on him, despite how angry he made me. No matter how I told myself this thing between us couldn't work, he made me want to go for it just the same.

We have a good thing going here, Rex, Santos was saying. *I don't want to screw that up because of some pesky deaf detective.*

Man, this guy just didn't like me at all. And how the hell did he know so much about me? It wasn't like I, or Metro, went around broadcasting that I was deaf.

Lane paced a while longer, then stopped and said something to his partner. I missed it because his face was angled too far in the other direction.

I swore under my breath.

Barlow shifted slightly. I wondered if that was his way of telling me to stay cool.

He might as well ask me to stop being deaf. Impossible.

He wouldn't dare risk exposure at this point. This from Santos. Who the hell was he talking about? Apparently I'd missed that part out of Lane.

...may be setting us up.

Again I missed part of what Lane said.

Santos shook his head. *No way. We're all in this together.*

There *was* someone else involved. A keen feeling of expectation stirred inside me. I needed a name. A location. Anything.

Lane abruptly looked away from Santos.

My pulse jumped when Santos turned in that same direction. Toward something I couldn't see on the other side of the room.

A woman stepped into view.

I froze. Surely this woman wasn't another intended victim.... They'd just killed a few hours ago.

I shut out all the static and focused fully on the scene evolving in front of me. I was here, illegally, with my boss standing right behind me. I needed to make the most of this since it might very well be my last undercover surveillance op, however unofficial it might be.

Santos moved across the room to get the woman a drink.

Lane pretty much ignored her. He appeared too agitated.

The woman was young, as was par for the course with these two. Long blond hair. Couldn't tell what color her eyes were. Very tall, very thin and more naked than not. She wore her panties and bra, neither of which covered a whole lot.

I didn't really have a problem with that. She had a terrific figure and wanted to show it off. It wasn't like she was parading around in public that way. My major concern was whether or not this woman was in danger. She, apparently, didn't believe she was. None of the victims had thought so, it appeared, since there were no signs of a struggle outside the ligature marks on their wrists and ankles. No sign of coercion at all. Of course, that didn't rule out the use of a weapon of some sort to gain their cooperation.

Behind me, Barlow shifted again. I couldn't take my eyes off the people inside long enough to worry about him.

The woman accepted the drink from Santos. So far the M.E. hadn't found any indications that the two utilized any sort of drug to incapacitate their victims. The women were, at least at first, willing partners in the sex.

I thought you were coming back to bed, she said to Santos as she draped herself on the sofa.

Was this the way it happened? If I managed to wrangle a search warrant would I find trace evidence from the dead women either here or at Lane's house? That would be the one and only nail these two would need in their coffins. I had a feeling about Lane. If pushed he would break. The only thing I needed was an official reason to bring the two in and interrogate them separately.

I loved the idea of playing good-cop-bad-cop with my new partner. Jesus, I really was turning into a cliché. God, I loved being a cop.

And I could think of all sorts of torture I'd like to inflict upon these two jerk-offs...oh, wait, torture would be violating their civil rights. Darn. I think I liked it better when I was a civilian and not bound by so many little annoying technicalities.

The woman's arrival had screwed up everything. The two men directed their responses to her and that left me unable to read their lips due to her position. And they sure as hell didn't appear to be talking about murder.

She suddenly stood, placed her glass on the sofa table and announced, *Let's take a swim. That should relax the two of you.*

I stiffened. Barlow tensed behind me, sensing something was up. Barlow can't hear through glass, right?

The pool was less than a dozen feet from our position. This could get hairy fast.

The water's too cold, Lane said.

I hoped his party-pooper attitude would keep them indoors. On the other hand, if they were outside, Barlow would be able to hear what they said. So much of the conversation was blocked from my view at this point.

You go ahead, Santos told her. *We'll be right there.*

I tensed. Careful what you wish for.

When the woman stepped outside the French doors she immediately stripped off her designer lingerie and dove into the pool. I didn't bother watching the show. I didn't want to miss whatever Santos and Lane said to each other.

We're in this together, Rex. Don't make a mistake. I'm not going down for this because you got nervous.

...think...scared her off...

Dammit. Lane had said something to Santos but I only got part of it.

I really don't think we'll have to worry about her anymore. She has nothing on us.

As the full impact of those words penetrated my brain, the two men walked outside, slid off what little they wore and got into the pool with their friend.

Had a woman died just to shake me up, to deliver a message that it could have just as easily been me?

I couldn't be absolutely certain, but it felt more and more like that with everything I learned.

My gaze zeroed in on the scumbags in the pool. Though there wasn't sufficient light around the water for me to attempt to get a good reading on their lips, I watched in hopes something one or both of them did next would give me the slightest hint of how to proceed with this investigation.

I knew Barlow would be listening and would get whatever they said now. Reading lips from a good distance, say thirty or forty feet, without the aid of binoculars was possible if there was adequate lighting. But with nothing illuminating them now but the mood lighting of the pool, I didn't stand a chance picking up on much of anything.

Still, I'd learned a lot in the last few minutes. Outrage rose all over again inside me at the idea of what these two had gotten away with.

Was this their first killing rampage? Had they done this before? Were these two the ones that got away four years ago? That still didn't feel right.

Although I had some confirmation of what I'd suspected, that fact didn't change a damned thing. I didn't have one shred of evidence on which to make a move to tie the scumbags to these murders. If I didn't get a break they would get off scot-free.

With a search warrant I could hope to tie the paper from the notes to them. One of the detectives assigned to the case with Patterson and me was working 24/7 to track down where the paper, which was not the usual generic stuff, had originated. If he could find the retail source, maybe he could track down the buyer, but that would take time. A search warrant would be so damned much faster. Simply take a sheet from both Lane's and Santos's personal and business computers and do a comparison. And then there were the hair samples. We only needed comparison samples.

But nothing about homicide was ever easy.

The play in the pool got a little rowdy. Though I couldn't hear the splashing sounds and banter between the three, I could see the enthusiasm that looked a whole hell of a lot like foreplay.

Oh, yeah. The play quickly turned into sex. The

rough, wild kind, but the woman didn't appear resistive at all.

The idea of just how long it had been since I'd had sex flitted evilly through my mind. The one orgasm I'd had about a year ago didn't count since we hadn't actually made love. And no, it hadn't been Barlow. Remember the bad guy I told my partner about? Mason Conrad. He and I…well…long story. Needless to say, that relationship had been doomed from the outset, as well.

I found myself looking away from the frantic movements in the pool and wishing Barlow wasn't pressed up so closely against me. Not to mention hoping a sudden spring breeze would blow through and cool things off. Hard as I tried I couldn't not look for long.

The woman leaned back against the edge of the pool, threw her head back and opened her mouth to cry out with what was clearly pleasure. Santos drove into her over and over. The waist-deep water did nothing to slow down his determination to make her as well as himself happy.

Lane stood by and watched. I couldn't see the expression on his face that well, but he didn't look displeased with the circumstances. Maybe he was used to going last.

Sweat rose on my skin and the heat of Barlow's body behind me made me want to step away from him or do an about-face and scale his amazing frame. But I didn't dare move. That he didn't make a move, either, told me he worried about the same thing.

Part of me wanted to get the hell out of here, but the detective in me wanted to hang around and see if the woman would need some help getting out of the situation.

Santos abruptly stopped his movements. Finished, I imagined, judging by the woman's expression. Hers was easier to see since her head was thrown back in the direction of the light from the French doors.

I watched to see if Lane would take over. Was this the way it began? But the woman wasn't restrained. Did that come later?

My mouth dropped open in surprise when Lane didn't move toward the woman. Instead he went into the arms of the other man, Santos.

Okay, this I could live the rest of my life without seeing.

I turned my back.

Barlow put his arms around me, whether to comfort me or restrain me, I wasn't sure.

For all of ten seconds I let myself enjoy the feel of his arms around me. I could stay like this—

I felt a change in him…a new kind of tension.

What the hell had I missed?

I looked back over my shoulder just to be sure I wasn't missing anything relevant. I doubted anything I saw at this point would surprise me.

I was dead wrong.

Chapter 12

I stared at the third man who, while my back was turned, had joined the fun and games in the pool.

Heath Woods.

For several moments my brain didn't assimilate what my eyes saw.

Heath, my ex-fiancé. The man whose girlfriend had been found murdered in my bed tonight. The same man who had supposedly been unreachable for more than a week now.

I felt Barlow's hands on my shoulders but I couldn't look away. He turned me around to face him. I didn't resist though part of me needed to keep looking, to somehow make sense of what I was seeing.

We have to get out of here.

I started to argue, but I didn't have the wherewithal

to follow through with it. I felt too stunned and confused.

Barlow kept a tight hold on my hand as if he feared that I would make a rash move that would alert the very private party to our presence.

We moved through the trees, retracing the path I'd used when I arrived, trespassed actually, on Santos's property. Beyond the bewilderment I felt at having just seen Heath naked and in that pool, I experienced a rush of amazement at Barlow's ability to anticipate exactly what I would do in a given situation.

He had known I would take the route through the treeline. That didn't take so much of a stretch. Any smart cop would have. But what really bugged me was that he'd probably sensed that I'd sneaked off to take this little illegal adventure even before someone mentioned to him that I'd claimed that I was going to my mother's.

When we reached the street, he didn't slow down until he came to his sporty car. I tried to slow his progress. My car was parked in a different direction. That's where I wanted to go. He had left his vehicle around the bend in the street that traveled away from where Santos's house sat. If I got in Barlow's car with him...

Too late. He opened the passenger-side door and ordered me to get in. I didn't actually make out each word in the sparse moonlight but I got the gist of what he said quite clearly. What I could see of his expression was arranged in a less-than-pleasant expression.

Not wanting to make a scene on the street this close to the Santos residence, I did as he asked. Thinking creatively wasn't exactly possible right now. I couldn't believe what I'd just seen. Somehow I needed to figure out what it meant. I couldn't do that if I stood around arguing with Barlow.

Barlow slid behind the wheel and started the engine. I sat there, attempting to piece the puzzle together in some sensible manner. What the hell would Heath be doing mixed up with those two creeps? Business, my logical side told me. But what I'd witnessed tonight had nothing at all to do with business.

Barlow didn't say a word to me, just let me stew over the newest nonconforming part of this mess that was supposed to be an investigation but felt more and more like a quiz show without any answers. Had Lucky Lane Productions had something to do with the new hit song Heath had written? I'd seen snippets of the video but I hadn't paid attention to who produced the thing. Did Heath know his friends had killed his girlfriend?

Dear God.

Was he the third man involved? The one Santos had referred to?

I looked up, dragged my thoughts back to the here and now as we reached our destination.

Barlow's place.

I'd never been inside, though I'd driven by just to see where he lived. That he'd brought me to his house startled me all over again. As if tonight hadn't already offered enough shockers.

I refused to let him see my uneasiness. Instead, I squared my shoulders and decided to let him know right now I wasn't sorry for what I'd done. Confused about the end results, maybe, but definitely not sorry. I'll admit I hadn't been thinking as rationally as I should have when I decided to sneak around, but that didn't change the fact that if we didn't make some headway soon another woman would likely die. Maybe even the one we'd left in that pool with Lane and Santos…and the man I'd once thought I would marry.

Barlow got out of the car before I could string together a demand to know why he'd brought me here. This didn't feel like a professional maneuver. He wouldn't let it be personal, I reminded myself. He was far too disciplined for that.

He moved around the hood and opened my door. My reactions were definitely in slow motion under the circumstances. I just couldn't shake off the distracting thoughts. I kept bouncing back and forth from the case to this thing between Barlow and me. I should have taken a firm stand and insisted that he take me back to get my car. Was this the beginning of shock? Had the cumulative effects of tonight's events finally gotten to me?

Might as well go inside, I decided after another look at the mounting irritation on his face. In a neighborhood like this someone would call the cops at the first sign of a disturbance. It didn't matter that we *were* cops. I started to say as much but another glance at his face kept me quiet. Oh, yeah, he was really p.o.'d.

Well, that made two of us. Might as well have this out right now. Let him say whatever it was he needed to say. Then I would have the same opportunity. Not that I had a legitimate excuse—I didn't. But I had my reasons. I felt certain that at some point in his career he had been right where I was now. I needed him to remember that time and understand how I felt.

I had to stop these guys. The means would simply have to justify the end…to the degree possible.

The image of my ex-fiancé flashed through my mind. What on earth was Heath doing with those scumbags? Well, he was pretty much a scumbag himself but in a totally different way. He didn't kill people.

At least, I didn't think he did. The image of his girlfriend being zipped into a body bag flashed into my mind. I shuddered.

The troubling question was momentarily shoved aside as Barlow opened his front door and stepped back for me to go inside. His house, a considerably larger one than mine, stood proudly on a highly coveted city lot on the west side. Very nice neighborhood. The brick ranch-style house wasn't new but it looked well kept from what I could tell. Inside, hardwood floors went a long way toward warming up the beige-walled living room. Brown leather furniture, massive and male-looking, sprawled around the well-proportioned space. A patchwork quilt, worn by age, draped one large chair. His favorite chair, I'd bet. I wondered if his mother or his grandmother had made that quilt by hand.

I closed my eyes a moment and wished I could hear his house. All houses make sounds, you know. Those soft creaking noises you hear in the middle of the night, or the soft hiss of the air-conditioning.

I sighed and opened my eyes. I liked this place. Despite the definite masculine slant to the decorating, it looked inviting and comfortable. I could imagine the two of us snuggled up under that lovely quilt.

Only one picture hung on the wall. A large, framed shot of his family.

I had only brothers. Barlow was blessed with two sisters. He'd told me a little about his family the first time we'd worked together. Like me, he was fortunate to still have both his mom and dad alive, though they were in Missouri. Like him, his sisters were attractive. The whole family had the same dark hair and amazing blue eyes. Very nice.

Tearing my gaze away from the picture I surveyed the room again and took a deep breath. The place smelled like him. Sexy, comfortable. Looked like him, too. Orderly and elegant with an understated hum of power.

Barlow came to stand in the middle of the room. The way he looked at me spelled trouble. Big trouble.

"I did what I had to do," I said before he could start. "I won't apologize for it. Lane and Santos admitted having killed at least one woman." I just didn't know which one. I held up a hand when he would have spoken. "Yes, I'm well aware I can't use that because I obtained it illegally. But it tells me I'm on the right track and that makes it worth it. I don't want to be wasting time here."

Are you finished?

I took another deep breath. "Yeah."

"You understand that if you'd been caught, assuming you'd survived the encounter, you would have brought a whole load of trouble down on Metro."

Okay, I guess I hadn't thought of that. I knew I'd be in trouble if I were caught. "I didn't think about that."

Of course you didn't. You weren't thinking at all.

His jaw flexed with the effort of holding back his temper. His posture looked rigid. He was seriously angry with me. I shifted my weight from one foot to the other. His stare didn't relent. He said nothing. Waited for me to explain myself further or admit defeat. Something.

I held up my hands in a classic surrender gesture but that was the farthest thing from my mind. "Just get it over with. If I'm in trouble, tell me how bad. Like I said, I don't want to waste any time. Those guys are guilty. I want to prove it."

He looked away as if his ability to hang on to control dictated that he take a moment.

I frowned. Hated that everything between us had to be so complicated. Then, unable to resist, I used the time to look at him. I stole moments like this to admire him. I shouldn't. It was detrimental to my ability to maintain my focus, but I just couldn't help myself.

It was past 2:00 a.m. I was tired. Maybe I didn't have the necessary energy to fight the desire to indulge myself as I usually did.

Even at this time of the morning, with a day's beard growth shadowing his jaw and his shirt beginning to wrinkle, he looked incredible. Sexy as hell and damned strong.

God, I could use both those things right now.

I squeezed my eyes shut again and blocked the images that tried to invade my brain. Lane and Santos. The woman. My ex. Unbelievable. The woman's face as Santos drove into her over and over.

Who was the most screwed-up? I wondered. Those who turned deviant and went to extremes for sexual gratification or those of us who deprived themselves for months and years, choosing to go without rather than take a chance. Okay, enough of that. At least my neglected sex life hadn't killed anybody.

Was this kinky, violent sexual behavior the real reason Heath had dropped me? Had my deafness just been a PC excuse to his way of thinking? Had he already been engaging in this sort of activity?

And why was I even wondering? We were over years ago.

I opened my eyes just in time to look Barlow square in the eyes as he stormed over to where I stood.

You could have gotten yourself killed tonight.

I didn't have time to answer. He grabbed me by the arms and pulled me close. *What do I have to do to get through to you?*

Though my heart pounded so hard I could scarcely breathe, somehow I managed to speak. "I'm not going to stop being who I am for you or anyone else."

We'd been over this already, but there was a panic in his eyes I hadn't seen before. As if he'd reached the end of his rope... Had I done this to him?

He released my arms, but those long fingers immediately plunged into my hair. He cupped my head, drew my face closer to his. *I know you won't stop being who you are.*

And then he did the one thing I'd waited almost a year for him to do...again.

He kissed me. No mere brush across my forehead. This was the real thing.

He tasted like coffee and mint and that male heat that made me ache to be skin to skin with him. God, it had been so very long since a man had touched me like this. I told myself not to melt against him, but I just couldn't help myself. My whole body vibrated with the need to be held more tightly against him.

I leaned closer... He held me more securely as if he knew just what I needed.

The moment was over far too quickly. He drew away. I groaned in protest. Couldn't take my eyes off his lips as much as I wanted to cover them with mine.

I'm sorry. He pressed his forehead against mine. *I lost my head. I brought you here because I want...I need to protect you. But...*

His breath caressed my skin, made me want to throw my arms around him and kiss him again. Made me want to promise him that everything would be all right. But it wouldn't.

We can't do this, he said. *As much as I want to.*

He was right. I knew that.

I told myself to pull it together. I was just tired. Not thinking straight.

I backed out of his arms. He didn't try to hold on but he didn't immediately let go, either. His hands slid along my arms as I moved away, giving the impression that he desperately wanted to maintain contact a little bit longer.

"I need to pick up my car and get back to work." I said this without allowing my eyes to meet his. For all the good getting back to work would do, I didn't add. I still had no new evidence. Yes, I'd had my suspicions confirmed, but fat lot of good that did me. The hopes and irrational motivation that had driven me abruptly deflated.

Wait.

There was Heath.

I knew him. Knew his weaknesses, or at least I had thought I did. The image of him in that pool made me shudder.

My former connection to him couldn't color my opinion. I needed my objectivity more now than ever. He was a new lead. I didn't care what he did behind closed doors, or in a pool as the case may be. He could help me with this case.

Whether he wanted to or not. Maybe he hadn't been unreachable at all this week, maybe he'd been avoiding me. His girlfriend was dead. His friends might have killed her. Surely that would motivate him to cooperate. If he was in this thick with Lane and Santos, he would know secrets.

You should get some sleep, Barlow suggested. *I have a guest room.*

No way. "I want to bring Heath in for questioning," I announced.

On what grounds? Barlow challenged. *That you trespassed on private property and saw him partying with your two main suspects?*

A couple of minutes ago I had reveled in that too-short kiss Barlow's temporary lapse in discipline had allowed. Now, I just wanted to punch him.

Even if he was right.

I opened my mouth to argue with him and inspiration stuck. I smiled. Oh, yeah, that would work.

"We can have a unit watch Santos's street. When Heath leaves, and he will eventually, if he were to be pulled over chances are he'd be under the influence of one thing or another."

Okay, so I was still skating a thin line. But women were dead. Four that I knew of. We had to stop these bastards.

"He's not going to want trouble with the law right now," I urged. With his career going so well I was certain he would be happy to cut a deal to keep himself out of trouble. Even if he didn't know anything significant, at this point any little thing would be helpful.

Barlow didn't look convinced. *He may not know anything,* he countered.

I held my ground. "We won't know if we don't ask."

My breath stalled in my lungs during the next five or so seconds as he made his decision.

All right. We'll try this your way.

Enthusiasm and determination were about all that was keeping me on my feet right now. I needed something to hang on to.

Barlow made the call. Officer Nichols, the same one who'd escorted me to the hospital and back, would do the honors.

I'll take you back to get your car if you agree to get some sleep. There isn't much else you can do until we have a report from the crime scene techs.

"I can rest at the office. The couch in the lounge isn't bad." That was the best compromise he was going to get out of me at this point.

All right.

As I started for the door, he stopped me with a hand on my arm. I allowed my gaze to meet his. I shivered inside at the memory of that kiss.

I should apologize again for...what happened. I was out of line. I didn't mean to take advantage of the situation.

There were a lot of things I could have said at that moment but I decided that nothing I could say would be quite right. So I handled the situation using something I'd learned from the Good Book in Sunday school when I was a kid. An eye for an eye...

I grabbed him by the face and pulled his mouth to mine. I kissed him long and hard, with all the tumultuous emotions churning inside me. His hands closed around mine but he made no move to pull them away. When I could no longer ignore my body's need for air,

I drew back, looked him in the eye and said, "Now we're even."

I walked out of his place without looking back. I don't think either of us knew what to say as he drove me back to where I'd left my car. What was there to say? Our positions in homicide dictated the boundaries of our personal relationship. End of story.

Why fight the inevitable? Working as a detective in homicide was what I wanted to do; it defined me more than anything I'd ever dreamed of doing in my entire life. Just as being chief did Barlow. We had the proverbial catch-22. There was nothing we could do.

"Thanks." I got out.

Barlow watched until I'd gotten into my car and taken off.

I didn't have time to have my heart feeling heavy like this. I couldn't dwell on that right now, but it was hard not to. I should never have let my emotions get so tangled up around a man I couldn't have.

There were far too many reasons why we didn't need each other that had nothing to do with work. Barlow deserved someone special with whom to spend his life. Someone he could have children with. Grow old with.

Don't get me wrong, I know I'm pretty special in my own way. But I still felt confused about my disability and the idea of having children.

No more. I kicked the crazy notions out of my head and focused on what I had to do.

First, I needed a change of clothes, but I didn't want

to go home and get in the way of things there. Disturbing any of my family was out of the question. No problem. I could drop by the nearest all-night supercenter and buy something.

I pulled into the Wal-Mart parking lot and hurried inside. Coffee would be my next order of business. This night was far from over.

Khaki slacks with a burgundy sweater plus underwear and socks would do the trick, along with a few personal hygiene products. Armed with my purchases, I returned to my Jetta and climbed inside.

I shoved the keys into the ignition and stilled. The gray sedan a dozen or so yards away snagged my attention.

Officer Jamison.

I thought about marching over there and asking him where he'd been when I needed him, but what was the point?

Like all my other personal feelings right now, I set that irritating one aside, as well. I drove to Metro, making a brief detour through a drive-thru for coffee, parked and went inside. Jamison had followed me most of the way but I guess when he confirmed that I was, indeed, headed to Metro, he'd taken a turn and disappeared into the night.

At three-thirty in the morning things were pretty quiet at Metro. I went to the ladies' room first and changed. Did what I could with my hair, brushed my teeth and swiped on some lip gloss. As my fingers glided across my lips, I stared at my reflection and found myself lost in thoughts of those kisses again. The one he'd laid on me and my cheap shot at revenge.

We had to stop torturing each other like this. We were way overdue for that long talk. Getting away and hashing things out would be good.

But first I had to get through this case.

Back at my desk, my phone rang. Detective Max Weisner, one of the other detectives assigned to the case, had an update for me.

There was news about the latest victim, the one found in my bed. My ex's girlfriend. I couldn't help wondering if he would be devastated by her death. Then I mentally kicked myself and remembered that he'd been in that pool having sex with another woman, not to mention two men. I doubted anything that didn't affect him directly would bother him much.

The M.E. had reported that the victim had had breast augmentation and one phone call to the hospital had confirmed that the surgeon of record was Dr. Xavier Santos. Next of kin, the victim's sister who also lived in Nashville, had confirmed that Miss Allen was a client of Rex Lane's, as well.

All four victims were clients of Lane's and all but one had undergone cosmetic surgery at the hands of Santos. Well, make that two. One victim hadn't lived long enough to get her planned surgery.

I knew for a fact that those two men had killed a woman. I'd read that dirty deed right off their lips. But my illegal entry onto Santos's property rendered that evidence null and void.

Other than that we had nothing except hair specimens from unidentified individuals.

Pretty thin case.

When I looked up from my notes, Barlow was headed in my direction. My pulse rate picked up. He'd changed, as well. Looked amazing as always.

Woods is here.

Anticipation zoomed through me, doing far more for my mood than a dozen cups of coffee.

"Can I lead the interrogation?"

Barlow thought about that for a moment, then said, *We'll conduct the interview together.*

The interrogation room where Heath was being held was small and plain white, walls and tiled floor to boot. The table and two chairs were standard-issue gray metal. The room had an empty, cold feel. Metro had a number of interrogation rooms, all were designed a little differently to better suit the situation.

I watched my ex-fiancé for a minute or two through the viewing mirror. He sat at the table, his hands folded in front of him. He needed a shave and he looked hungover. I knew that look all too well. I'd seen it plenty of times before he finally admitted we were through.

A tap on my shoulder drew my attention to Barlow who stood beside me. *You sure you're up to this?*

I nodded. Heath and I had been over for almost three years. It didn't hurt anymore, just chafed my pride.

Barlow and I exited the viewing room. He waylaid me in the corridor outside the interrogation room once more. *I'll take the lead.*

I shrugged. "You're the boss."

I was pretty sick of thinking how right he was every time he made a decision, but he was.

I opened the door and entered the interrogation room and Heath's head shot up.

He blinked, looked immensely relieved. *Merri...I...*

Have you been advised of your rights, Mr. Woods? Barlow kept his expression impassive, absolutely free of compassion.

Yes, Heath said, *I...* His gaze swung to me. *Merri, I don't understand why I'm here. I didn't have that much to drink.*

Mr. Woods, can you tell us where you were tonight? Heath's gaze moved cautiously from me to Barlow.

I was at a party with friends.

A party. I almost smirked.

Do you have any witnesses to prove your whereabouts?

Oh, I saw where Barlow was going with this.

Panic claimed my ex's face. I had to admit I was getting a little glee out of the whole situation. Okay, where was that objectivity I'd sworn I had?

Well, my friends are private people with reputations to protect. I'm...not sure...

You either have an alibi we can confirm or you don't, Mr. Woods.

He squirmed in his chair a little. *I was at...ah...the home of Dr. Xavier Santos.* He swallowed hard, the difficulty visible along the muscles of his throat.

Will Dr. Santos confirm your story?

Heath looked uncertain. *Well, ah…Rex Lane and Riana Saunders were there, too. I'm certain they'll back me up.*

He definitely didn't look certain.

Why don't you give me their numbers and I'll try to reach them now?

His right leg started to bounce nervously.

My turn, I decided.

"Heath."

His attention swung to me and the relief he felt at hearing my voice was palpable.

"Did you know Gail Allen?"

He blinked, looked uncertain of how he should answer.

"According to the tabloids the two of you were involved," I said when he didn't readily answer.

We parted ways a couple of months ago. He shrugged. *She decided she preferred a singer over a songwriter.*

I didn't have to press the issue. He was telling the truth. I knew that damaged-ego look.

"When was the last time you saw her?"

He frowned. *I don't know. Maybe a couple weeks ago at one of Rex's parties. Why?*

All the murders appeared to revolve around this social circle.

"She's dead," I told him. "Murdered."

While the shock settled over him I turned back to Barlow who said, *We still need to verify his whereabouts last night during the time of her murder.*

That Heath and Gail Allen were no longer involved, changed nothing. We still needed whatever he could give us on Santos and Lane.

Heath looked from me to Barlow and back. *You're going to call my friends?* He didn't look happy with the prospect. *I swear I don't know anything about her anymore. You know I wouldn't kill anyone.*

"I tried to reach you earlier this week, Heath," I said with as much accusation as I could infuse into my tone. "What exactly does *unreachable* mean?"

He swallowed hard. Looked scared to half death. *I had a little cosmetic surgery.* He patted his stomach. *You know how demanding this business is. No one wants a fat guy writing their songs. I didn't tell anyone where I was going.*

We'll need confirmation, Barlow insisted.

"Maybe there's another way."

Barlow stepped forward to garner my attention. He held his cell phone in his hand. *Excuse me, I have a call.*

I nodded, wondered if he really did have a call.

When Barlow had left the room I turned back to Heath. "I can help you, Heath, maybe keep this whole mess off your record, if you help us."

What the hell is going on here, Merri? I didn't do anything wrong. Maybe had a little too much to drink. But I sure didn't kill anyone. His expression appeared to soften a little. *You look great, by the way.*

I ignored his compliment, folded my arms over my chest in a stern manner. "Your friends, Santos and Lane, are in very serious trouble."

Worry lined his brow. *What do you mean, serious trouble?*

I walked closer to the table. "We have four murder victims," I said carefully. "Including your ex-girlfriend Gail."

From the corner of my eye I watched his anxiety heighten.

"All four were clients of Lane's. Three of the four were patients of Santos."

Heath's anxiety level lessened slightly but visibly. *Well, that's not that unusual, Merri. Those two point potential clients in each other's direction.* He shrugged. *That's what friends do.*

I did the shrugging this time. "Maybe. But I have a material witness who's willing to testify that there was bad blood between Lane and one of the victims."

I wasn't sure Barlow had intended for me to go this far but since he didn't come in and intervene, I ran with it.

It's the nature of the beast in this business, Heath challenged. *You make enemies. That doesn't mean he's a killer.*

His cockiness started to rear its ugly head. "There's much more than that, Heath. I simply can't share the rest with you." That announcement appeared to take him down a notch or two. "The reason you're here rather than in a holding tank awaiting formal charges—"

The color drained from his face during my pause.

"—is because we think you can help us. You help

us and we'll make sure this all goes away. I'm sure you'll call yourself a cab the next time you have a little too much to drink."

He nodded. *Definitely.* Then he let out a big breath. *The problem is, I don't see how I can help you. I don't know anything about any murders. If Santos and Lane are involved in anything other than savvy business tactics I'm not aware of it. I've seen the news and honestly I didn't even know these women were connected to Santos or Lane. They've never mentioned anything about them to me and we're pretty tight.*

So he didn't know anything useful. Damn. He could know things that he didn't realize were useful, but digging up that kind of information took time. We didn't have time.

"What I need you to do for me, Heath," I began, the idea gaining momentum as I spoke, "is help me find a way to put some pressure on Lane and Santos. If we apply the right pressure maybe we'll get the right reaction."

How?

I could understand his hesitancy. But I had no sympathy for him. I thought of him naked in that pool and I just got outraged all over again.

"When will you be seeing one or both again?"

He filtered a hand through his hair. *Tonight, I guess. I'm having a party at my place.* He shrugged. *You know, to celebrate my new song staying at number one for six weeks in a row.*

Six? I was behind a week or two.

They're supposed to be there. His gaze met mine. *Rex is the one who did the video.*

I figured as much. This was how Heath had gotten involved with the two. "You say you're having the party at your place?" I remembered his place pretty well and it wasn't anything like the homes of Lane and Santos. I couldn't imagine Heath pulling off that kind of party at his digs.

His expression turned sheepish. *I have a new place now.*

"Really?"

He nodded, then gave me the address. The only thing that kept my jaw off the floor was the way my teeth were clenched together. High Point was *the* place to live now. The newest, swankiest development in Nashville. Looked like Heath had definitely come into his own.

He pushed up from his chair, yanking my attention back to him. *Merri, if there're still any hard feelings between us—*

"There aren't," I cut him off. His innuendo made me furious. I tried not to show it since I understood exactly what he would presume. "I need an invitation to this party, Heath. And I need you to do exactly as I say."

The door opened and Barlow walked in. From the look he arrowed my way I knew he wasn't happy with where I'd taken this.

Too bad. We were out of time. We were desperate.

Okay. Heath looked from me to Barlow and back. *I can do that. No problem. Anything you say.*

Detective Walters, I need to speak privately with you.

I gave Barlow a look that said "in a minute."

"I'll need to disguise my identity," I said to Heath.

He nodded quickly. *That'll work out. I hired some celebrity impersonators to mingle and keep the party lively. You could do that.*

Perfect.

"Have a seat, Heath," I said to him. "Chief Barlow and I have to discuss this before I can promise you complete immunity."

At the word *immunity,* Heath's eyes rounded in fear, but he didn't argue.

Once I'd turned my back to him I smiled. Oh, yes, this was the perfect revenge. I could get the bad guys and make my ex squirm at the same time.

The door to the viewing room had no more closed than Barlow wheeled on me.

What the hell do you think you're doing?

"Whatever it takes, Chief. Don't you want to get these guys?"

He went toe to toe with me. *You know I do.*

"Do you see any other way to do this?"

Since your partner is out of commission, I'll stand in. If you're going in, so am I.

My head was shaking before the words were completely out of his mouth. "No way. We can't risk that they'll spot one of us. I'll have a tough enough time keeping my own identity under wraps."

For three beats I was certain he would put his foot down and say no. I watched the battle on his face. His emotions were on the surface like I'd never seen before. In the end, he relented.

We'll do this your way. The rigidity of his jaw gave away just how badly he did not want to do this. *But you'll have backup both in and out of the house.*

When he could see I was about to argue he held up a hand. *We'll make sure they blend in and stay out of the way. And you'll be wearing a wire.*

This compromise was as good as it was going to get. Besides, as usual, he was right about the wire. If I didn't live to pass on what Santos or Lane said, at least someone else would have heard it.

"Fine."

We glared at each other for another minute or two.

"What about that Fed, Stratton?" I suddenly realized he needed to be made aware of this latest victim. God, he would pitch a hissy fit if he found out we hadn't let him know the deal in a timely fashion. He would also want to know about the party plan.

He called. I brought him up to speed.

So, the phone call had been real. Maybe Barlow hadn't intended I have so much slack in there with Heath. I remembered the simmering animosity between Barlow and Stratton that day. "What's the deal between you two?"

Barlow's gaze warned me even before his words that the bitterness went deep. *He was the agent in charge of the Hammond case.*

The Hammond case had been my first official operation with Metro. The Feds weren't involved. But years before, they had been. They'd fallen down on the job and Hammond had gotten away with his murderous ways for a few more years. Barlow blamed Stratton for letting that happen. I knew the story, I just hadn't known the Fed. If I had my guess, Barlow blamed Stratton for the death of Hammond's girlfriend, Heather, the woman who had agreed to help Barlow bring Hammond down. The worst part was, to some extent Barlow still blamed himself, as well. Maybe that's why he was so damned protective of me.

Speaking of which…it was past time I told him I was on to him completely.

"I have a bone to pick with you, Barlow." Might as well shift the conversation to him before he came up with another reason I shouldn't do this undercover operation. If he dwelled on Stratton and Heather too long, it might just go there.

Those blues eyes settled on mine. He looked tired. And amazing, I had to add. How was it that I could love looking at the man so? How in the world did I expect ever to keep my objectivity where he was concerned?

What's that?

So calm, so open, as if he had nothing to hide.

"Look." I planted my hands on my hips and prepared for battle. "I know you have this thing about protecting me, but you really need to give the guy a break. He's tried, I'll give him that, but he wasn't there when I needed him most. I'm kind of disappointed that you didn't do a better job selecting my tail." Maybe the guy had to sleep, maybe that's why he'd missed all the excitement every time I was in trouble.

Genuine confusion crept into Barlow's expression. *What're you talking about, Merri?*

Uneasiness trickled through me. "Don't try to pretend, Steven." I used his first name to level the playing field, but part of me couldn't get past the sincere confusion I saw in his eyes.

He moved his head slowly from side to side. *I don't know what you're talking about. Who's been watching you? Besides the detail assigned to your house?*

I swallowed, the unexpected tightening in my throat working against me. "Officer Jamison, the Murfreesboro cop you've got watching me." I shrugged stiffly. "He follows me practically day and night."

Barlow took me by the shoulders, the worry in his eyes only heightening the fear mounting inside me. *Merri, I didn't order anyone to follow you around. Only the unit that sits outside your house at night.*

That was impossible. "But he said you—"

He lied. I don't know any Officer Jamison.

Chapter 13

Officer Waylon Jamison did not exist.

The Murfreesboro Police Department had never heard of anyone by that name. Jamison wasn't in any database we had access to, including the DMV.

We'd spent hours driving around in search of Jamison or whoever the hell he was. I'd driven my Jetta as if this were any other excursion. Jamison couldn't know his cover was busted. But we hadn't found him. Maybe the APB would.

I'd spent the last hour with a sketch artist coming up with a likeness of the guy. The artist did an amazing job. It was as if she'd snapped a photo. Whoever he was, we would find him. His picture would hit the airwaves later that afternoon.

Since the discovery of the third victim and my press-conference fiasco, the top brass had been taking care of all media issues. Metro was keeping such a close hold on information that we hadn't even had the first newshound show up at a scene. That had to be some kind of record.

My cell phone vibrated and I dragged it from the pocket of my Wal-Mart jacket. I smiled. I recognized the hospital's number.

Patterson.

"What's up, partner?"

What's this I hear about you being stalked by some make-believe cop? Why didn't you tell me?

I sighed. Okay, here's the thing. I've never had a partner. I wasn't up on the partner etiquette. I guess I was supposed to tell him stuff like this. But since I had this pegged as being a part of that thing between me and Barlow, I suppose I considered it personal.

"He…" This would be a big admission for me. Patterson had already noticed something was up with me and Barlow. "The guy, Jamison, told me that Barlow had hired him to keep an eye on me. His badge looked real. And Barlow's always trying to protect me and the whole idea made me furious so I didn't mention it." I hoped that last part didn't sound as lame to him as it did to me.

Be careful, Walters. I haven't been able to sleep for thinking about this case. We're missing something, I'm sure of it.

Funny thing was, I had the same feeling. With every victim it was the same. Every aspect of the MO was repeated. And yet, something had changed with the victims after the first one. Two hairs, just two, from two different individuals other than the victim had been found by the M.E. Even stranger, the hairs were found in the same spot, amid the victim's pubic hair as if they'd been planted there.

If we were dealing with two killers here, why would they purposely plant evidence? And, in both cases, the extraneous hairs were from the same two individuals. The match was perfect.

Had to be Santos and Lane, with a third party setting up one or both. But why?

"You just take it easy, Patterson. I'll be fine."

I laughed as he told me about his adventures with the nurses. The guy had a great sense of humor. As we talked I felt a sense of completeness with this new aspect of my career. I liked having a partner. A friend.

That was just another part of this case that didn't make complete sense. What motivated two wealthy bisexual men, close friends and confidants, to commit such heinous homicides over and over?

I'd looked into the backgrounds of both men and nothing jumped out at me. The two appeared to have it all.

But maybe having it all just wasn't enough.

Patterson reminded me again to be careful. I appreciated his concern, but he needn't worry; Barlow wouldn't let me out of his sight…or, at least, out of hearing range.

I looked up to find the chief headed my way. He

stopped in front of me, assessed me a moment, then said, *Nothing on Jamison just yet, but we will catch him. I've got three other detectives on this case doing all they can.*

I knew this was headed someplace I wouldn't like, but I didn't interrupt.

There's no reason for you to be here right now. You need some down time to prepare for tonight's op.

I folded my arms over my chest, tapped my forefinger to my lips and considered all that he'd just told me. Then I looked him dead in the eye and said, "Have you sent any of the other detectives who've worked through the night home already?"

A muscle flexed in his rigid jaw.

I looked around the bull pen. Most of my peers were out beating the bushes. But no one else, as far as I knew, had gone home to rest.

None of the other detectives will be performing as you will be tonight. Undercover work is always sticky business but the players in this op make things even dicier. Lane and Santos are highly intelligent suspects. One mistake and they will see through you.

I had to admit he had a point there. He somehow always managed to have one.

There's nothing else you can do here, he added. *I need you in top form tonight.*

"Okay." That came out easier than I'd expected. "Should I expect a tail?" Might as well know up front. I didn't want any repeat performances of the Jamison fiasco.

Yes.

No clarification or qualification. Just plain old yes. End of story.

I reached for the file on my desk. I planned to study a few details while I rested. I managed a smile for him despite the tension coiling inside me. "I'll see you tonight."

I meant what I said.

His statement stalled me when I would have walked past him. "Which time?" I tried to pretend I had no idea what he meant, but I knew exactly what he was talking about.

When this is done, we have things to settle.

I didn't argue with him. He was right, as usual. We couldn't keep dancing around this thing. We had to settle it once and for all.

I drove to my house and sat in the driveway for a long while just staring at the crime scene tape draped across my front door.

I could go in. I had the authority. The question was, did I want to? Would I ever be able to live here again and not think of that poor woman lying in my bed? For sure, a new bed was in order.

A rush of loneliness washed over me and I couldn't deny it, as hard as I tried. I needed to talk to someone who would understand how I felt.

I got out of my car and strode up to my front door. I unlocked the door and pushed the tape aside far enough to go inside. I found the bags of goodies for my niece and went right back out again. I didn't even breathe. Didn't want to inhale the stench of death lingering in my home.

Shuddering, I locked the door and went back to my car.

I could always count on Sarah for an objective opinion. For rational advice. I needed that voice of reason now.

The drive to Brentwood was pleasant. I blocked all thoughts of the case from my head. That I could was testimony to my state of exhaustion. Otherwise, nothing short of death would have wrestled the details from my brain.

Remembering my manners about halfway there, I called Sarah to warn her that I was on my way. She sounded thrilled at the prospect of having adult company.

Her home was spotless as usual. It amazed me that a brand-new mother could find the time to keep her house in order, too. If I ever had children that was going to be my excuse to let everything go.

Not that I would likely ever have any.

I wasn't even sure how I felt about that. What if I couldn't take care of a child? How would I hear it cry? On some level I knew technology existed to take care of most any situation, but I couldn't help feeling anxious about the idea. It was totally stupid. I wasn't even romantically involved, not really. How had childbearing horned into the picture?

I couldn't believe how much Sasha had grown in the few days since she'd been born. She was even more beautiful than I remembered. Holding her was amazing.

Are you sure you're all right, Merri?

Lord, not Sarah, too. I gave her a look that said as much. "I'm fine. I'm trained for this sort of thing, you know."

She looked worried and I hated that anything I did or said would make her do that.

I can't believe the body was left in your bed. She shivered. *That had to be terrifying.*

I wasn't sure the full impact had hit me yet. I had this case to obsess about—not much else got past that wall. The idea that the woman found in my bed had been involved with my ex only made it sicker.

Sarah put her hand to her forehead. *I heard about Clarence Johnson, too. That was a close one, Merri.*

Maybe I should tell her about Jamison, who was still on the loose, and give her something else to fret about. Knowing what I knew now, I believed he'd let me catch him that first time. He'd wanted me to know he was following me. Had wanted to lay out that alibi about Barlow having ordered him to.

"So, how's motherhood?" I had to get our conversation off the case and onto more neutral territory. For my own peace of mind.

She took the baby from me. *It's just like we always thought it would be. Incredible.*

The way she looked at the baby…the way the baby stretched and made funny little faces…all of it took my breath away. It didn't take much of an imagination to know it would be nothing short of incredible to have one of my own. I scolded myself for going there.

I know you're skeptical about motherhood now, she said, seeming to read my mind. *Just...keep an open mind.*

I nodded. Something squeezed in my chest.

So, what's really bothering you, Merri?

Sarah looked at me the way she had twenty some years ago when I'd first met her in kindergarten. She'd wanted to know how my hair got so red and curly. I kept those curls tamed to some degree nowadays. But back then I'd looked like Little Orphan Annie. We'd been friends ever since.

"It's Barlow." I traced my finger over the silky hair on Sasha's perfect little head. "He's driving me crazy."

You know he's in love with you, don't you?

Her pronouncement startled me a little. I had considered that maybe his feelings were fairly profound...but that someone else would say the words out loud...

I shook my head. "No, he can't be in love with me."

This was one of those situations when you pretty much agreed with what someone had concluded but you needed additional confirmation. Needed to hear them say it again. So, you fished for it.

Sarah lifted her chin in defiance and said, *He's been in love with you since the Hammond case. If Kent hadn't made him chief...* She shook her head. *That's the only reason he backed off. It was what he had to do.*

I rested my chin in my hands and closed my eyes a moment. I really was exhausted. Barlow was right. I needed sleep. A patrol unit sat right outside. It was safe to take a break here. Sarah wouldn't mind...

Opening my eyes, I looked at her once more. "He wants to talk when this is over."

She nodded. *When he accepted the position I think he thought he could put his feelings for you aside, the same way he'd been doing with his personal feelings for everything. But it didn't work.*

I didn't know what to say. This was too much for me to absorb right now.

You need to consider how you feel about that, Merri. Do you love him?

Did I love Steven Barlow? I was pretty sure I did. I loved looking at him...loved the way he smelled, the way he moved. Everything. I yearned to be with him, but, like him, I had learned to deal with it.

Until now.

Had he broken first or had I? I wasn't sure. He'd voiced it first...

But what if Sarah was wrong?

Maybe he just wanted me out of his division so he didn't have to worry about the deaf detective anymore. No, I knew that wasn't true.

I know what you're doing, Sarah said. *You're trying to decide if he really cares about you or if he's just worried that you can't handle yourself in the field.*

My sister-in-law the mind reader.

"What if that's the bottom line?"

Please, Merri, you have eyes. You can surely see how he feels about you.

"Okay," I admitted. "I'm in love with him, I think." Was I really uncertain or was this a self-preservation instinct kicking in? I couldn't seem to commit fully to the concept. I kept qualifying it with *I think.*

Sarah got up and put the baby, who'd fallen asleep, in her bassinet. She came back over to me and held out her hand. I looked up at her, confused.

You're going to get some sleep. You're exhausted. We can talk about this some more later.

I stood, then I hugged her. "Thank you."

She ushered me to her guest room and I crawled into bed, scarcely taking the time to kick off my shoes. I felt certain I wouldn't be able to sleep for dwelling on the case or on Barlow, but I was wrong. I went to sleep almost immediately.

And I dreamed.

Mostly about Barlow and the strange woman who wouldn't get out of my bed. It was as if she were trying to tell me something…or maybe she just wanted me to catch her killer.

As soon as I wake up, I promised, I'll get it done. No matter what.

By seven I was in costume and at Heath's new house.

When he'd given me the location I had known the place would be a mansion, but I hadn't been prepared for palatial. Could one damned hit song give a guy this kind of money?

Evidently so.

Barlow and three other men were stationed outside, all listening via the wire I wore.

After guests had begun to arrive, two female detectives would move into place. One as a waitress, the other as a guest.

I was Marilyn Monroe, complete with blond wig and colored contacts to shield my green eyes. The white dress I wore was an off-the-rack reproduction of the one Marilyn had worn in her most famous pose over the subway air vent in *The Seven Year Itch*. You know the one where her dress gets blown up to reveal her great legs? Well, my legs weren't quite that great so there wouldn't be any blowing up of the dress. Besides, I wore a thigh holster complete with weapon.

I wandered around the downstairs, noting the details that made up the home's personality, the baby grand piano, the framed and autographed pictures of dozens of country music stars. I just couldn't get right with the thought of Heath living here, amid all this luxury. It wasn't so much that it wasn't him…it just didn't feel real.

As if my musings had summoned him he walked into the room. He'd changed into elegant black slacks and a red button-down shirt that looked good on him. He still wore his hair a little long. Still as handsome as ever.

I thought of him in that pool and I shuddered inwardly. Surely he hadn't been into that kind of thing when we'd been together.

If I have to be involved with this, I'm glad it's you that's here, he said to me.

That Barlow was listening crossed my mind but I had no control over that.

"How long have you been involved with Lane and Santos?" We'd talked all around this early this morning.

He shrugged offhandedly. *A couple of years, I guess.*

"What about the more personal side of your relationship, when did that develop?" I couldn't exactly tell him that I'd watched them in the pool that morning. Not if I wanted to avoid legal difficulties.

It's not what you think. He didn't avert his gaze, which surprised me. *There are some things you just have to do if you want to be accepted in this business.*

I wanted to remind him that this was Nashville, Tennessee. What I'd witnessed in Santos's pool was not widely accepted in these parts. At least not openly. He surely understood the risk he was taking.

"You understand what you have to do tonight?" I needed to be sure that he followed through with his end of this.

He nodded. *I tell Rex that I was hauled in this morning and questioned about him and Xavier. I mention that you kept bringing up some piece of evidence you had.*

"Be sure you do it in the open. Discreetly, of course. But I don't want them to hear this behind closed doors. I need to be able to see them."

I'll make sure you're within eye shot.

I glanced at my wristwatch communicator. Guests would start to arrive soon. A flurry of activity was going on in the massive kitchen. Other faux-celeb hosts were taking tours of the house so they knew where everything was.

I'm not sure I ever told you, Heath said, dragging my full attention back to him, *but I'm truly sorry I hurt you. I just couldn't get past the reality of what your hearing loss meant. I know now that was wrong. I hope you can forgive me someday.*

I was pretty sure I already had, but why give him the satisfaction?

The wicked-female side of me wondered what Barlow thought of Heath's abrupt confession. He and three other detectives were listening to every word I, as well as anyone within a dozen feet of me who spoke at a certain decibel or above, said.

"If we're clear on how this is going down, I should probably get into character."

From the look on Heath's face he would have liked to push for a response regarding his apology but something drew his attention to the front door.

The doorbell, I presumed.

He glanced back at me. *We'll talk about this later.*

Something he and Barlow had in common, they both wanted to talk about *us* later.

I thought about Sarah's insistence that Barlow was in love with me. That foolish tingly sensation that I had been certain I would never again feel flittered through me. Barlow was the first man since my breakup with

Heath to make me feel that way. Mason Conrad had given me a thrill, too, but not like Barlow.

Not smart, Merri. Whatever Barlow and I felt for each other was pretty much doomed if we planned to keep our careers. I couldn't imagine him walking away from his and I damn sure wasn't going to walk away from mine.

I couldn't. I'd lost too much in the past. Given up so much of myself that I'd almost disappeared. This job—my work at Metro, period—had helped me rediscover and recreate who I am. I cannot walk away from that. No matter how badly I wanted more with Steven Barlow.

Within the next half hour the mansion filled with guests. Most were members of the country music industry, ranging from the behind-the-scenes sound technicians to the performers themselves.

I was impressed.

Heath had come a long, long way.

I stopped star-watching when Rex Lane and Dr. Xavier Santos arrived. The lovely young lady who'd frolicked in the pool with them last night had one man on each arm. Made me wonder who was in charge of their little threesome.

Also made me wonder if those triple-D cups were real or designed by the lover on her left, Santos.

I watched as the couple plus one strolled across the marble entry hall and joined the growing crowd in the massive great room turned ballroom.

Since my cover included mingling, I smiled and

said hello to anyone I encountered. The only folks in costume were the ones acting as hosts, glorified waiters and waitresses actually. Some served drinks, while others ensured that everyone had whatever they needed.

I also kept an eye out for Jamison. Even though I knew he wasn't really a cop, I didn't know his real name so I used the one I did know.

It crossed my mind that maybe Santos and Lane had hired the guy to follow me. The idea wasn't impossible. I'd mentioned it to Barlow, who considered it a plausible option. The fact was we wouldn't know anything until we knew who the man was. He wasn't a family member of any of the victims, that much we were pretty sure of.

Santos and Lane moved through the crowd as if they owned the place. Even the most high-profile celebrity went out of his or her way to schmooze with the two.

I resisted the urge to shake my head. How had these two scumbags managed to make it to the top of the heap? Just didn't make sense.

Unless, of course, they had something on all these glamorous people. I surveyed one A-list face after the other. Most people had skeletons in their closets of one sort or another. Was that what bound these beautiful people?

What did Heath owe them?

I regarded my ex-fiancé for a time. He'd finally made his mark in the business, something he'd longed to do for as long as I had known him. What had snagging that brass ring cost him?

Maybe I was just being cynical.

Who knew? Oh, well, time to mingle.

I dismissed all else from my mind and focused on what I'd come here for…nailing Santos and Lane.

I shook off the cop persona and relaxed. Swayed my hips just the way Marilyn would have as I floated around the room. A wide smile spread across my lips as several of the male guests made eye contact. A raised eyebrow, a brief nod, the slightest tilting of one corner of a mouth. I had to admit, the attention was flattering.

Lane's gaze collided with mine and in that immeasurable space in time before his brain assimilated what his eyes saw, my heart stalled with anticipation.

If he recognized me the jig was up…

Lane smiled and winked.

My heart started to beat once more.

Neither fear nor fury registered on his face, leaving me in the clear.

Lane turned back to his sweetie-pie at his side. Santos appeared deep in conversation with a man I didn't recognize. Probably someone from behind the scenes of Music City's major export, or perhaps another parts man who kept the stars looking good.

I watched the two men talk for a moment and decided the latter was the correct answer since the discussion revolved around silicone versus saline implants.

A full hour passed before Heath made his way to rub shoulders with his two pool pals.

These stilettos were killing me, but I kept the smile spackled on my face. The full skirt of my dress was perfect for concealing the thigh holster on my right leg. The weight of it felt comforting.

My scalp itched beneath the blond wig, which, so far, appeared to be totally unnecessary since most of the people who stared at me didn't get past the enormous cleavage offered by virtue of the mega lift of the super padded bra. I was pretty sure the other guests had me pegged as one of Santos's patients.

As I covertly observed their movements, Heath, Lane and Santos moved to a quiet corner of the room. I wondered if Heath had had someone holding that spot for him. If so I had to give the guy credit for advance planning.

But not that much.

Heath, dividing his attention between the two laid out the story I'd given him. *I'm telling you,* he said, *for some reason they're trying to connect you two to these murders.*

That's ludicrous, Lane argued, his expression going instantly from disbelief to outrage.

They're desperate, Santos said, his expression remaining oddly calm. *They need someone to pin it on so they've selected us because it's the only connection they have.*

I just thought you should know, Heath said with such sincerity that he almost fooled me.

That's when I knew he hadn't really changed. He could still lie straight-faced and never flinch. Unless the man you want to spend the rest of your life with is a cop, a soldier or an actor, this is not a desirable trait.

It's that deaf detective, Lane suggested as he stretched his neck side to side. Apparently that tie was beginning to bind. *She practically accused me of being involved.*

I smiled as I considered that nervous tension had kicked in. Santos still looked unfazed.

Heath patted Lane on the back and excused himself.

I didn't take my eyes off Santos and Lane now that Heath had made his exit.

She's going to be trouble, Lane said, his fury having given way to something like defeat.

We've taken care of trouble before.

My pulse jumped at Santos's statement.

Now we were getting somewhere. I didn't dare move closer in an attempt to get their words going across my commo's air waves. I'd just have to act as reader and recorder.

You said, Lane snapped, his expression vehement, *that we wouldn't have to do that again. Never again.*

I found myself holding my breath, hoping one of them would mention a name…something…anything I could use against them.

We won't do anything, Santos assured him. *She doesn't have anything on us. We're in the clear. All we have to do is stay calm.*

Lane's expressive face turned suspicious. *I'm not sure that's working.*

The tension was growing between these two. I wanted Lane to snap.

I'm getting tired of your obsessing. Stop worrying. Santos looked around the room. *We're totally in the clear.*

During the next two hours I kept Santos and Lane under close surveillance. Neither, to my knowledge, talked about anything related to the case. And ironically, the two didn't speak to each other at all during that time. The bimbo who'd arrived with them had latched onto the latest country music heartthrob. I recognized him from a television commercial promoting his new CD. Cute, maybe too cute. Guys like him were far too much trouble. Other women would constantly be after him, single or married. It was the nature of the beast.

When Santos wandered off into the kitchen I followed. The watch on my wrist vibrated. The message: *B careful.*

Obviously one of the other cops embedded inside had passed along my movements to those listening.

Maybe I should have stayed with Lane, but my instincts had warned all along that Santos was the one. His comments had confirmed my assessment.

I surveyed both commercial-size refrigerators as if I'd been sent in search of lemons or olives. As I did, Santos stared out the window over the sink a moment. Eventually he set his glass on the granite counter top then took the back stairs.

"Second floor," I murmured before turning to follow the route he'd taken.

At the bottom of the stairs I slipped off my stilettos and padded barefoot up the stairs as quickly as I dared.

Most of the upstairs rooms were dark. I hadn't topped the stairs in time to see which one Santos had disappeared into. A bathroom wasn't his destination since there were two downstairs.

I started to think as I searched for the scumbag that he'd likely learned all he knew about me from Heath. Fury bubbled up inside me. I should have thought about that before. Heath had probably laughed about his ex-girlfriend the deaf cop. Jerk. If I found out—

Strong fingers wrapped around my upper arm and pulled me around. I dropped my shoes to the carpeted floor in a show of surprise.

Santos leaned in the open doorway of one of the bedrooms. His hold on my arm turned brutal. *If God had intended for you to be a blond, you wouldn't have been born with that amazing red hair.*

His offhanded compliment turned my stomach. I tried to jerk out of his hold but he dug in deeper. "This is no way to get on my good side, Doc," I said hostilely. But then, this confrontation was exactly what I'd been hoping for.

He wheeled me around and pinned me against the door facing. *Maybe I like your bad side, Detective.* He cocked his head and seemed to listen. *You hear that, Detective? That could be our song. Why don't we dance?* He pressed his forehead to mine. *Oh, that's right, you can't hear the music, can you? You can't hear anything.*

He knew I'd be wearing a wire. He was playing with me.

"I don't need to be able to hear to know a loser when I see one, Doc." I smiled knowingly. "You're not going to win this game. I know you've killed…all I have to do is prove it."

The watch on my wrist vibrated madly but I ignored it.

During the five seconds that followed my summation, a white-hot fury flamed in Santos's eyes, but I wasn't afraid. The fingers of my free hand were already inching down the skirt of my dress.

I would love to shoot this bastard right between the eyes.

His hand clamped around my throat. His face twisted with anger as he spoke, *Don't come near me again, Detective. Next time I'll press harassment charges.* His fingers tightened, very nearly cutting off my breath.

"Come on, Doc, is that the best you've got? Can't get the job done without a rope? Come on," I baited, "show me what you've got."

For a moment I thought he'd take me up on my challenge, but realization struck and he stopped. His grip on my throat and arm relaxed. He dropped one hand down to mine, felt the weapon I'd almost reached and then the sick SOB smiled.

What? And give you an excuse to shoot me? I don't think so, Detective. He grabbed my hand and pressed it to his crotch to show me how hard he'd gotten. *But*

*if there's anything else I can do for you, you just let
me know.*

I jerked my hand free of his. "No, thanks, Doc. I like
to continue breathing after an orgasm. Your lady friends
appear to have a problem with that."

I'll be contacting my attorney, he threatened before
walking away.

I took a moment to compose myself after he stormed
off. Jesus, that hadn't gone as planned. I'd let it get personal. Big mistake.

I sensed someone looking at me and I opened my
eyes expecting to find one of the other cops headed in
my direction.

Jamison.

He stood at the other end of the upstairs hall, near
the top of the front staircase.

Our gazes connected, and in that nanosecond before
he pivoted and double-timed it downward I saw something I couldn't quite label. Maybe he'd been too far
away. Maybe I'd just been too rattled. But I could have
sworn he looked furious.

I ran after him, shoeless, my throat still throbbing
from Santos's brutal grip.

"Heads up, boys and girls," I said for the benefit of
those listening, "Jamison is on the premises. I repeat,
Jamison is on the premises. Headed down to the party.
I'm on the main staircase after him."

He disappeared into the crowd. I tried to plow
through as he had done, but I wasn't so fortunate.

Then he was just gone.

I couldn't find him.

I turned all the way around in the ballroom. I'd lost Jamison.

Now where the hell were Santos and Lane?

And my backup?

Chapter 14

We lost him.

Jamison got away clean. No one but me even saw him. And neither of the female cops inside the house had come to my aid, not that I'd needed their help with Santos, but it wouldn't have mattered anyway—they had both been disabled.

One had been left unconscious in the butler's pantry while the other had been locked in the wine cellar.

Neither one had gotten a look at their assailant but since Santos had been with me, it had to be either Jamison or Lane.

My money was on Jamison, or whoever the hell he was.

I couldn't shake that feeling I'd gotten when our

gazes connected. A kind of admiration mixed with fury? I just didn't know.

Thankfully no one at the party had realized anything untoward had gone down. The three men outside with Barlow had searched the grounds for Jamison while Barlow himself had come inside to see after the women. I told myself it wasn't that whole macho thing, but I felt reasonably certain that in my case it was.

Once he'd seen I was undamaged, Barlow had ordered me to get back to the party to keep an eye on Santos and Lane. I had a feeling that he had things to say to Heath. I hadn't liked the look in Barlow's eyes when I'd left him alone with my ex, but I figured Heath would just have to fend for himself.

Santos glanced at me once after I'd drifted back into the party. He hadn't smiled but he'd given me one of those looks that said, *I've got you right where I want you.*

I wanted him to keep believing that fairy tale.

For the first time in my life I understood what blood lust felt like, because I sure as hell wanted to see this man go down any way necessary to get the job done.

As much as I'd despised Luther Hammond, my first official case, once I'd found out what he really was, I hadn't felt this fierce need to hurt him the way I wanted to hurt Lane and Santos. Particularly Santos.

As if he'd read my mind, Santos left soon after that, Lane in tow.

"The Bobbsey Twins are on the move," I said quietly. My wristwatch vibrated and I checked the display. *Got 'em.*

I couldn't see any reason to hang around here now that my targets were gone. I needed to take up surveillance with Detective Weisner. He'd followed the two when they left.

Barlow and Heath appeared and I moved in that direction. Heath cut a trail before I reached their position. Probably just as well. I still wanted to punch him for talking to Santos about me.

This night is over for you, Barlow said to me. *Pratt and Weisner will maintain surveillance on Santos and Lane tonight. I'm taking you home with me. No arguments.*

I started to argue, despite his warning, but I just couldn't summon the stamina. I was tired. I needed to sleep. And, how could I turn down an offer to go home with the man I'd been falling for since the first time I read one of his case files?

I couldn't. That's why I followed him out of my ex's house, climbed into his sporty car and let him drive me wherever he wanted to.

I needed to decompress. Forget all about murder for just a little while.

At his place, Barlow turned on the lights and showed me to the guest room. *You should find everything you need in the bathroom.* He thought for a moment. *I'll get you a shirt to sleep in.*

He left me standing in the tastefully decorated room. Comfy looking full-size bed. Neat dresser and a matching side chair. I walked over to the bed and sat down on the edge of the mattress. It felt good to get off my feet. I stared down at the shoes I'd worn for this op. I could only assume that women who wore shoes like this had some gene I didn't have. My feet were killing me.

Barlow came back into the room and I quickly stood.

I hope this'll do.

He handed me a clean white shirt. One of his. I held it against me and images of him unbuttoning that white shirt and sliding it off his broad shoulders flitted through my mind.

"Thank you," I managed somehow. My throat had gone bone-dry.

He shoved his hands into his pockets. *Get some rest. I'll wake you if there's any news.*

I could look at him like this all night. The black suit and crisp white shirt. He looked wonderful.

When I still stood there mooning over him, he said, *Good night.*

"Barlow."

At the door he turned back to me. *Yes?*

"What did you talk to Heath about?" That question had been burning inside me since they'd disappeared into Heath's study together.

I told him to keep us informed as to anything he learns regarding Santos or Lane.

I nodded.

He started to go, but he hesitated again. My heart fluttered. I prayed he would be strong tonight because I was pretty sure I wouldn't be able to be.

I also told him to stay away from you. His gaze locked with mine. *I don't want him anywhere near you.*

With that said he left, closing the door behind him.

I stripped off my costume and the wig. Then I removed the contacts and washed my face.

Rest was what I needed but after lying in bed for half an hour I wondered if it would happen. I kept thinking about what Sarah had told me, then fast-forwarding to the way Barlow had just behaved.

It was crazy. What was crazier was the fact that I didn't have time to think about this. This case had to have my full attention.

Jamison elbowed his way into my thoughts and I wondered again who the hell he was. Was he the killer we were looking for? He hadn't felt like a killer, but was I misjudging him?

At some point I went to sleep.

I snuggled into the pillows and wished it was Barlow's skin next to mine, not just his shirt.

The next morning Barlow treated me to breakfast, after he'd taken me by my house to pick up something to wear, that is. He was all business and so damned confusing. How was I supposed to figure out this thing between us if he waffled back and forth?

Detectives Weisner and Pratt had turned over Santos's and Lane's surveillance to a new shift. Both men were still at home this morning.

Still nothing on Jamison.

I called to check on my partner. He was being released today but wouldn't be able to return to work for another three weeks. I wasn't sure I could survive three more weeks of having Barlow for a part-time stand-in.

When Barlow had gone off to preside over a press conference related to our case, one I was forbidden to attend, I decided I needed to do something besides reading autopsy reports and statements from witnesses.

Boring stuff considering none of it gave me a damned clue to point at anyone.

Santos and Lane were guilty, I was certain of it. But I couldn't do a damned thing about it.

I grabbed my purse. My .9-millimeter was strapped onto my shoulder beneath my jacket. I was good to go. Knowing Barlow would have a cow if I didn't, I put in a call to Officer Nichols. At least if he followed me around Barlow couldn't complain about me getting back out into the field. I couldn't just sit around here waiting for the killer to come to me.

I went in no particular order.

Gail Allen's place first. I walked through slowly. Had the techs missed anything that might be relevant to who she was or why someone would want to kill her? I didn't see even a single picture of her and Heath together.

Dr. Ammon had called to confirm that the MO for her murder had been carried out in exactly the same way as the others.

I wasn't surprised. I doubted anyone else in homicide was, either. And still, this case didn't feel like a serial killer case. It was like the victims were unrelated on some level I couldn't quite see yet. Yet they shared certain milestones in their lives, like working in music videos and cosmetic surgery—all except Reba Harrison.

I picked up framed photographs and studied them. I kept hoping I would see someone matching Jamison's description and that would explain his strange presence in this case.

After Gail's place, I went to Mallory Wells's home. Nothing. Just that same stark loneliness that speaks of total emptiness. I knew that feeling. The final dishes the victims had used still sat in the sinks. Their beds remained unmade. A magazine lying here, a discarded blouse there. Not one had suspected their home would come under the intense scrutiny of half a dozen people. Not one had left home that last time expecting to die.

When this case finally closed, someone would pack up the belongings of the victims and a new tenant or owner would take over the property and life would go on.

Delia Decker was apparently still at the radio station, I decided when I stopped by Ryland's place. I didn't bother calling her—I just used the key she always left under the welcome mat. She'd told me last time to feel free to come in any time I needed to.

This victim's life in Nashville had narrowed down to the one room a friend allowed her to call home. Stuffed animals and family photos littered the room.

Patricia Ryland had been the most innocent of the victims in my opinion. So painfully young and still clinging to beloved objects from her childhood. It just wasn't fair that she'd died such a horrible death.

The idea that two lowlifes like Santos and Lane had taken advantage of her made me want to strangle them with my bare hands. But that was too good for them, would probably allow them to die during orgasm. I'd read about and, of course, seen characters in movies who enjoyed pain and who dabbled in the more bizarre aspects of sex. What made intelligent men who seemingly had it all go this far?

Had the murders been intentional or accidental?

Did it matter to me? Not really. I wanted them to pay regardless of how the murders had come about. All the remorse in the world—not that Lane or Santos appeared to have any—wouldn't bring the victims back. And I wanted whoever else was involved to pay, as well.

I drove to Reba Harrison's place next. Nichols followed. I found myself watching for that gray sedan Jamison drove, but I didn't think he would be stupid enough to let me spot him. He was damned good at staying out of sight.

The question was, if he wasn't a cop, how had he learned to tail a target so covertly? Who the hell was he? And why had he gotten so close in Heath's house last night? He knew we were on to him now, his likeness had been flashed on the news. Still he'd risked getting that close during my intense moment with Santos.

Didn't make sense.

Then again, maybe to him it did. That's what the Metro shrink said, anyway.

Reba's home had sat empty for fourteen days now. The closed-up smell had settled deep into the fabrics and upholstery. Reba, at twenty-seven, was the oldest of the four victims. Pictures of her performing in clubs and at malls hung proudly on the walls. One closet held her stage wear. Rhinestone shirts, bejeweled jeans and silk dresses.

I rolled my eyes at all those damned stilettos holding court in her closet. What was wrong with women? Didn't they know shoe manufacturers would just keep making those things as long as they bought them?

In Reba's bedroom I scanned each framed photograph carefully. Lots and lots of pictures. I picked up one small frame from the collage on her bedside table. I studied the faces in the crowd gathered around a birthday cake. The big twenty-five on the cake had me assuming this was a birthday celebration for her.

My heart slammed against my rib cage.

I examined the photo more closely. I looked at each face. One man, his profile to the camera, was difficult to see clearly. And then I recognized him. Walt Kennard…the silent partner who'd disappeared fourteen months ago.

My pulse throbbing with anticipation I set the photo aside and hurried to look through more. The same man appeared to be in several but his face wasn't clear in any of them.

Photo albums. I needed to find more pictures. I opened drawer after drawer, rifled through her stuff until I found two photo albums. I sat down on the floor and flipped through the first one. On the very first page I found what I was looking for...a full frontal view of the man.

Definitely Walt Kennard.

He was in dozens of pictures, some dating back to Reba's childhood. Kennard hadn't been some godfather in name only; he'd been real family to her.

My head was spinning by the time I pulled out my phone and put in a call to Barlow.

"Kennard was very close to Reba Harrison. Like a father. I don't know exactly what it means yet but I think I'm on to something."

Barlow said he'd send over Detective Pratt to help me go through Reba Harrison's things more thoroughly. Maybe we could find a letter or something that would tell us more about her relationship with Kennard and what that had to do with her relationship with Lane.

Pratt arrived and the two of us systematically deconstructed Reba's home and put it back together once more. We found nothing that gave us any more than we already had. Just as frustration set in, my cell phone vibrated. It was Barlow calling from his own cell phone.

"Walters."

I watched the display as Barlow's words formed. *Meet me at Santos residence.*

Why did he want me to meet him at Santos's place? Was he finally ready to confront the man?

Pratt returned to Metro to follow up on the additional thread we had on Kennard. I followed Barlow's orders and met him at the Santos residence.

Two police cruisers were already there. So was the medial examiner's van.

I climbed out of my car and walked up the cobblestone path leading to the front door with tension roiling inside me. Had Santos killed his friend from the pool the other night? Had he finally screwed up and failed to follow through with his clean-up work?

Or had he and Lane killed each other?

I'd never be that lucky.

Good thing this wasn't a pop quiz otherwise I would have failed.

Dr. Xavier Santos was dead in his luxurious bed.

The gruesome way his life had ended made me feel ill. I tried not to feel any sympathy since I was reasonably sure he deserved every moment of the pain he'd endured, but I couldn't help it.

From the condition of his lower anatomy he'd apparently indulged in a hefty dose of Viagra.

Can't say I've ever seen that before, Detective Weisner commented.

I knew I hadn't. The twisted tiara that had been wrapped around his still-stiff penis was definitely different.

But even worse than that was the rudimentary breast augmentation someone had attempted. The incisions had been made in approximately the proper places and rocks had been shoved beneath the skin.

Clownish makeup had been applied, along with what could only be called an overdose of collagen or a similar plumping agent in his lips. His face was so thoroughly devoid of expression that his skin looked as though thick wax had been stretched over a skull.

Not a pretty way to die.

Especially for a man who prided himself on creating beauty.

The crime scene techs and the M.E. were already deep into their work. I stayed out of the way.

Barlow tapped me on the shoulder and said, *We should talk.*

I followed him from the master suite to the kitchen. So far as I'd seen the rest of the house appeared undisturbed.

According to Lane, Barlow began, *Santos had called for a companion from a local service after they left the party last night. Lane had been upset so he refused to stay. Detective Weisner leaned on the owner of the service and he admitted that his man never made it to the Santos residence. Someone worked him over right out there on the street.*

"Anyone able to ID the guy who did the working over?"

Barlow nodded. *Just vague details though. The guy from the companion service didn't really get a look at him since he came upon him from behind, just a couple of fleeting glances. But from what he described I'm reasonably sure it was Jamison.*

"Lane has an alibi?" Though I couldn't see him

doing anything this gruesome without help, I felt compelled to ask.

He was with the pool girl all night.

"She could be lying." Though I doubted it. Lane just didn't strike me as a guy who could be so brutal without someone to prod him. Especially considering Santos was his friend.

Maybe. I have a unit watching his house.

I shuddered when images of Santos's body filtered through my mind.

"You know," I said, the idea only just occurring to me, "if this is Jamison's work, what's the motive? Why was he following me around?"

Barlow allowed me to see the concern troubling him. *I can't answer either of those questions, but I'm convinced that Jamison is a part of this.*

"Lane needs round-the-clock protection," I suggested. "If we're going to keep him alive. Maybe this Jamison person is that third partner we suspected."

Perhaps.

I knew what I had to do then.

"I should stay with Lane. Be the one inside."

I fully expected Barlow to challenge my suggestion but, incredibly, he didn't.

I think that's the best course of action for now. Nichols can go with you.

Wow. Was Barlow finally letting go of his obsession about keeping me safe?

But how did that impact his personal feelings for me?

Maybe Sarah was wrong, maybe he didn't care quite

so much. Of course, that meant all my little fantasies were wrong, as well.

Regret pricked me.

Damn, I was a mess. First I was ticked off that he was too protective, then I was sorry when he let me do what I really wanted to do.

I seriously needed to get a grip on my own emotions.

How do you feel about the things Woods said to you?

If he'd asked me what color panties I had on I wouldn't have been more surprised.

"What?"

He apologized for causing you pain. Sounded sincere. Barlow shrugged. *How do you feel about that? Perhaps there's room for reconciliation.*

Okay, now I was really confused.

"He's a jerk. I don't care what he meant to do or didn't mean to do." I considered the relationship Heath and I had shared and then my life now. "He did me a favor." That was the truest statement I'd ever made. I wouldn't be here now if Heath hadn't been a selfish ass.

Thank God.

Amusement twitched Barlow's lips. I tried not to dwell on it but since I had to stare at them to understand what he said next, well I might as well enjoy it.

I'm glad you feel that way.

As he was about to turn away, I asked, "Why?"

He hadn't expected that.

I liked that I had startled him.

We'll talk when this is over.

Ah, his noncommittal promise.

I folded my arms over my chest. "Why can't we talk now? What difference does it make how I feel about Heath? Do you have a personal interest?"

There, I'd said it.

As the words reverberated inside me, I blinked, shocked that I would go that far.

He considered my questions a moment. The man always thought before he spoke. I remembered the few and brief kisses we'd shared and I decided that he usually thought before he spoke or acted, but not always. Gee, I guess that meant Barlow was only human, too.

Yes, he admitted. *I do have a personal interest and when this is over we're going to talk about it.*

And that was that.

With Nichols as my shadow I drove to Rex Lane's Franklin residence. As Barlow had said, a police cruiser sat outside the front of his house. I instructed Nichols to cover the rear of the property. I imagined Lane was pacing the floors inside, scared to death that whoever killed his buddy would be after him next.

Once again I was wrong.

Why are you here? he demanded the instant the door closed behind me. *I don't want you here.*

I studied him a moment. He was fully dressed in casual slacks and a lightweight pullover sweater. He looked as if he'd just stepped out of a salon. Probably had his own stylist at his beck and call.

"You have no idea why I'm here, Mr. Lane?" As I asked this question I moved toward him.

He backed away from me, moving farther down the entry hall. *What do you think I am, stupid? Of course I know why you're here. You think I had something to do with Xavier's murder.*

The moisture that gathered in his eyes as he said this confirmed my suspicions that there was no way Lane could have orchestrated such a brutal murder on his own.

"I'm here, Mr. Lane, because you're in danger."

Any color that had remained in his complexion drained away in an instant. *What're you saying?*

I stopped less than three feet from him. "I believe that whoever murdered Santos might come after you next."

Lane's head started shaking the moment I said the word *murdered. But why? We didn't do anything.*

My phone vibrated. "Excuse me," I said annoyed at the interruption and with his persistent lying.

"Walters."

I watched as the words spilled across the display. An update from Barlow regarding the M.E.'s preliminary conclusions.

I thanked him and disconnected. When I'd put the phone away I turned back to Lane. Time to get dirty.

"Did Chief Barlow explain to you the circumstances of your friend's death?"

Lane waved both hands at me. *I don't want to hear this. He said it was brutal. That's enough for me.*

"Well, you're going to hear it whether you want to or not."

Lane abruptly wheeled around, giving me his back, and all but ran up the stairs.

What the hell?

Jesus. The bastard was a real wimp.

Getting madder with each step, I stormed up the stairs after him. I found him in his bedroom searching through his dresser drawers.

"What're you doing, Lane?" I demanded. My fingers itched to curl around the butt of my own weapon. The guy could be looking for a gun.

He stopped long enough to look at me. *I don't want to die. I'm not going to let him kill me.*

Yep, he was looking for a gun.

"Maybe he won't even bother with you. Santos was probably the one, right?" I shrugged. "That's my thinking. Especially considering the killer twisted a tiara around his dick and gave him a boob job using rocks."

Grimacing, Lane held up his hands again. *I told you I didn't want to hear this.*

"That's not even the worst," I went on. "Whoever did this used some sort of blunt instrument to brutally rape him, if you know what I mean."

Lane's eyes grew wider and his mouth dropped open.

"Then he washed him nice and clean. That's why there wasn't any blood. And he borrowed some of that Botox Santos kept around for parties and gave him so many facial injections that he looked all—"

Stop! Lane braced himself against his dresser and wept.

There I went feeling sorry for him. He had just lost his best friend and lover. But they were killers. Whether Lane did the worst of the physical damage or not, he'd still participated.

"Tell me the truth, Lane." I moved toward him. "You and Santos killed your silent partner, Walt Kennard. That was the beginning, wasn't it? Is that why Reba Harrison got involved with Lane Productions?"

His gaze swung to mine. *I...I don't know what you're talking about.*

"Sure you do. He didn't like your new illegal ventures and you got rid of him before he could cause trouble. Where'd you hide the body? Is that why this whole thing started? Did you have to kill Reba, too? She was his goddaughter, you know. Was that how all this insanity got going?"

He thrust his hands back into the top dresser drawer and pulled out a gun.

I had snagged mine, as well. The proverbial Mexican standoff. Not a predicament I liked finding myself in.

It was his idea. He waved the gun as he spoke, didn't actually aim it at me. *He said if we didn't get rid of Kennard he would ruin everything. I didn't mean for it to happen—it just did. Xavier and I were desperate.* He shook his head. *Xavier hid the body. And no one ever suspected.*

"Where did he hide the body?" I suddenly wished I was wearing a wire so someone else could hear this.

You'll never find it. He hid it too well. I don't even know where all of it is.

My stomach tightened. That Santos had been one sick puppy. "Why kill Reba Harrison and—"

She tried to fool us! Lane charged, his fingers tightening on his weapon. *She wormed her way into our lives just so she could try and find out what happened to the old man. He'd treated her like his own daughter and she wanted to know the truth. Wanted revenge.* He scrubbed his free hand over his face. *I didn't want to do it. But Xavier insisted it was the only way.*

Something about his story didn't click. "Wait." I was careful to keep my weapon steady. He didn't seem to notice. "If you killed Kennard to keep him quiet and Reba Harrison because she suspected you had done so, why kill all the others? Were you trying to throw us off track?" The man was talking in circles. I needed him to calm down and give me the facts before one of us ended up dead.

Lane flung his arms madly. *You don't understand,* he railed. *We didn't kill them. We had nothing to do with any of that. It was him!*

"You're talking about the other murders? The ones after Reba Harrison?" He nodded dramatically as if I should have known that. I frowned. "Who exactly is this *him* you're saying killed the others?"

Lane looked startled. *You don't know?*

Okay. This guy really had gone off the deep end. "No, I'm afraid not. We thought it was you and Santos."

His confusion visibly escalated. *You think we killed all those women?* He started to laugh hysterically at that idea.

I reached for my cell phone. Might as well call for backup while he was distracted. Clearly the guy had come completely unglued. He might do anything.

As I waited for dispatch to pick up, Lane's laughter ceased. His expression turned somber.

We shouldn't have killed her. That's what started all of this. But we didn't have any other choice. Making her murder look as if she were one of the Starlet victims was the only way to cover up what we'd done.

I closed my phone, had to hear the rest of this while he was still talking. I shoved it into my pocket. "Was that Xavier's idea, too?"

Lane nodded. *We had no idea that it would start something we couldn't stop.*

"I don't understand—what did it start?"

He blinked, peered past me in abrupt horror. I whipped around, leveled my weapon on the first thing that moved.

Jamison.

The weapon he had trained on me left me with few options. Shoot and take my chances or see what he had to say. Curiosity had always been one of my shortfalls.

Funny thing was he hadn't felt like a killer. How could my instincts have been so off?

Lane stalked up to the man I had known as Jamison and shook his finger in his face while the weapon in his hand hung loosely at his side. *It was you! You killed them.* Pain twisted his face. *You killed Xavier.*

I wondered vaguely if Lane's weapon was even loaded. He kept waving it around, but Jamison, or whoever the hell he was, didn't appear to be bothered by it. Or me, for that matter.

"I need both of you to put your weapons down," I announced, firming my aim at Jamison since I considered him the greater threat.

Lane looked at me as if I just didn't get it.

Jamison unexpectedly shifted his aim, putting a bullet in Lane's head, ending his misery once and for all.

The blast sent blood and brain matter splattering every nearby surface, including me, before Lane's body crumpled to the floor.

Shock had me staring at Lane in disbelief for a fraction of a second before my cop sense kicked in. I summoned my scattered courage and glared at the bastard. "Put your weapon down."

As if I hadn't spoken at all, he stepped over the dead man and walked straight up to me. I should have pulled the trigger then. Wished like hell I had. Couldn't say exactly why I didn't.

"Don't make me have to shoot you," I warned.

He smiled, that same pleasant, all-American-boy charmer he'd flashed me when I'd first nailed him for following me. *If you were going to shoot me, Detective, you already would have.* He shook his head. *I really liked you. I hate that it has to end this way.*

As if he fully expected me to stand there and let him do what he would, he pressed the muzzle to my forehead, dead center. *Such a shame. I spared you once, you know.*

I managed a little laugh, it was probably brittle and horribly dry, but I coughed it up just the same. "What's that supposed to mean?" I refused to call him Jamison since I knew that likely wasn't his name. I told myself again to shoot—to end this before he could. But I couldn't.

Don't you know who I am, Detective?

I stared directly into his eyes. Evil lurked there. Why hadn't I seen that before? Had he been that good at disguising himself?

I took a chance, shook my head. "Don't have a clue."

Fury and something like indignation twisted the features of his face. *I'm the one that got away four years ago.*

Another wave of shock radiated through me, but I kept it inside. The Starlet murderer. Jesus Christ. My hand shook, but I quickly tightened my grip on my weapon. Just shoot. Why wouldn't my fingers cooperate?

This fool, he glanced at Lane as he went on, *and his friend thought they could get away with pinning their dirty deed on me. Well, I couldn't have that.* His gaze settled on me once more. *I gave you clues but still you failed. I'm sorely disappointed in you, Detective.*

The hairs…he'd planted them. I didn't have to see lab results to know they would belong to Lane and Santos.

Something he'd said slammed back into my brain. "What do you mean, you spared me once before?" My heart was pumping like mad. I needed backup. I needed a plan.

He smiled, it wasn't pleasant. *Remember who my victims were four years ago? You and your Mr. Woods were quite an item. But when I came for you, you'd gotten sick. I couldn't follow through with it. You were special, a survivor…you deserved to live. So I walked away, didn't kill again until,* he glared at Lane once more, *they forced me to avenge myself.*

"That's why you've been following me around this time," I said more to myself than to him. I'd become some sort of obsession to him. "It was you who came into my house," I realized aloud. "And pushed me into that tool room with Johnson." I blinked. "You killed him!"

He shrugged. *He would have killed you. And you were still useful to me at that point. I'd been keeping an eye on you, keeping you safe so you could do what had to be done. I needed you to uncover what Lane and Santos had done. As for your modest little home, I've never met a lock I couldn't open with ease,* he said with a smirk. *Or a cop I couldn't elude. I assure you, Detective, you've never met anyone quite like me.*

And if he had anything to do with it, I likely never would again. I knew his secrets now. What his confession meant wasn't lost on me. What I needed was to keep him talking just a little bit longer.

"No one is ever going to believe a guy like you got past the surveillance posted outside my house."

Fury claimed his expression again but he quickly

reined it back in. *That's the beauty of me. No one ever realizes who I am until it's too late.* He pressed the muzzle of the weapon against my forehead. *No one ever—*

He never got to finish the sentence. Survival mode finally kicked in. I depressed the trigger of my .9-millimeter twice without another split second's hesitation.

I didn't get any glee from the look of surprise on his face. I was too damned thankful that he didn't reflexively fire off a round or two from his own weapon.

He dropped like a rock, landing haphazardly across the man he'd murdered right in front of me.

I might never know exactly who he was, but at least I was alive to talk about it. Thank God my courage hadn't deserted me completely. I'd never had to kill a man....

I took a breath and reached for my cell phone. I called Barlow. I needed to hear his voice.

Minutes later I was once again surrounded by crime scene technicians and cops.

I didn't have all the answers, but I did understand it was over.

I was glad.

Chapter 15

Forty-eight hours after the confrontation in Lane's bedroom I sat on my sofa at home and let the calm and quiet keep me company.

The first thirty-six hours had been a whirlwind of activity. The M.E. had confirmed that the planted hairs on victims two, three and four had come from Lane and Santos, clearing up that little mystery. I couldn't help feeling just a little bit sorry for Lane and Santos, but only for about two seconds. In an effort to cover their greedy, selfish murder of a silent partner, they had unknowingly awakened a monster who would ultimately destroy them.

Therein lay the biggest mystery of all: the true identity of the serial killer. The FBI was still looking into that. His prints weren't on file anywhere, nor was his face. So far absolutely nothing about him had been found. It was as if he'd never existed. But he had. A creepy, highly intelligent man who could move about like smoke and who killed so efficiently and for unknown reasons. No way could a whole team of shrinks know all there was to know about a man like that. He'd been inside my home…inside my head.

I shook off the disturbing thoughts. It was over. The case, as far as Metro was concerned, was closed.

I snuggled more deeply into my blanket and reached for my hot chocolate. I didn't want to think about killers and crime scenes anymore.

I wanted to forget.

Forget I'd killed a man before he could kill me.

I'd done the right thing. I knew that. Barlow and Chief Kent had assured me the kill was righteous. Even Internal Affairs had cleared me in record time.

But I couldn't get the idea out of my head that I wouldn't have known Jamison was a killer. Hadn't seen that one coming. And, literally wouldn't have known he'd entered Lane's bedroom if I hadn't seen the look on Lane's face.

Did that make me an unreliable cop?

I couldn't hear the enemy coming. Barlow had harped on that for over a year.

I relied heavily upon my other senses, especially my instincts. But those instincts had failed me in some respects this time. Luckily I'd still come out alive, but that might not be the case next time.

I cradled my hot mug in hopes of funneling some of that warmth to my chilled bones.

It wasn't so much that I understood I could be dead right now had things not turned out the way they had. No. I'd understood that risk from the day I'd signed on to be a cop. What troubled me most was the idea that a partner could be relying on me in a situation just like that and I might fail.

My swaggering confidence had cooled considerably.

The doorbell caused the warning light on the wall to flash, letting me know someone was at the door.

I set aside my hot chocolate and threw back my cover. If my mother came by one more time I was going to scream. God knows I love her, but she was getting on my last nerve.

And if I got wind of another family dinner that included an invited guest, always male and usually the son of one of my mother's friends, I was going to have to stop attending myself.

I tightened the sash on my favorite robe, a big old worn-out terry-cloth one I'd had forever, and then opened the door.

Patterson, on crutches, a huge bouquet of flowers clutched in one hand.

He held them out. *For you,* he said.

"Thank you." I took the mixed arrangement and inhaled deeply. I loved spring flowers. And the vase was lovely, as well, not the generic one usually provided with arrangements. This one was white porcelain with hand-painted flowers in the colors from the arrangement.

"Come in." I stepped back, inviting him in. "Have a seat while I put these on the table."

He limped into my living room and studied the framed photographs on my sofa table. I smiled as I positioned the arrangement on my dining table. Lovely. Partners were really nice.

"I'm not sick, you know," I said to Patterson as I trudged back over to the couch.

He had leaned the crutches against the wall and relaxed in the big clunky chair I'd rescued from the side of the road. I'd reupholstered it myself in a lovely yellow shade that fit in nicely with my other furnishings.

Are you really taking two weeks off? he queried.

"What do you care?" I teased. "You're on leave all that time."

He lifted one shoulder in a nonchalant shrug that wasn't nonchalant at all. *I guess I was just worried that you'd changed your mind about being a homicide detective.*

I wanted to tell him he was barking up the wrong tree or that he could just stop worrying, but, unfortunately he'd hit the nail right on the head.

"I have to think, Patterson." For the first time in my soundless life I worried that I couldn't do all the things I'd assured myself I could. I was different now. Handicapped. I had to face that. "I have to consider what's right for the people I work with."

You're talking about me, he returned pointedly. *I'm your partner and I can't think of anyone in the whole division I'd rather work with.*

Emotion clogged my throat but I had to say this. "I could get you killed, Patterson. I see that now."

Nobody's perfect, Walters. It happens sometimes in this line of work even to people who have no physical shortcoming to blame. The fact of the matter is, I'll take my chances with you.

How could I walk away from that?

I smiled. "All right. We'll go back to work the same day."

His face brightened. *Good. When I considered the turkeys I could have been stuck with I got worried. A guy like me doesn't fit in with just anyone.*

We talked for a while. Patterson was a good guy. We made a terrific team. And I didn't have to worry about sexual attraction becoming an issue.

When I opened the door to see Patterson out I discovered Steven Barlow standing on my stoop. He, too, arrived bearing flowers. Red roses. At least three dozen. Wow!

He and Patterson exchanged chitchat before Patterson made his way down the walk. He winked as he waved to me before climbing into his new sleek luxury car. His healing left leg obviously wasn't stopping him for getting around. I guess he'd decided he didn't need a macho SUV anymore since he wasn't worried about pretending to be something he wasn't with me. Good. I hated climbing into that huge vehicle, not to mention it sucked down enough gas to fuel a third world country for at least a week.

May I come in?

I redirected my attention to Barlow. As usual he looked damn good. Wore a classic-looking charcoal suit with a black shirt and tie. Very nice.

"Sure." I went through the same routine with him. Took the flowers, told him to have a seat, then set the flowers on the table next to Patterson's. Admittedly, Barlow's huge bouquet had it all over my partner's, but it was the thought that counted. Considering he'd gotten red roses, I decided Barlow's thoughts were far more intimate.

My heart started that pitty-pat thing that I always experienced whenever I was alone with Barlow. As I sat down across from him I promised myself I wouldn't stare. But it was damn hard. The guy looked amazing.

You look good, Merri.

I barely restrained the need to look around the room and see if there was another Merri present. I looked like hell. My unruly hair was bunched up in a clip—far too many strands had worked their way loose to look sexy. Pretty much I just looked messy.

The idea that I was naked under the robe abruptly rammed into my brain. I'd dragged out of a long soak and just tugged on my robe.

Now why hadn't I thought of that while Patterson was here? Because he was like one of the girls, I didn't have to worry. But Barlow…he definitely wasn't one of the girls.

"Would you care for something to drink?" I could deal with something stronger than hot chocolate, that was for sure. My pulse skipped erratically and I felt suddenly hot. No more chilled bones.

He shook his head. *I'm here to talk.*

My heart kicked into a faster rhythm. "Am I in trouble?" I told myself he was here about work. I knew we'd said we were going to talk about personal issues when this case was over but we'd agreed to have that talk on neutral territory. This wasn't exactly the way I'd pictured it. Especially the part with me in the tattered bathrobe.

This isn't about work, exactly.

I looked into those blue eyes then and I felt my insides start to melt. I loved his eyes. Loved the way he looked at me as if nothing else on the planet mattered more.

"We agreed to have this talk on neutral territory," I reminded, my breath coming too fast now. Sarah's words echoed in my head. *You know he's in love with you, don't you?*

I'd promised myself I wouldn't take this kind of chance with my heart again. Not until I was completely sure. I was far from completely sure. As much as I cared about Barlow, loved him actually, my whole life was still confusing to me on some levels. Sure I went weeks and months feeling utterly complete, but then a moment like this would come and shake everything up all over again.

I just didn't know.

Neutral territory won't be necessary, he explained.

This made no sense whatsoever. Was he about to tell me that he didn't feel the way I thought he did?

Since we met, he went on, *my emotions have been in a turmoil.*

I definitely understood how that felt.

I know how much your work means to you. I fully understand how my being in the position of your division chief has hampered your need to grow in your chosen profession.

The very rush of my blood seemingly stilled as his words filtered through me. He was going to end this once and for all. All the hope I'd promised myself I wouldn't let build, all the feelings I'd kept tightly compartmentalized imploded at once. I couldn't bear it if he said this thing neither of us had fully acknowledged was over.

So—I held my breath—*I've resigned my position as Chief of Homicide. I'll be going back to being a detective. That's where I belong.*

At first I didn't get it. He had stepped down from the position of Chief of Homicide? He'd decided to be a detective again? Okay, I sounded like an echo here, but I was stunned.

"Are you sure that's what you want to do?" I couldn't think what else to say…it was too unbelievable. He was a great chief. The right man for the job. And he'd deserved that promotion.

I didn't want him to do this for me…. I wanted him to do the right thing for him. This felt wrong.

The decision is made. It's what I want. I prefer being out in the field. He smiled, that one-sided charmer that made my heart do more of those strange acrobatics. *Like you.*

I closed my hands between my knees to keep them from fidgeting. "But I was considering moving into profiling after all." I shrugged. "Maybe being a detective is not the best fit."

I'd said it out loud. To Barlow of all people. But, God, I couldn't have him resigning as chief. And I had been considering that maybe I'd made a mistake.

He closed the distance between us, making me sweat, then crouched in front of me and took my hands in his. *Merri, you're a hell of a detective. You don't need to change. I need the change. I can do without the politics. It's not who I am. I'm about catching killers. That's where I belong.*

I held on tightly to those strong hands as I searched his eyes. "You're sure your decision isn't about me?"

He smiled again, so sweetly it made me ache inside.

Merri, every breath I take is about you. How could I possibly separate who I am from that? I want every minute of every day from this moment forward to be about us. I want you in my life. He cupped my face in his hands. *I want you, period.*

Okay, I was convinced.

"Then stop talking and take me," I murmured.

I watched as his mouth moved toward mine. I didn't breathe again until he'd kissed me so thoroughly I thought I might just pass out with the incredible pleasure of it.

He stood, took my hand in his and pulled me toward my bedroom. Not once during the journey did he take his eyes off mine. I felt myself getting more and more lost in that blue gaze.

I'd waited three long years to take this plunge again. But I'd waited an entire lifetime for a man like Steven Barlow.

He frowned as he surveyed my bedroom. *Where's your bed?*

"I had it taken away," I explained. I just couldn't sleep on it again, not after…well, you know. "The new one won't be here until tomorrow."

He looked from me to the mound of pillows on the carpet and then back. *I guess we'll just have to make do.*

"Not a problem." I released my sash and let the robe fall to the floor.

Every mile I'd ever run, every set of crunches I'd ever endured were worth the trouble for this one moment. The way he looked at me made me glad to be a woman.

I took the two steps between us and pushed the jacket off his broad shoulders. My body hummed with need as my hands slid over the crisp cotton of his shirt.

The tie went next. Then, together, we unbuttoned and peeled off the shirt. I dropped to my knees and pulled his shoes off his feet, the left, then the right. With those out of the way the socks rolled off next.

He reached for his fly, I pushed his hands away and did the honors myself. I wanted to enjoy the reveal…to admire him the way he'd admired me.

The trousers dropped to his ankles. He kicked them aside. I didn't wait. I grabbed the waistband of his boxer briefs and dragged them down his muscled legs.

The feel of his skin beneath my fingertips made me desperate to have him down here with me.

I sat back on my heels and admired his gorgeous body. I had known he would be just amazing beneath those classy clothes and I'd been right.

He lowered himself down to his knees, reached out to take the clip from my hair and allow all those tangled tresses to fall down around my shoulders.

We kissed again. Kissed until my head spun. He lowered me to the mound of pillows and lay over me. The feel of his warm skin against mine made me restless…made me want to touch him all over. I loved the pressure of his weight.

He took his time, learning my body, ensuring I was primed and ready before the next step. When I could bear the torture no longer, I pushed him onto his back and straddled his waist.

"My turn now."

Before he could argue I sank down onto him. He shuddered. I did the same. For several seconds I couldn't move…couldn't speak…couldn't even think.

He pulled me down to him. The move shifted the pressure to just the right spot and I almost climaxed. He kissed my lips, my nose, my eyes and then he rolled me onto my back and made love to me the way I'd longed for him to do for far too long.

We came together, not once but three times. Then we ordered food to be delivered, made love again, ate and fell asleep.

It was amazing.

Everything I'd hoped it would be.

Shadows had gathered in the room as I lay there looking at him. I was pretty sure he was asleep but I wasn't taking bets on it. Part of him was definitely ready to go. I glanced down to that semi-aroused penis and I got wet all over again. I wanted to wake up next to him like this every day for the rest of my life.

He hadn't proposed, but judging by all that he'd said and done, I felt reasonably certain that it was only a matter of time before we crossed that bridge.

Sarah had been right.

Steven Barlow was in love with me.

And I was very much in love with him.

We could go to work together, make beautiful babies together. My breath caught. Where had that thought come from?

I turned over the idea, thought about how it felt to hold my niece. Maybe, as Sarah had said, I would keep an open mind.

The light over my door was flashing quickly, indicating that I'd missed a call. The flash patterns for doorbell, ringing phone and missed call were different, making life considerably easier. I slipped away from my lover and crawled on all fours to the phone sitting on my bedside table.

The caller ID listed the call as out of area. I depressed the playback button and the message played aloud as well as appeared on the display screen.

The words that tumbled across the display had the oxygen evacuating my lungs.

Merri, it's Mason. I'm back in Nashville. When can I see you?

Mason Conrad. Talk about a blast from the past. I sat there, stunned. Whatever had taken place between us one year ago, I had mixed emotions about hearing from him now. We'd connected physically during the Hammond case. Mason had saved my life. But he'd been one of the bad guys. He'd turned state's evidence and gotten a certain level of immunity.

He'd apparently done his time.

And now he was back in town.

Ready to pursue that connection we'd shared.

I glanced back at where Barlow lay.

My heart stumbled. He'd propped himself up on one arm and was watching me. I wished now I hadn't played the message. I didn't want anything to ruin this special moment.

Come over here, he said.

How could I resist? I couldn't. He was the man I wanted to be with. Mason Conrad was a ghost from the past. He had no place in my life now.

As I went back into Barlow's arms I refused to let the tiny nagging feeling of uncertainty take root.

This was where I wanted to be.

Tonight and always.

At Silhouette Bombshell, the excitement
never stops, and the compelling heroines never
give up 'til they get their men, good and bad.
We're dedicated to bringing you
innovative stories that will keep you riveted!
Turn the page for a sneak peek at one of
next month's compelling reads:

TRACE OF INNOCENCE

by Erica Orloff

Available January 2006
at your favorite retail outlet.

Chapter 1

Blood spatter was artfully arranged.

Photographs from crime scenes, in stark black and white, were matted and framed, lining a long hallway, with hardwood floors that squeaked as I walked.

I had stopped thinking of the photos as gruesome or even odd two years ago when I started working for Lewis LeBarge, my boss at New Jersey's Genetic Testing Laboratory and collector of all things macabre. He told me once it came with the territory. "Spend enough time around the dead," he had said to me, his New Orleans accent giving him a certain Southern charm, "and eventually you come up with ways to mock the Grim Reaper—just to let him know he hasn't won...yet." Lewis regularly talked to the Reaper, like an old friend, asking him just how or why a dead body had met its maker.

"Lewis?" I called out from the hallway. I had let myself in the front door to his old duplex in Hoboken.

"Up here," he called out. "The office."

I climbed the stairs. There were just two small bedrooms on the second story. One was the master bedroom, and the other he used as a home office, complete with Internet links to our database in the lab.

I poked my head in. "Ready?"

"For you, darlin', always." He winked at me, his prematurely gray hair giving him a distinguished look, belying his forty years.

I spied a new photo on the wall. The blood puddle next to a gunshot victim looked like black syrup. "Has anyone ever suggested to you that perhaps the reason you never make it past the first date with a woman is your taste in art?"

"Now, Billie, I'm just waitin' for you to realize we're the ones meant to be together. And until then," he sighed, "I remain alone and desperately lonely in this cold northern city."

"Don't give me that...your New Orleans–gentleman charm is a magnet for women. I've seen them clustered around you like bees buzzing around a flower."

"I never hurt for first dates, as you so kindly pointed out. It's getting to date number two that's difficult."

I looked at the aquarium tank on the shelf, which housed an enormous tarantula he'd named Ripper, after the serial killer he once wrote a thesis on. I'm not squeamish—can't be, working in a forensics lab—but spiders give me the creeps. Especially hairy ones.

"Maybe you should try telling them you do something sane. Boring even. Ever try saying you're an accountant? Working with numbers all day is certainly an improvement over saying you spend all day examining brain matter."

"Eventually, I'd be found out. And with the exception of you, there's not many women who enjoy discussin' blow flies on dead bodies and the rate of maggot infestation over a lovely supper of jambalaya."

"Really? I would have thought some women would love to hear all about it. Especially while eating." I rolled my eyes. "I've got you figured out. You, dear Lewis, love to scare them off."

"Perhaps I do." He winked at me. "How's that cop you've been dating?"

"Good…when he's on the wagon."

"And when he's not?"

"Come on, Lewis, neither of us has a stellar track record in the love department."

"We're both married to the job."

"I suppose we are. You ready?"

"Darlin', I wouldn't miss this chance to mingle with the underworld of New Jersey for anything. Your family is like an anthropological field study."

"Shut up," I snapped, but grinned at him as he stood up, ducking his head slightly to avoid hitting the overhead lamp. Lewis stood a lanky six foot two inches in his custom cowboy boots. He wore his standard-issue black Levis and white oxford-cloth shirt, well-worn at the elbows, with a pair of black onyx cuff links he was never without. He turned off the lamp and the two of us made our way downstairs and out the door. My big maroon Lincoln was parked on the street.

"Still driving the Sherman land tank, I see."

"I can't part with it, despite how much gas this thing guzzles. My uncle Sam left it to me when he went inside."

"'Inside,'" Lewis mused, as he climbed into the car after I unlocked the doors. "I do love how the Quinn family has such special euphemisms—like this party we're going to."

"What? It's a welcome-home party for my father. What's wrong with that?"

"You mean a welcome-home from *Rahway Prison* party. But no doubt your aunt Gloria will make one of her wonderful cheesecakes for the occasion. I'm fond of the strawberry one. Very moist."

"Lewis, it's still a coming-home party, no matter where he was prior to actually coming home. Besides, this time was really stupid. A parole violation…busted at an illegal card game. I mean, come off it. You sometimes sit in with them, too."

I started the car and pulled away from the curb, biting my lip in irritation for a minute. There was nothing I hated more than cops going after bullshit crimes when murderers and child rapists were a plague.

Lewis leaned back against the plush velour seats. "Well, all I can say is family parties with you-all is like stepping into a Scorcese film. I love bein' around your relatives. They are quite entertainin'."

I drove out of Hoboken and eventually steered onto

the Jersey Turnpike, which was loaded with eighteen-wheelers and heavy traffic.

"But you know, Billie, I've still never understood how it is you managed to turn out honest and law-abiding, if a little unusual around the edges."

I shrugged, staring ahead at the highway. "I don't know."

"Come on, you've thought about it. You must have some explanation."

I had thought about it. Endlessly. Until my head hurt sometimes. My mother had disappeared when I was nine. The cops had bungled the case, more interested in focusing on my father—head of an Irish crime family—than in uncovering the truth. When her body turned up six months later—nothing left but bones and the shreds of her dress—they arrested the wrong man, eventually freeing him without the case going to trial.

"I don't know. I wanted to solve murders. And if I became a cop, my family would have disowned me. So working for you is about as close as I can get to fighting the bad guys legally."

* * * * *

Meet Billie Quinn, criminalist. She's caught between her loving but shady family and her will to bring the bad guys down. And she's about to face the hardest decision of her life, one that will determine whether a man lives or dies.
Don't miss TRACE OF INNOCENCE!

THE IT GIRLS

Rich, fabulous...and dangerously underestimated.

*They're heiresses with connections,
glamour girls with the inside track.*

*And they're going undercover to fight
high-society crime in high style.*

Catch The It Girls in these six books
by some of your favorite Bombshell authors:

THE GOLDEN GIRL by Erica Orloff, September 2005

FLAWLESS by Michele Hauf, October 2005

LETHALLY BLONDE by Nancy Bartholomew, November 2005

MS. LONGSHOT by Sylvie Kurtz, December 2005

A MODEL SPY by Natalie Dunbar, January 2006

BULLETPROOF PRINCESS by Vicki Hinze, February 2006

Available at your favorite retail outlet.

Lucia Garza suspected she'd made
a deal with the devil when she opened her
detective agency. And the red envelopes
containing tricky assignments kept coming
from her shadowy bankroller. Now Lucia was
an unwilling pawn—in a battle to control
the future of the world.

RED LETTER DAYS:
YOU'LL NEVER BELIEVE
WHAT'S INSIDE

DEVIL'S DUE
by Rachel Caine

Available January wherever books are sold.

If you enjoyed what you just read,
then we've got an offer you can't resist!

Take 2 bestselling
love stories FREE!

Plus get a FREE surprise gift!

Clip this page and mail it to Silhouette Reader Service®

IN U.S.A.
3010 Walden Ave.
P.O. Box 1867
Buffalo, N.Y. 14240-1867

IN CANADA
P.O. Box 609
Fort Erie, Ontario
L2A 5X3

YES! Please send me 2 free Silhouette Bombshell™ novels and my free surprise gift. After receiving them, if I don't wish to receive any more, I can return the shipping statement marked cancel. If I don't cancel, I will receive 4 brand-new novels every month, before they're available in stores! In the U.S.A., bill me at the bargain price of $4.69 plus 25¢ shipping & handling per book and applicable sales tax, if any*. In Canada, bill me at the bargain price of $5.24 plus 25¢ shipping & handling per book and applicable taxes**. That's the complete price and a savings of 10% off the cover prices—what a great deal! I understand that accepting the 2 free books and gift places me under no obligation ever to buy any books. I can always return a shipment and cancel at any time. Even if I never buy another book from Silhouettte, the 2 free books and gift are mine to keep forever.

200 HDN D34H
300 HDN D34J

Name	(PLEASE PRINT)	
Address	Apt.#	
City	State/Prov.	Zip/Postal Code

Not valid to current Silhouette Bombshell™ subscribers.

Want to try another series?
Call 1-800-873-8635 or visit www.morefreebooks.com.

* Terms and prices subject to change without notice. Sales tax applicable in N.Y.
** Canadian residents will be charged applicable provincial taxes and GST.
  All orders subject to approval. Offer limited to one per household.
® and ™ are registered trademarks owned and used by the trademark owner and
or its licensee.

BOMB04   ©2004 Harlequin Enterprises Limited

COMING NEXT MONTH

#73 DEVIL'S DUE—Rachel Caine
Red Letter Days
Lucia Garza suspected she'd made a deal with the devil when
she opened her detective agency. And the red envelopes
containing tricky assignments kept coming from her shadowy
bankroller. Every order Lucia followed—or disobeyed—could
mean someone's life or death. But as she made her move to
get out, Lucia learned that her backer and his enemy were using
Lucia and her team as pawns in a battle to control the future of
the world. And if she left, there might not be a future at all....

#74 A MODEL SPY—Natalie Dunbar
The It Girls
As a former supermodel from a wealthy family, Vanessa Dawson
was the perfect fit for the Gotham Roses's latest society
crime-fighting mission. Two Miami models were dead, and
all signs pointed to a drug ring operating from high fashion's
highest precincts. Was hip-hop mogul Hot T involved? Vanessa
went undercover as a swimsuit model to find out, but soon
shoot-outs replaced fashion shoots as the order of the day....

#75 TRACE OF INNOCENCE—Erica Orloff
A Billie Quinn Case
For criminologist Billie Quinn, using DNA evidence to nail the
bad guys was a personal crusade—after all, her own mother
had been murdered by a serial killer. But sometimes DNA proved
innocence, and Billie knew—in her *heart*—that the wrong man
was in prison for the infamous Suicide King killings. When her
ex-lover fought to keep the wrong man behind bars, Billie had
to ask herself—who was the real Suicide King?

#76 THE BIG BURN—Terry Watkins
After a daring California wildfire rescue, smoke jumper
Anna Quick was a little burned-out. But fire waits on no woman,
and Special Ops team leader John Brock needed her—now!—
for a dangerous secret mission in Malaysia. Anna expected
the "routine" challenges of fighting a big blaze. Instead, she
discovered deception, smoke screens…and incendiary
revelations about the war on terror and her own family.

SBCNM1205